TWELVE ANGRY LIBRARIANS

A Cat in the Stacks Mystery

TWELVE ANGRY LIBRARIANS

Miranda James

Berkley Prime Crime
New York

BERKLEY PRIME CRIME
Published by Berkley
An imprint of Penguin Random House LLC
375 Hudson Street, New York, New York 10014

Copyright © 2017 by Dean James
Penguin Random House supports copyright. Copyright fuels creativity, encourages diverse
voices, promotes free speech, and creates a vibrant culture. Thank you for buying an authorized
edition of this book and for complying with copyright laws by not reproducing, scanning, or
distributing any part of it in any form without permission. You are supporting writers and
allowing Penguin Random House to continue to publish books for every reader.

BERKLEY is a registered trademark and BERKLEY PRIME CRIME and the B colophon
are trademarks of Penguin Random House LLC.

Library of Congress Cataloging-in-Publication Data

Names: James, Miranda, author.
Title: Twelve angry librarians / Miranda James.
Description: First edition. | New York : Berkley Prime Crime, 2017. | Series:
Cat in the stacks mystery ; 8
Identifiers: LCCN 2016042276 (print) | LCCN 2016048829 (ebook) | ISBN
9780425277768 (hardback) | ISBN 9780698181991 (ebook)
Subjects: LCSH: Librarians—Mississippi—Fiction. |
Libraries—Mississippi—Fiction. | Murder—Investigation—Fiction. |
BISAC: FICTION / Mystery & Detective / Women Sleuths. | GSAFD:
Mystery fiction.
Classification: LCC PS3610.A43 T93 2017 (print) | LCC PS3610.A43 (ebook) |
DDC 813/.6—dc23
LC record available at https://lccn.loc.gov/2016042276

First Edition: February 2017

Printed in the United States of America
1 3 5 7 9 10 8 6 4 2

Cover art by Dan Craig
Cover design by Lesley Worrell and Katie Anderson
Book design by Tiffany Estreicher

For a decade of unfailing support, encouragement, and enthusiasm, I dedicate this book with boundless gratitude to my wonderful editor, Michelle Vega.

Truly, sine qua non.

ACKNOWLEDGMENTS

Thanks as always to the usual suspects: my agent, Nancy Yost; and her associates: Sarah E. Younger, Natanya Wheeler, and Amy Rosenbaum for all they do; the team at Berkley: Michelle Vega, Bethany Blair, and Roxanne Jones for constant support and help in numerous ways; the art department for consistently beautiful covers; and the copyeditors who always work so hard to catch my mistakes and lapses in logic.

My dear friends Patricia Orr and Terry Farmer read and encouraged as the chapters popped up in their e-mail boxes, and I can never thank them enough for what they do.

Finally, special thanks to Patrick B. Kyle, PhD, DABCC, director of clinical chemistry and toxicology, at the University of Mississippi Medical Center, for graciously answering questions about poison that came to his e-mail inbox out of the blue. He is not responsible for any errors or misinterpretations that I have made based on his answers to my questions.

TWELVE ANGRY LIBRARIANS

ONE

||||||||||||||||||||||

"But I don't *want* to do it."

I glared at my administrative assistant and longtime friend, Melba Gilley. "You know how much I hate public speaking. Why can't Forrest Wyatt do it? College presidents do this kind of thing all the time."

"Forrest will be welcoming everyone to open the conference. If you'd actually *read* the schedule instead of whining like a three-year-old you'd see that." Melba Gilley glared right back at me.

My Maine Coon cat, Diesel, obviously disturbed by the sudden tension between two of his favorite people, started meowing loudly. He butted his head against my leg, and I immediately felt exactly like the three-year-old Melba labeled me. I rubbed the cat's head to reassure him. The meowing slowed and softened in volume.

"Sorry." I sighed as I skimmed the first page of the document Melba gave me a few minutes ago. Surely I wouldn't be expected to give a lengthy speech. "You're right. Forrest is speaking before me, I see. How long do I have to talk?"

"Only two or three minutes," Melba said. "If you look at the times on the schedule, you can see that there's only ten minutes allotted for both you and Forrest."

"He'll probably talk for nine and a half of the ten." I grinned. "So I can have thirty seconds to say 'Welcome to Athena and have a nice time.' That ought to do it."

Diesel warbled as if he agreed with me, and Melba laughed.

"I think you should say more than *that*."

"We'll see. How many people usually attend this meeting?" I asked.

Melba shrugged. "We hosted it ten years ago, and as I recall, there were about three hundred people. Nowadays with travel budgets being cut, fewer people may attend."

I glanced at the header of the document. "Southern Academic Library Association. I've heard some of the other librarians talk about it." I shrugged. "I had my fill of library meetings from my days in the public library system in Houston. The Texas Library Association Annual Conference is about the largest of its kind in the country, and I went to over twenty of them. I thought I was done with them when I moved back here."

"Stop trying to sound so dang pathetic." Melba cocked her head to the right and frowned at me. I knew that look. No more whining, or she'd get *really* testy with me.

"Yes, *ma'am*," I said in a pert tone. Diesel chirped, and Melba's expression relaxed into a grin.

"At least you've only got a couple days to worry about what you're going to say, with everything starting on Thursday."

I forbore to comment. I skimmed through the schedule. After

an opening reception Thursday evening, the conference ran from Friday morning through Sunday at noon. I spotted several names I recognized. People I'd gone to library school with nearly thirty years before. We hadn't kept in touch, but I figured it might be interesting to see them again.

Then my eyes lighted on the name of the speaker for the Friday luncheon keynote. *Gavin Fong.*

Surely there couldn't be two of them, although I hoped there were. The Gavin Fong from library school days had been a jerk, a condescending snot who thought he was intellectually superior to the rest of us. He always talked as if he were slumming by earning a master's degree in library science.

"What's wrong, Charlie?" Melba asked. "You're looking like you stepped in something nasty and can't get it off your shoe."

I laughed. "Great metaphor." I glanced at Gavin Fong's name on the page again. Before I could continue, however, the phone on Melba's desk rang, and she disappeared to answer it.

Moments later my phone buzzed, and I picked up the handset. "Yes?"

"Lisa Krause for you," Melba replied before she transferred the call.

I picked up the receiver. "Good morning, Lisa. What can I do for you?" Lisa was head of the reference department at the library.

After returning my greeting, Lisa said, "I'm sorry about the short notice, but I have to go over to the Farrington House to deal with some last-minute issues about the SALA meeting. I'm chair of the local arrangements committee. I'm not sure how long it's going to take, so I might not be back in time for our meeting at one."

"That's not a problem," I said. "We can always talk later. I'm afraid I haven't paid much attention to the conference and who's doing what."

Lisa chuckled. "You've had far more important things to deal with, and better you than me. I hope you're not still pulling your hair out over the budget mess."

I grimaced, even though she couldn't see me. The *budget mess* was a legacy from the former director who had failed to keep a tight rein on things, and much of my time since I'd been named interim director had been spent in meetings with the college board and the chief financial officer.

"I have a few stray hairs left," I said. "I hope you can get your problems at the hotel solved more easily."

"If a certain jackass weren't coming to the meeting as a plenary speaker, my job would be a lot easier," Lisa said. I could hear the frustration in her voice.

"Let me guess," I said. "Gavin Fong."

"How did you figure that out?" Lisa asked, obviously surprised. "Do you know him?"

"I did, years ago," I replied. "We went to library school together. I didn't care for him in the least and was happy to see the last of him. He wouldn't deign to work in a public library."

"I think you'd have to look a long time to find someone who does care for him." Lisa giggled. "Everyone in SALA loathes him and has done for years. I can't figure out why on earth the program committee chose him as a featured speaker. He'll just stand there and go on and on for an hour about how wonderful he is and all the innovative things he's into."

"About what I would expect," I said. "What library is he with now?"

Lisa named a school. "It's in Alabama. He's the director."

"I've never heard of it," I said. "I figured he'd be heading one of the big university libraries. You know, dean of libraries, or vice provost of something-or-other by now."

"The way I've heard it, he started at one of the Ivy League schools as some kind of hotshot right out of library school, but after that he moved down the ladder instead of up. And down, and down." Lisa giggled. "Which is why he's at this tiny school in Alabama that nobody's ever heard of."

I had to admit my baser nature found great satisfaction in hearing that. "If that's the best he can do, he must have gotten even more obnoxious than he was when I knew him."

"Obnoxious doesn't even *begin* to describe him," Lisa said. "I'll have to show you the list of demands he sent. I swear you'd think he was some opera prima donna. He has to have a certain kind of bottled water, and his room has to be kept at a certain temperature, and he can only eat certain foods, and, well, you get the gist."

"What a twit." I laughed. "I'm sorry you're having to deal with this infantile behavior."

"It's only for a few days." Lisa sighed. "Don't be surprised if I don't make it in on Monday, though. I may be under my bed, sucking my thumb and clutching my blankie by the time this is over with."

"Once he gives his speech, I wouldn't pay any more attention to his demands. If he isn't happy, he can go back to Alabama, and good riddance."

"I like the way you think, Charlie." Lisa chuckled. "Well, I'd better get on over to the hotel. Thanks for the encouraging words."

"Good luck."

Melba ambled back into my office right after I hung up the

5

phone. "What was all that about? Lisa sounded in a tizzy when I answered the phone."

I explained, and Melba grimaced. "Sounds to me like somebody needs to take that guy out behind the woodshed and give him a good talking-to. With a horsewhip."

"Are you volunteering?" I asked. Diesel chose that moment to speak up with a loud meow.

"You reckon he's saying he'll help me?" Melba laughed. "If this jerk gets in my way, you'd better bet I'll be telling him what he can do with his bottled water."

"I'd pay good money to see you give him what for," I said. "I hope he's not going to disrupt the whole conference. There's no telling what he might say when he gets up in front of a captive audience of librarians."

"I'll see about having a supply of tar and feathers on hand."

I laughed. "You do that."

The phone rang again, and Melba disappeared to answer it.

Diesel tapped my leg with a large paw, and I rubbed his head. I glanced at the clock on my desk. Nearly noon. Time to head home for lunch. The cat could tell time as well as I could.

"Okay, boy, let me finish this e-mail, and we'll go home."

Diesel chattered at me, a mixture of chirps and trills, and I knew he understood what I had said. He stared at me the whole time I typed at the keyboard, as if he were afraid I would leave without him.

A few minutes later, with Diesel harnessed and on the leash, we ambled down the sidewalk toward home. The late April sunshine bore down, but thanks to the low humidity, the heat was not uncomfortable. Trees shaded our way for the short trip to the house. As we drew close, I spotted a familiar car in the driveway.

"Laura is here," I told Diesel, and he tugged against the leash in his eagerness to get into the house. He adored Laura, and she adored him.

We found her in the kitchen, seated at the table, chatting happily with my housekeeper, Azalea Berry. I unhooked the leash, and Diesel trotted over to my daughter. He put his front paws on her leg and rubbed his head against her belly. She scratched his head and laughed.

I bent to kiss her cheek. "How are you feeling? Ready to have that baby?"

Laura rolled her eyes. "Only six weeks to go, and I am so ready not to be pregnant anymore."

Azalea had her eyes fixed on Diesel as he continued to rub against Laura. "I swear that cat knows you're going to have a baby, Miss Laura. I've never seen the like."

"He's a smart boy." Laura rubbed Diesel's head. The cat responded with a loud meow. "See, he agrees with me."

"He's as anxious to meet the baby as the rest of us." I went to the sink to wash my hands. "Are you having lunch with us, sweetheart?"

"There's plenty," Azalea said.

"I could manage to eat a little." Laura grinned. "I have to keep up my strength, you know." Then she sobered. "Before we eat though, Dad, I have something to tell you. I hope it won't ruin your appetite."

I laid aside the dish towel I had used to dry my hands and came back to the table. My hands on the back of my usual chair, I stared at my daughter, suddenly apprehensive. "What's wrong? Is it something to do with the baby?"

Laura shook her head. "No, Dad, it's not that." She paused, as if gathering her nerve to continue. "You know Frank's been out of town for a couple of days?"

I nodded. Frank Salisbury, Laura's husband, taught in the theater department at Athena College. "He's home again?"

"Yes," Laura said. "We didn't tell you, but he went to Virginia on a job interview."

I suddenly lost my appetite. "And?"

Laura looked upset. "They've offered him the job, and he's thinking seriously about taking it."

TWO

My fingers ached from my tight grip on the back of the chair. I let go, pulled the chair out, and sat, all the while staring at my daughter. I tried to form a response, but my brain refused to cooperate.

Laura easily read my thoughts in my expression, however, and her tone turned defensive. "I knew you'd hate the idea, Dad." She paused, and her lower lip trembled. "I'm not crazy about it myself, but it's such a great opportunity for Frank."

I heard the whispers of doubt in my daughter's voice. For her sake, I had to keep calm and try to look at the issue with a clear mind. Diesel sensed my agitation, however, and came over to my chair. He rubbed against my legs and meowed. I stroked his head to reassure him.

When I could speak, I was pleased that my voice didn't wobble. "Tell me about this great opportunity."

Laura looked at me doubtfully, as if surprised at my seeming lack of emotion. "Well, it's a much bigger department with a bigger budget, and the salary is about twenty percent higher than what he earns here. He would have graduate students as well, and he would get to teach theater history courses. He can't do that here, at least not until Professor Thayer retires."

"Those are powerful inducements to taking the job." My heart ached at the thought of my daughter and her husband moving to Virginia not long after the birth of my first grandchild. I had so looked forward to seeing little Charles Franklin Salisbury grow up here in my hometown. I realized that was selfish, though, because Frank had his family and his career to consider, and this opportunity sounded like an excellent one. "What do you think about it?"

"Since I decided to stay at home with the baby for at least the first three years," Laura said, "the increase in salary will help make up for the loss of income." She frowned. "Frank hasn't said anything, but I know he's worried about how we'll manage on his salary alone if we stay here."

"Has he discussed this with his department head here?" I asked. "From what you and Frank have said, she thinks highly of Frank. If she wants to keep him here, maybe she can come up with more money."

"She leans on him a lot," Laura said. "They don't have an extensive budget, though. They have to get grants for most of the productions as it is, and when I quit at the end of this semester, she's not going to be allowed to rehire for my position."

My daughter sounded more upset the longer we discussed the situation. Diesel left me to go to her. She looked down at him and smiled briefly. She stroked his head for a moment, then focused her gaze on me again.

"I don't want to move, Dad. I don't want to leave you all. I'm terrified of trying to cope with a baby and finding a new place to live and packing up and moving and . . ." She threw up her hands. "But we have to think about our future, and in the long run Frank's taking this job and our moving to Virginia makes perfect sense. I'm simply feeling a bit overwhelmed."

I didn't want to add any pressure to Laura's already overburdened emotions. Frank's and her needs—present and future—came before mine. She deserved honesty, too, but honesty phrased as tactfully as I could manage. I noticed Azalea standing by with her hands clasped as if in prayer, and I hoped she was praying for guidance for us all.

"Frank is a good man." I tried to keep my voice steady, but I struggled. "I'm proud of his accomplishments and his dedication to you and the baby. If he truly thinks that taking this job in Virginia is the best course for you—and if you agree with that decision—then I will support you with all my heart." I paused. "Of course I would love to have you all here in Athena, but what I want most of all is what's best for the three of you."

"Thank you, Daddy," Laura said, her smile tremulous. "You and Mom always told Sean and me to follow our dreams, and you allowed us to make our own decisions, even when they didn't turn out so well. Frank and I still have a lot to discuss, but I didn't want to go any further before I told you."

She pushed back from the table and stood, holding on to the table as she did so. "If you'll excuse me, I need the bathroom." She moved slowly out of the room and into the hall.

Azalea and I looked at each other. I could see she was fighting back tears.

"Oh, Mr. Charlie, I can't hardly bear thinking about that child being all alone in Virginia with her baby and nobody there to look after them." She dabbed at her eyes with the hem of her apron.

I was ready to cry myself. "I can't bear it, either, but this is their decision, hers and Frank's. I know Frank will make sure that Laura and the baby have everything they need, no matter where they are."

"I'll be praying for them," Azalea said. "The Lord will provide."

I nodded, my throat too tight for me to be able to get words out. I stared down at the table through a mist of tears. Diesel meowed anxiously and put a large paw on my knee. He hated it when I was upset about anything, and this was probably the most worried or anxious I'd been in a long time.

He continued to meow and mutter while I rubbed his head. I didn't think my attentions convinced him that all was well. I certainly didn't feel it myself.

I cleared my throat and pulled my handkerchief out to wipe my eyes. "Let's try to perk up." I spoke for Azalea's benefit as much as my own. "We don't want to cause Laura any distress, and I know she's already worried about how we're taking this news."

"I'll try." Azalea moved to the sink to wash her hands and, I suspected, dab her face with cold water.

By the time Laura returned a couple of minutes later, I had better control of my emotions, and Diesel had settled down by my feet. He moved over to sit beside Laura, however, when she resumed her place at the table.

"You'd best be eating something, Mr. Charlie, before you have to go back to work." Azalea set a plate in front of me, and then placed one before Laura. "You, too, Miss Laura. You need your strength."

Laura offered a wan smile of thanks. I looked down at my

plate, my appetite nearly nonexistent. I knew, however, I needed to eat or Laura would see the lack of appetite as a symptom of distress on my part. The chicken and rice casserole, one of Azalea's standards, was a favorite of mine. I had a bite, then another, at first having to force myself, but then my appetite revived, and I ended up eating the entire serving, along with two buttered rolls and some green beans almondine.

Diesel went off to the utility room for a snack of his own. He couldn't have any of the casserole because it had onions and garlic in it, and both of those were no-no ingredients for cats. He did occasionally get treats from the table, but I was careful about their contents.

Azalea excused herself, after being sure we had everything we needed, and headed upstairs to clean.

Laura and I chatted about my job as interim director at the college library. Focusing on that, rather than her possible impending departure to Virginia, made it easier to get through the meal.

"So you really don't want the job yourself?" Laura asked. "I have to say, Dad, you seem really engaged in it, and you've been, well, I suppose *livelier* is the word I'm looking for."

I frowned. "I didn't exactly sit around like a lump all the time before I agreed to—or rather, was coerced into—taking the job."

"No," Laura said. "But you were awfully quiet a lot of the time. Unless you were involved in a murder investigation, of course. With those you're always perky." She grinned.

"I've had enough of those," I said. "I'm not anxious to repeat the experience anytime soon." Diesel chirped loudly, and Laura and I both laughed.

"Seriously, though, haven't you at least thought about the job?" Laura patted her lips with her napkin.

"Yes, I have." I hadn't discussed this yet with anyone, but I had been thinking more about the job as a permanent thing. When I first agreed to do it, I really believed I didn't want to be a full-time library director again. And that was still true, at least partly.

One part of me, however, found the challenge interesting, not only intellectually, but emotionally as well. This was my alma mater, the college at which I had spent four wonderful, happy years and for which I maintained a strong affection. When I first went off to library school in Texas I had nourished the fantasy of returning to Athena one day and working in the college library. My wife would have been happy with that, too. Then came Sean, and not long after, Laura, and we found ourselves putting down roots in Houston. There we stayed, until my wife died and Sean and Laura had left home.

I delayed my answer to Laura's question a bit too long, I supposed, because she said, "I can see you've been considering it, Dad. What would be so terrible about going back to work full-time? I'm sure they would let Diesel go to work with you still, if that's what you're worried about."

"I wouldn't take the job if he couldn't come to the office with me," I said without thinking clearly about the implications of my words.

"Aha." Laura grinned.

"All right," I said with a rueful grin. "You got me. I *am* thinking seriously about it. But I haven't officially put my name in. I have to see if they would even consider me, because I have no background in academic libraries, other than as a student. My experience was all public libraries."

"I see what you mean," Laura said. "I guess I was thinking

that running a library is, well, running a library, but there are differences whenever academia and academic types are involved."

"Yes, and some academic institutions want the head of their library, or libraries in some cases, to have a doctorate and to have publications to their credit. I have neither of those."

"That could be a problem, then," Laura said. "If they have any brains, they'll ignore that and hire you anyway. I'm sure the staff would rather have you than anyone else."

"That I don't know," I said. "They're a great group, overall, but I'm a bit of an outsider to them, in some ways." I folded my napkin and laid it by my plate after a glance at my watch. "I have to be getting back to the office, sweetheart. I'm sorry I can't stay and talk longer."

I pushed back from the table and then went to kiss her cheek. "I need to get home and take a nap," Laura said. "Frank will probably be wondering where I am."

"Drive carefully." I decided not to mention the decision about Frank's job. I knew they would let me know once they had figured it out. I felt convinced they would move. Suddenly the food refused to settle in my stomach.

"I will, Dad," Laura said. "You go on back to the library and don't worry about me. I need to ask Azalea something before I go."

"Okay. Come on, Diesel," I said. "Time to go back to work."

The cat gave Laura a few last chirps and warbles but then followed me to the back door.

On the walk back to the office, I couldn't stop thinking about this move to Virginia. I felt sure that Frank wouldn't be able to resist taking the job. He had every right to make that choice, but I wanted to be sure that Laura agreed with him.

My lunch turned to lead in my stomach as I considered what life would be like with my grandson and his parents in Virginia. I had reached the age where I hated long driving trips, but I would have to get used to them if I wanted to see my family often. They would be too busy for trips home except for the holidays.

If I seriously pursued the job at Athena, I realized, I would have a far from flexible schedule myself. I wouldn't be able to take off for Virginia when I wanted.

When Diesel and I reached the office, we found it empty. Melba must have been on her way back from lunch.

I opened my e-mail and scanned the list of new messages while Diesel circled around several times in his chair before settling down to nap. I saw that there was one from Forrest Wyatt, and I clicked on it.

As I read, that lump of lead in my stomach began to dance around, and I felt sick—and then furious. There was an attachment to the message—the résumé of one Gavin Fong, who had just today applied to be the director of the college library.

THREE

I scanned Forrest Wyatt's e-mail message a second time to make sure I hadn't misunderstood the import. No, I decided once I finished, I hadn't made a mistake. According to Forrest, Gavin Fong submitted his letter of application and résumé earlier today. Forrest asked that I make a recommendation whether this candidate should receive further consideration by the entire search committee. The next meeting was set for tomorrow morning.

My initial—but mental only—response to this request consisted of words that would have my aunt Dottie and my grandmothers rolling in their graves. I doubted Melba would be shocked. I'd heard her use the occasional earthy expression herself. I, on the other hand, rarely ever did.

Gavin Fong deserved the profanity, at least in my mind. I decided I couldn't respond right away to Forrest's message. I had to let my temper cool before I tried to frame a coherent, reasoned reply.

Diesel's loud meowing finally penetrated my focus on the e-mail on my screen. "Everything's okay, boy." I scratched his head and repeated my words. After a moment, he evidently decided things were fine. He went back to the nearby chair, jumped into it, and curled up for a nap. I knew he missed the window ledge in my office upstairs, but he had found a new favorite spot in this office.

I forced myself to open the attachment with Gavin Fong's résumé. I couldn't, in all fairness, write a response to the college president without having at least examined the man's qualifications. I couldn't simply tell Forrest I despised the man for his behavior nearly thirty years ago in graduate school.

The résumé followed a standard format, and I read through it fairly quickly, despite the fact that it was twelve pages long. To my surprise I discovered that Fong had earned a doctorate in education five years ago. I didn't recognize the name of the institution, but there were many online schools these days offering degrees of all kinds.

Over the years since our graduate school days Fong had published a number of articles and three book chapters, the most recent one dated two years ago. None of the titles sounded remotely interesting to me, but they were—mostly—published in respected library science journals.

I examined his job experience a second time. As Lisa Krause told me during our phone conversation before lunch, Fong's career began on a high note with a position at an Ivy League university library. He stayed there for nearly five years, but I noticed when I read further down the list that those five years constituted his longest tenure of any position. He changed jobs about every three years. Again, as Lisa told me, the prestige of the institutions declined steadily from the first job, even as the level of responsibility of the position rose.

Red flags went up for me whenever I saw such frequent job

changing, especially on such a consistent schedule. I counted, and Fong had worked at ten different libraries including his present one since leaving graduate school in Texas. The fact that several of the job changes resulted in higher-level positions didn't seem to me sufficient motive—not when the schools were all small, relatively unknown ones.

I, on the other hand, spent twenty-five years in the city public library system in Houston. I worked at several different branches over the course of those twenty-five years, but I ended my career as a branch manager, a position I held for seventeen years.

In my reply to Forrest Wyatt, I cited this job-hopping as a major negative. I did say that I had gone to library school with Fong but that I'd had no contact with him since. I concluded by saying that I did not consider his application worth further consideration.

I sent the message and leaned back in my chair, eyes closed. My head ached, and I tried to relax. I hadn't realized how tense I'd become over this one e-mail message.

My brain wouldn't let go of the fact that Gavin Fong applied for the position I currently held. I wasn't sure I really wanted it myself. I had doubts whether the search committee would consider me qualified for the position permanently, but I certainly didn't want Gavin Fong to get the job. If Forrest and the rest of the committee decided to ignore my recommendation and Fong somehow ended up in the position, I would retire. I wouldn't work for him. I would be able to travel back and forth to Virginia when I wanted.

I checked Fong's references again to see if any of the names rang a bell. He listed four people, three women and one man. I didn't recognize any of them.

With only a vague purpose in mind, I went through the list of Fong's publications again, more slowly this time. Most of them were coauthored, I saw, and among his coauthors I spotted two names I knew. We had all gone to library school together. Marisue Pickard and Randi Grant.

As I recalled, Marisue Pickard was my own age, early fifties. Randi Grant was possibly a decade older. Unlike Marisue and me, she had come to library school for a second career. Randi, Marisue, and I shared many classes together, along with Gavin Fong. Among the students in the program with whom I shared classes, the only two I came to know more than superficially were Randi Grant and Marisue Pickard. We kept touch in desultory fashion over the years, and I ought to have e-mail addresses for them. They had both migrated east in recent years, Randi from Colorado and Marisue from Kansas, and had ended up working together in Florida. I checked the conference program again and saw that I remembered correctly. They were giving a presentation on Sunday morning, and the affiliation listed was the same institution.

I opened the browser on my computer and typed in the URL of my webmail account. Once I logged in, I checked the address book and found the two e-mail addresses I wanted.

Then I paused. What was I doing? What was the point of e-mailing Randi and Marisue to ask for dirt on Gavin Fong? They had coauthored articles with him, one apiece, and I suspected that meant each had worked with him at the time.

I included them both in one e-mail message.

Dear Randi and Marisue, I'm delighted to see that you are both attending the SALA meeting this week. I look forward to catching up with both of you and hearing about life in Florida. Will you have time in your schedule for dinner with me? If not, I understand, but I'd love to spend an evening with y'all. I see

another of our classmates is attending—I was surprised to see
that Gavin Fong, of all people, is giving one of the keynotes. I
haven't thought about him in years. Well, safe travels, and I'll see
you later this week.

I signed it and then hit Send. That was subtle enough, I thought.
Mentioning Gavin Fong opened the door for one or both of them
to respond with a comment about him. I wondered whether their
opinions of him had changed since library school, enough so that
they had felt comfortable coauthoring articles with him.

Time to focus on the job the college was paying me to do. I had a
stack of invoices to approve, and I might as well get on with it. I hated
dealing with invoices and spreadsheets, though I had done so years
ago. Staring at the stack of paper on my desk, I wondered again why
I was tempted to apply to have this job on a permanent basis.

After I finished with the invoices—signing them and checking
their amounts against the spreadsheets—I glanced at my webmail
account, still open on the browser.

I had a new message. Marisue Pickard had replied to my
e-mail.

Charlie! Great hearing from you. Of course Randi and I would
love to have dinner with you. Lots of things to catch up about,
and we want to hear all about that cat of yours. He sounds
adorable. A friend of mine has a Maine Coon, and she's the
sweetest thing. How about dinner on Friday night? That should
work for both of us. Love, Marisue

Two smiley face icons followed her name.
Another e-mail, again from Marisue, appeared in my inbox.

Re: the matter of GF, why would you even want to think about that creep? Keep your mind clean. Randi and I have a few things we could tell you. Maybe, with enough wine at dinner, we will.

That was intriguing, I thought. There was obviously dirt, and I didn't think I'd have to ply Marisue and Randi with much wine before they started dishing on Gavin Fong.

I shut down the browser and checked my work e-mail.

Three new messages, and one of them came from Gavin Fong. Why on earth was he e-mailing me? Probably something to do with the job, I supposed.

I made a face at the screen and clicked on his message to open it.

Dear Charlie, been a long time, hasn't it? Easy to forget certain things after all these years, but yet, some things do tend to stick with you. I have absolutely clear memories of you and our interactions—one in particular. We'll have to chat about it when I arrive in Athena. I'm coming in early to have a look around your campus. I'll drop by your office—which I hope will soon be my office. I'm ready to get out of this hick town to a school with the kind of reputation Athena College has. I'm sure I can count on your support, right? You certainly wouldn't want to derail my chances, I'm sure. Especially once we've had a chance to discuss old times, eh?

The message ended with the standard professional institutional signature.

Fong's message both irritated and confused me. I wasn't surprised by the sheer gall of his words. They were pure Gavin Fong. His assumption that I would support his candidacy for the position was ludicrous. As for talking over old times, I couldn't remember any that he and I had shared that were worth discussing.

What the heck was he hinting at? His e-mail could be interpreted as blackmail. Or was it extortion? But what could he possibly have to use as ammunition to force me to support him for this job?

I mulled this over for a few minutes, thinking back to the events of over twenty-five years ago. I had tried to keep out of his way as much as possible, because in those days I hadn't yet learned to manage my temper effectively. My late wife, Jackie, whom I married right after graduation from Athena College, helped me learn to hold back and not pop off without thinking about what I was saying or doing.

Jackie . . . I frowned. Something about Jackie, me, and Gavin Fong. What was it?

Then the memory came flooding back, and I felt my stomach twist into a knot.

FOUR

I hated recalling the stupid things I did in my youth because of my quick temper. I prided myself on the fact that I had matured enough to master my feelings before I turned thirty. I still got angry on occasion, as did most human beings. The difference was, I could keep that anger from erupting into intemperate speech or action—almost all the time.

In my early twenties, however, I had not yet learned the lessons I needed to learn. The incident with Gavin Fong gave me one of those lessons, and my stomach knotted with embarrassment from simply recalling what happened.

While I worked on my master's degree in library science, my wife, Jackie, worked on a master's degree in history part-time. She taught as a substitute in the local public school system to help offset expenses not covered by our savings, student loans, and my own part-time job at the university library. I spent every day on campus while Jackie attended classes twice a week. On the days she came to campus, we lunched together.

The incident with Gavin Fong occurred on one such day. I was running late that day, and by the time I reached the student union where we met, I found Jackie in conversation with Gavin Fong. He had pestered her with his attentions before, but in the past I had been able to laugh it off. I knew Jackie found him amusing, in a creepy sort of way, and he posed no threat to our marriage. That day, as I approached the table in the crowded room, I saw him put his hand on her arm and pull her toward him. She tried to jerk her arm away, but he held on.

I already disliked Gavin Fong intensely for his pseudo-intellectual superiority and his rude comments about our professors and their intelligence. I had managed to keep my hands to myself on those occasions. That day, however, I felt no such restraint.

In my memories of the incident, a roaring in my head blocked out other sounds. I don't think I'd ever been so angry in my life. I dimly remembered dropping my lunch bag and briefcase on the table before I grabbed Gavin Fong by his hair and jerked him away from my wife.

He screamed and let go as he found himself stumbling backward into the next table. Before he could recover, I had my face in his. I think I said to him, *If I ever catch you near my wife again, I'll beat you into a bloody pulp.* Or some similar macho threat.

Several of the young women seated nearby clapped, and one of them poured a cold drink over Gavin's head. He sputtered as the liquid and ice hit him, and then he yelped when he slipped and landed hard on his rear.

I stood over him and glowered. He looked up at me with

loathing—and fear. He never said a word in response. He got up, shot me the bird, and walked away.

After that he never came near Jackie, and he steered a wide berth around me. Jackie scolded me later for overreacting, but I wasn't repentant at the time. I knew she tried her best to stop him, but he was too aggressive. My temper took over, and I let it. I felt embarrassed later on by my own aggression and violent behavior. I could have handled the situation more calmly, but I didn't. Lesson learned, however.

I wondered what Gavin thought he had to gain by threatening to reveal this incident to Forrest Wyatt and members of the search committee if I didn't recommend him for the job. Did he seriously think I would let that stop me from giving my honest opinion of him?

If he did think that, then he would be deeply disappointed. The incident didn't reflect well on either of us, but I wouldn't shy away from telling my side of the story. I certainly ought to have more credibility with the search committee, most of whom I had known for some years, than a rank outsider like Gavin Fong could.

I was tempted to reply to Gavin's e-mail with two words. The first word would be a verb in the imperative—and not a nice verb—followed by the word *you*. That was my temper's idea. I knew better though I was itching to do it. He brought out the worst in me.

My response to Gavin could wait. I looked at the other two messages that arrived along with his. One of them was from Randi Grant, and I clicked on it.

Charlie my darling, how the heck are you? Marisue and I are delighted that we'll be seeing you soon. It's been way too long.

Dinner would be great. You'd better know a fabulous restaurant, one with a superb wine list. You know the two of us love us some wine.

Now, about that waste of space otherwise known as Gavin Fong, I will have plenty to say. In person, though, not in an e-mail. Au revoir, *cher* Charlie!

I couldn't help but grin while I read Randi's message. I could hear her voice in my head. I couldn't wait to see her and Marisue again—and not because they had dirt on Gavin.

The other e-mail came from a researcher in Louisiana who wanted to come to the archive to delve into the personal papers of several Athena families prominent during the antebellum and post–Civil War years. He gave two sets of dates when he could make the trip and asked if I could accommodate the request.

The dates were for two-week stretches, one in early July, the other in early August. While I served as interim library director the archives were closed. I had no staff member to spare to open the archives for scholars. I had three vacant positions that were on hold until a new director was hired, and those openings left two areas understaffed. The proposed dates were three to four months away, however, and by then I could be back at my desk upstairs. I knew Forrest Wyatt wanted a permanent director in place before the beginning of the fall semester, but if I got the job, the archives position would have to be filled.

I hated to deny the researcher. I was familiar with the collections he wanted to examine, and I knew they were both rich with details of local history and daily life in Athena for a period of over sixty years. After mulling it over a few minutes, I wrote back to the man that the August dates would be best. Somehow I would see that he had the access he needed, no matter what happened with the director's job. Laura's baby would be close to two months old by then, and she and Frank would probably be in Virginia.

Depressed by that thought, I leaned back in the chair and stared at the window across the room. I had been able to avoid thinking about Laura and Frank leaving Athena for a while, but now I could think of nothing else. Had Laura discussed this with Sean before she told me? Most likely she had, because she and her brother were close and always had been, even during the difficult teenage years. I knew Sean would hate to see her move, even though he would have more than enough to occupy his thoughts with the impending birth of his own child later in the fall.

Six years ago I thought I had lost my daughter to Hollywood forever. A talented actress, she left to find her future in California at twenty-two. The first couple of years brought little success, but a small guest part in a long-running drama gave her the foothold she needed. The jobs turned up more frequently, and she had a respectable body of work by the time she came back to Athena some eighteen months ago for a one-semester teaching gig. After meeting Frank Salisbury, a young assistant professor in the theater department, and then getting married, Laura had decided to stay in Athena. The lure of Hollywood stardom, so difficult to achieve for even the most talented, took second place to a new husband and a new career.

I had never really considered the idea that they might leave. Both she and Frank seemed content at Athena College. But circumstances changed, as did career paths. Faced with a tempting offer, Frank had every right to accept it. Taking Laura and my grandson with him.

My gaze dropped to the nearby chair where Diesel napped. As if he sensed my focus on him, he opened his eyes, blinked, and yawned. Then he stretched, his front legs extended off the seat of the chair that was barely large enough to contain him when he curled up. He offered me a couple of interrogatory chirps and a meow, and I smiled at him. He slipped down from the chair and padded over to me. He climbed into my lap and butted his head against my chin. I stroked his head and murmured to him what a sweet boy he was. He meowed again and butted my chin when I stopped my attentions to his head. I resumed, and he began to purr, that loud, rumbling sound that had earned him his name.

I realized I couldn't allow myself to wallow in self-pity over my daughter's possible move to another state. No good would come of it, and I had more than enough to do to keep up with the demands of the interim director job. I gave Diesel a last few strokes on his head, then informed him gently that I needed to get back to work.

He meowed once in seeming protest, but he climbed down from my lap and headed to the nearby closet where I had installed a litter box and food and drink bowls for him. I heard him lapping water as I turned my attention back to my desk and the work that awaited me.

My phone rang, and I picked up the handset. "Yes?"

Melba said, "I've got Lisa Krause on line one. She needs to speak with you for a minute."

"Sure." I punched the button. "Hi, Lisa. What's up?"

"Charlie, I hate to do this, but I got an e-mail a few minutes ago from one of the out-of-state librarians who was going to be moderating one of the panel discussions. She's had a family emergency and can't come. Could you possibly take over for her? I can brief you on the panel and the participants later. It's on Saturday morning."

I had no desire to participate in a panel discussion, even as a moderator, but I could hear the tiredness and the frustration in Lisa's voice.

"I'll be happy to do it for you," I said.

"Oh, that's wonderful. I can't tell you how relieved I am. The panel's on cataloging in the academic library, so I think you'll find it interesting. I can come by later this afternoon, if that's convenient."

"Sure. I'll be in the office until five or five thirty."

Lisa thanked me again, and I ended the call.

A panel on cataloging ought to be interesting, I thought. I delved among the papers on my desk to look at the details of the session. Saturday morning, Lisa had said. I flipped a couple of pages, and there it was. The title of the session was *Cataloging for the Digital World: Absolute Necessity or Waste of Time?*

I frowned. I didn't care for the title. I considered cataloging still a vital part of the *digital world*. The discussion ought to prove lively, I figured. I wondered who might be arguing that it was a waste of time.

My gaze lighted on the list of participants. I dropped the schedule on my desk and closed my eyes. Gavin Fong was one of the panel members.

FIVE

Two afternoons later, I stood on the dais of the Farrington House ballroom with Lisa Krause waiting for Forrest Wyatt to arrive. The conference started in five minutes, and Forrest had a welcome speech to deliver. If he didn't show, I imagined I would have to fill in, and I hadn't prepared for such a situation. I had my two minutes and nothing more.

"I'm sure he'll be here," Lisa said in an undertone. "His administrative assistant assured me that she would let me know immediately if something came up and he couldn't get here."

"He's cutting it too close for my comfort." I shifted my weight from one leg to the other. My collar felt tight, and I fiddled with my tie. *Should I loosen it before I had to speak? Or would I look sloppy if I did that?*

I had a horror of appearing unkempt in front of a crowd like this, even in these days of increasing informality of dress no matter the occasion. My parents had been unfailingly particular in their dress for any kind of public event, and that habit was too ingrained for me to ignore it. So I stood on the dais in my best suit and tie, shoes freshly polished, and hair cut the day before. I knew I must look presentable because Lisa complimented me when I found her several minutes ago, waiting to mount the dais.

"Relax, Charlie, here he comes." Lisa nodded toward the center aisle of chairs that occupied much of the ballroom floor.

Tall, thin, dark of hair, and tanned of skin, Forrest Wyatt looked every inch the successful executive he was. He had been at the helm of Athena College for nearly two years, and he seemed to have a magic touch with potential donors. The endowment was growing, and alumni and board alike were happy with his leadership.

He greeted Lisa and me with an affable smile. "I'm always worried I'll forget at the last minute, right before I start talking, exactly who the audience is and give the wrong speech." His eyes twinkled, and Lisa and I chuckled in response. He checked his watch and glanced at Lisa. She nodded, then stepped to the podium.

"Good afternoon, ladies and gentlemen." Lisa paused to let her gaze sweep the room. "I am Lisa Krause, head of access services at the Athena College Library and chair of the local arrangements committee for this meeting. It is my great pleasure to introduce the president of the college, Dr. Forrest Wyatt, who is here to offer you an official greeting." She briefly listed Forrest's academic credentials and past experiences, then stepped aside.

Forrest moved to the podium. After thanking Lisa for the introduction, he faced the audience. "We at Athena College are delighted to welcome the Southern Academic Library Association Annual Conference back to Athena. Libraries are an integral part of any institution of higher learning, and over the next few days

I know you will be discussing the exciting changes and trends in academic libraries."

He continued in this vein for about five minutes more, and his talk evinced more knowledge of those exciting changes and trends in academic libraries than I realized he possessed. I hadn't briefed him, and thus I was duly impressed by his comments.

His welcome complete, he said, "It is now my pleasure to introduce the interim director of the Athena College Library, Mr. Charles Harris. Mr. Harris has recently been guiding the library ably through a period of transition, and we are fortunate to have a man of his experience and knowledge serving in this capacity."

I imagined that many in the audience were well aware of the events that led up to the *period of transition*, and, ever the diplomat, Forrest put the best spin possible on it.

Suddenly I realized Forrest had stepped back from the podium, and I stepped up to the microphone. "Thank you, President Wyatt, for those kind remarks. On behalf of the faculty and staff of the Athena College Library, I am delighted to welcome you all to the elegant, historical Farrington House. I know Ms. Krause and her committee have worked hard to make this a successful event. We have an exciting slate of presentations and panel discussions ahead of us, and I trust we will all come away from the conference energized by fresh ideas and new connections. We hope you will find time to visit our beautiful campus and the library." I smiled and stepped away from the microphone.

I made it through the short speech without stumbling, even as I gazed out at the blur of faces, some two hundred twenty-odd of them. Lisa murmured, "Well done, Charlie," and took my place at the microphone. She made a couple of announcements, and we were done.

Forrest made a speedy exit from the room. No doubt he had another meeting to attend. I would have to remember to thank him for the fine welcome he had extended to the conference.

I walked down the three steps from the podium to the ballroom floor and moved a couple of feet away. I needed to be back in the office by five to pick up Diesel. He stayed with Melba this afternoon while I came to the hotel to attend the opening of the conference. He protested when I left him, even though he loved Melba. I had to assure him a couple of times that I would be coming back for him before he stopped meowing and chirping indignantly.

"He's got a sassy mouth on him." Melba had grinned at me as I eased out of her office to head to the parking lot behind the building.

The drive back to campus would take all of seven or eight minutes, and I had plenty of time to look for Randi and Marisue before I needed to leave.

I glanced around the room, searching for them. I had hoped they would come find me, but at the moment I didn't see them anywhere. I also hadn't spotted Gavin Fong, and that was fine with me. The longer I went without contact with the toad, the happier I would be.

"Hi, there, Mr. Harris."

I turned to see a tall, willowy blonde approach me. She appeared to be in her midsixties and wore a tailored suit in a shade of aquamarine that suited her figure and coloring admirably. I had never seen her before that I could recall.

She extended a hand, and I took it. "Good afternoon." I smiled. "I must apologize. If we have met before, I'm afraid I don't remember it."

The stranger laughed, a pleasant, throaty sound. "No need to apologize. We've not met before. I'm Nancy Dunlap. I'm director of the library at a school in Louisiana. I was hoping to meet you, and to meet that wonderful Maine Coon cat of yours. I've heard about him, you see."

"I'm afraid he doesn't do well in large crowds," I replied. "He's back in the office with my administrative assistant. He's quite friendly, but too many people at once tend to overwhelm him."

Nancy Dunlap inclined her head. "Of course, and I should have realized that had I given it much thought. I was excited about the opportunity. Both of you are apparently rather well-known here in Athena."

Oh dear, I thought. *She's heard about the murders I've been involved in and is going to pump me for details.*

I must have betrayed my dismay in my expression. She waved a hand in my direction. "No, no, not to worry. I'm not going to ask about anything to do with murder. Not my cup of tea."

"Thank you," I said. "I must admit to being curious as to how you heard about Diesel."

She laughed again. "One of my dearest friends lives here in Athena. Has done for many years. I don't imagine you know her. Sandra Wallesch. We exchange letters regularly, and she's written about you and your cat."

I searched my memory, but I couldn't recall ever having met the woman.

Nancy Dunlap continued before I could reply. "I believe she is a friend of a friend of yours. A woman named Melba Gilley."

I smiled. "I don't believe I've ever met your friend, though Melba might have mentioned her to me at some point. I've known Melba since childhood, and she has so many friends it's impossible to keep track of them all."

I was about to continue with an invitation for Nancy Dunlap to drop by my office tomorrow morning, but before I could get the words out, she scowled. What had I done to offend her?

"You'll have to excuse me," she said in a rush of words. "I see someone coming toward us that I have no desire whatsoever to talk to. I'm sure I'll run into you again."

With that she turned and hurried away. I glanced in the direction she had been looking before her departure, and I spotted Gavin Fong loping toward me.

I was tempted to walk off as if I hadn't seen him, but I was too late. Seconds later he halted about two feet from me. He was as reed thin as he was the last time I saw him, over twenty-five years ago. He blinked at me through thick glasses, and his hair, once jet-black, was now threaded with gray. His skin looked sallow and unhealthy, and his shoulders hunched forward like those of a much older man. His neck and head jutted forward as though he were a turtle. I had to look down to meet his gaze. He seemed to have shrunk a couple of inches since I'd last seen him. Maybe it was the atrocious posture, probably the result of too many hours spent peering at a computer screen. He had been more interested in computers than in his fellow human beings back when I knew him, and I doubted that had changed in the years since.

His baleful gaze didn't bother me. He pushed his glasses up the bridge of his nose with a middle finger. I wanted to roll my eyes at such a childish display, but I refrained. I waited for him to speak.

"Where's your wife? I figured she'd be here with you." His voice still sounded high and whiny.

"Dead."

That disconcerted him. Either his acting had improved significantly, or he honestly hadn't been aware of Jackie's death several years ago.

"Uh, sorry." Then Gavin mumbled for a moment, and I couldn't make out the words.

"Sorry, I didn't catch that," I said.

Gavin shrugged. "I wasn't talking to you."

Had he said a brief prayer? I wondered. *Or was he responding to a voice in his head?*

I started to edge away from him, and he held out a hand, almost—but not quite—touching my arm. "Hang on," he said.

"What is it you want, Gavin?" I knew I sounded irritable, but at the moment I didn't care whether anyone overheard us.

"You never did respond to my e-mail." Gavin blinked at me, his eyes eerily magnified by his lenses. "You aren't qualified to keep the job permanently. You don't have any publications to your credit that I could find. Your background is public libraries. You're simply not a worthy candidate."

"Unlike you?" I invested those two words with every ounce of sarcasm I could muster, but I had forgotten how oblivious Gavin was to such responses.

"Most assuredly." He began to recite the positions he had held and tick them off on his fingers. I waited until he was nearly done before I interrupted.

"Do you *seriously* think a school like Athena College is going to be impressed with your pathetic record of moving from one job to another every three years? It's painfully obvious to anyone with even a quarter of a brain that you weren't fit for the positions you managed to wangle yourself into somehow." I paused for a breath. "You're either grossly incompetent or impossible to get along with, or perhaps both, and I'll be skating on ice in the underworld before you get anywhere *near* the job."

Even a man as obtuse as Gavin couldn't help but understand me. I had obviously managed to penetrate the fog of self-importance that clung to him. He scowled, took one step back, and swung at me.

I had anticipated him, though, and easily stepped away. He came at me again, and once more I moved out of reach. The third time he tried to hit me, I'd had enough. My temper took over, and I decked him with a swift right to the jaw.

SIX

Luckily for both of us, I hadn't hit Gavin as hard as I could have. He landed on his rear, his glasses askew but still on his head. I stood looking down at him, watching lest he try to come after me again.

As the moments passed and he stayed sitting on the floor, my temper began to cool. I started to feel sorry for him. I had spoken harshly and provocatively, and I realized belatedly I had baited him, hoping he would attack. Well, my temper had won that round.

"Sorry, Gavin, I shouldn't have done that." I extended a hand to help him up.

Instead of taking the proffered hand, he scooted away from me, still on his rear, until he was several feet back from where I stood. I shrugged and watched while he slowly got to his feet, after first having straightened his glasses.

"Oh, Gavin, you poor thing." A woman rushed up to Gavin and clutched his arm. "Are you all right? I saw the whole thing."

Gavin rubbed his jaw and glared balefully at me. "I'm okay,

Maxine." He brushed her arm away. "I'm glad you saw this unprovoked attack on me. You can be my witness when I bring charges for assault against this ape."

"But you tried to hit him first." The woman, who looked to be about forty-five, hovered anxiously around Gavin. She made no further attempt to touch him, however. "That's not going to look good, and you know what Dr. Elmwood told you the last time you tried to hit someone."

Interesting, I thought. How many other incidents like this had Gavin been involved in recently?

"Yeah, yeah. Elmwood is an ass," Gavin said. "I can't help it if I try to defend myself against Neanderthals all the time. I'm getting so freaking tired of these threats and attacks, I don't know what I'm going to do." He took a couple of steps toward me. "You can rest assured, Charlie, I'll be taking this up with the president of Athena *and* with the local authorities. Maxine is my witness."

He strode away with the rather dowdily dressed Maxine right behind him.

I didn't bother calling after him with a response. There was no point.

After a moment I became uneasily aware that a number of people nearby stood watching me. One of them, a bald, tall, muscular young man who sported double earrings in each ear as well as heavily tattooed forearms, came up to me.

He extended a hand. "Bob Coben, Mr. Harris. I am happy to shake your hand. I work with Dr. Fong, and I can't tell you how many times I've wanted to do exactly what you just did. I'll be happy to serve as a witness for you, that he swung at you three times before you retaliated. Plus I'll be happy to tell whoever it is what a complete and utter jerk he is."

I shook his hand. He had a firm grip, and I tried not to wince. "Thank you, Mr. Coben. I appreciate that. I provoked him, however, so it really was my fault."

Coben shrugged. "I didn't hear what you said to him, but frankly, it doesn't take much to provoke him. He's always convinced everyone is out to get him, and he lashes out all the time. He's lucky he's still employed. Actually, the word going around on campus is that he's gone as soon as the semester's over. Our president loathes him, just like everyone else who's ever spent more than five minutes with him."

Another person approached while Bob was talking. A woman of average height, she sported dark, curly locks and a warm smile. She extended her hand.

"Hello, Mr. Harris, I'm Cathleen Matera. Sorry, but I couldn't help overhearing what you two were discussing. I also saw what happened and would be happy to be a witness for you, if necessary."

I shook her hand and returned her smile. "Thank you, Ms. Matera. I regret I displayed such poor behavior in front of you all. Sometimes my temper gets the better of me."

Cathleen Matera laughed. "I worked with Gavin in Colorado, mercifully for me only for about three years. We had a party after he left our library."

Bob Coben snorted with laughter. "I'm looking forward to a party like that myself."

"I went to library school with him, lo these many years ago," I said. "He never endeared himself to his fellow students, I have to say. It's rather sad to see he has never learned to get along with people."

"He is rather pathetic," Cathleen Matera said. "He is his own worst enemy, of course, but he's such a narcissist he will never understand that."

"Yeah, he's always frustrated that the rest of the world can't see and appreciate his genius." Bob Coben ran a hand over his smooth pate. "I have to go now, got to meet someone for dinner, Mr. Harris, but don't forget my offer." He dug in the pocket of his jeans and pulled out a business card.

I accepted the card and thanked him. He nodded and sauntered off. I turned to Cathleen Matera, who was digging in her handbag. She, too, pulled out a business card for me.

"I appreciate this," I told her. "I'm sorry, but I don't have any cards with me."

"Not to worry." Her cheeks dimpled when she smiled, I noticed. "I think I know where to find you. I need to get going myself. Talk to you later."

As she walked away I realized the small crowd that had been watching us had dispersed. I felt considerably relieved. I hoped I didn't have to talk to anyone else for a while about my poor behavior.

I headed for the door, intent on getting back to the office, collecting Diesel, and going home. I was surprised that I hadn't seen either Marisue or Randi, but perhaps they had decided to skip the welcome. There was a reception later that I had to attend. I had enough time to get Diesel home and freshen up, however, before I had to be back for it. I'd rather stay home, of course, but duty called.

Yet another reason to rethink my interest in the job as a permanent part of my life.

I managed to reach my car without being further detained. During the short drive back to campus, I thought about Gavin's threat to denounce me to Forrest Wyatt and the *local authorities*. Would he really follow through on that? He well might, I decided.

He was probably vengeful enough. If he did, I would turn the matter over to my lawyer, my son, Sean. He could handle it. I refused to worry about it for now.

Diesel and I made it home shortly after five. I made sure he had fresh food and water, and I left him happily munching his favorite dry food while I went upstairs to undress and freshen up.

I decided a hot shower was in order, and when I finished I found Diesel snoozing on the bed. I sat down by him for a few minutes to cool down before getting dressed. He turned on his back for me to rub his belly. He purred while I did so.

"I've got to go out again in a little while," I said. "You're going to have to stay here, though." He meowed, and I felt sure he understood me. "Stewart and Haskell are going to be here with you, though, and Dante, too." Dante was Stewart's little poodle. He and Diesel were good friends. "They'll take care of you until I get home again." Diesel meowed again while I continued to stroke.

Stewart Delacorte, a chemistry professor at Athena, and his partner, Haskell Bates, a deputy in the Athena County Sheriff's Department, occupied an apartment on the third floor of my house. Haskell had only recently moved in, and I frankly felt more secure having both him and Stewart in the house with me, now that both my children were married and living in homes of their own. My young boarder, Justin Wardlaw, would soon be back after a semester in England. He had one final year at Athena, and then he would no doubt move on. I would certainly miss him, and so would Diesel.

That thought led me back to the possibility that Laura and Frank and my grandson might be headed for Virginia over the summer. I really didn't want to think about that at the moment. It was too depressing.

I forced my mind back to the conference and my responsibilities. I looked forward even less than before to that cataloging panel on Saturday morning, now that I'd had a run-in with Gavin. Having to sit with him on a panel wasn't a prospect calculated to fill me with anything but disquiet, not to mention loathing. I had no choice, however. I had to hope that he wouldn't kick up a ruckus when he saw me there.

Perhaps I should discuss this with Lisa Krause, tell her about the incident, and help her find someone to take my place on Saturday morning. Yes, I decided, that was what I needed to do. No point in exacerbating an already tense situation by putting Gavin and me together in a public setting again.

Diesel tapped my hand—the hand that had stopped stroking his belly. I smiled and rubbed a little more. "You've had enough of that," I told the cat. "Time for me to get dressed, though I really don't want to put on another suit and tie and go out again." My dry-cleaning bills had gone up considerably, and I was at the point of having to buy a couple of new suits. Not to mention a few new ties. I had given most of mine away once I retired from the public library, and now I had only three. And maybe a few new dress shirts to go along with the new suits and ties. I could probably use another pair of shoes as well.

I sighed. This job was getting expensive. I gave Diesel one last rub and a scratch of the chin, and went to finish dressing.

Downstairs, Diesel and I found Stewart and Haskell in the kitchen. Haskell sat at the table, sipping a beer, while Stewart worked at the stove, adding ingredients to a large pot. Dante, his poodle, left his side and came to greet Diesel with a few licks. Diesel tolerated them for a moment, then put a paw on the dog's head to stop him. He moved away from Dante and went to sit beside Haskell's chair. Dante turned his attention back to Stewart, his eyes riveted on the stove.

"What's for dinner?" I asked, chuckling at the two animals.

"Chili," Stewart said. "There will be plenty of leftovers. Sorry you can't stay and eat with us tonight."

"Me, too," I said. "I'm sure it will be much better than the finger food they'll serve at the reception. I'll probably help myself to a bowl or two later on when I get home."

Diesel meowed loudly, and Haskell cracked a grin. He reached out to rub the cat's head. "Better set aside a dish for Mr. Big here, too."

"No, he can't have any," Stewart and I said in unison.

"Why not?" Haskell asked.

"Onions," Stewart said. "They're toxic to cats and dogs both, so Dante can't have any, either."

"I forgot that." Haskell downed the rest of his beer. "I guess I'm not used to having these four-legged critters around much. My dad was allergic to cats, and my mama was afraid of dogs, so we didn't have any around when I was growing up."

"That's a shame," I said. "They're a lot of company."

"I'm getting used to it." Haskell grinned. "Luckily for me, I'm not allergic or afraid."

"You certainly are getting used to it." Stewart turned and waved the ladle in his partner's direction. "I'm not getting rid of my dog for anyone."

Haskell looked at me, one eyebrow raised. "Guess I know where I stand now."

I grinned. "Never try to come between a man and his dog. Or his cat."

Haskell laughed, and Stewart rolled his eyes at him.

My cell phone rang, and I pulled it out of my pocket. I recognized the number. Forrest Wyatt's office. I had a sick feeling I knew why he was calling.

"Hello." I identified myself, then waited for Forrest to speak.

Instead of Forrest, however, it was his administrative assistant, Margaret Foxwell. "Hello, Charlie. Sorry to bother you this evening, but Dr. Wyatt needs to see you in his office first thing tomorrow morning. Something serious has come up, he says. Can you be here at eight thirty?"

SEVEN

||||||||||||||||||||||||||||||||

"Yes, I can be there. Eight thirty," I repeated to let Margaret Foxwell know I had the correct time.

"Thank you. See you then."

She ended the call before I had the chance to ask her why Forrest wanted to see me. I figured it had to be about the incident with Gavin Fong, but I could hope that it was something else entirely. Foolish, of course.

"What's wrong? From the look on your face, it's bad news." Stewart frowned at me.

I stuck the phone back in my pocket. "Forrest Wyatt wants to see me in his office first thing in the morning."

"Uh-oh, what have you done?" Stewart waggled the ladle in my direction, and Dante barked.

"Something really stupid." I gave him and Haskell the bare outlines of my fight with Gavin Fong and a brief history of what led up to it. When I finished, they exchanged a glance, and then both started laughing.

"What's so funny?" I asked, nettled by their response.

"I'd give anything to have seen you deck that guy." Stewart shook his head, still grinning. "I'm surprised at you, Charlie Harris. I never suspected you of being a brawler. What are your children going to say when they hear about it?"

"And you soon to be a grandpa." Haskell smirked at me.

"Ha-ha." I felt like a complete idiot now. "I'm glad I could entertain you both." I immediately regretted my snide comment. "Sorry, guys, I don't know what's come over me."

"You're not the first guy who's taken a swing at a jerk," Haskell said. "He might press charges, but you've got a good lawyer. Sean will take care of it."

"I know it's embarrassing, Charlie, and we didn't help by laughing." Stewart appeared contrite. "But Haskell's right. I don't imagine Forrest is going to fire you over this. Admonish you, maybe, but once you tell him the background to all this, I think he'll be understanding. He's not a jerk himself."

"No, you're right," I said, feeling a bit relieved. "Still, I should have had better control of my temper. There's just something about that guy that really gets under my skin."

"Yeah, I know the type," Haskell said. "Guys like that don't have a clue how obnoxious they are. Nothing is ever their fault. Somebody's always got it in for them because they're smarter than everyone else."

"That's Gavin all right." I shook my head. "I'll be happy when this conference is over, and he's gone back to Podunk, Alabama. Well, thanks, guys, for looking after Diesel. I need to get going."

Diesel and Dante had curled up together near the stove to keep a close watch on Stewart. I gave them both a few head scratches before I left. Diesel meowed when I headed for the back door but otherwise didn't appear overly upset at being left with his buddy Dante and the two human cat-sitters.

During the drive back to the Farrington House for the reception I counseled myself to steer clear of Gavin Fong this evening. Surely in a crowd of a couple hundred people I could manage that. Surely he would be as eager to stay away from me.

I found a spot for my car in the parking lot behind the hotel and made my way inside through a back entrance. As I approached the foyer to the ballroom I spotted Lisa Krause in conversation with a tall woman with light brown hair. I recognized her as Donna Evans, the catering manager at the hotel. As I neared them, Donna nodded and moved toward the closed ballroom doors. She opened one and slipped inside. Lisa turned in my direction. She came toward me with a tired smile.

"Hi, Charlie, you just getting here?"

I nodded. "I went home to freshen up and change after the opening ceremony. How are things going?"

"As far as the food and the service for the reception, everything is fine. You know how efficient and well organized Donna is." Lisa sounded pleased, but she suddenly frowned.

"Yes, I do know," I said. "But something seems to be bothering you. What is it?"

"I'll give you one guess." Lisa sighed.

"Gavin Fong."

She nodded. "He's a gigantic pain in the derriere, that's for sure. He tracked me down about thirty minutes ago with a couple of complaints. The refrigerator in his room wasn't working properly, and one of the lights was on the fritz and kept blinking on and off. I think he expected me to attend to them personally."

"Instead of simply notifying someone at the front desk?"

"Yes. I told him that's what he should have done because I am neither an electrician nor a refrigerator repair person. Then he had the nerve to tell me it was *my* job to deal with menials like repairmen, that *he* had far more important things to do. Then he just turned and walked off." She made a growling sound. "If I'd had something to hit him over the head with, I swear I would have done it right then and there."

"I've tried it, and it doesn't work," I said in a rueful tone.

"What do you mean?" Lisa asked.

I told her briefly about the incident earlier in the afternoon. She giggled when I finished. "Oh, Charlie, I'd give anything to have seen that. I may end up doing it myself before this conference is over."

"I wouldn't recommend it," I said. "I've been called to a meeting first thing in the morning with Forrest Wyatt, and I have no doubt what it's about."

"He's certainly not going to fire you over this," Lisa said. "At least, I don't think he would. I'll be happy to tell Dr. Wyatt what an absolute jerk Gavin Fong is."

"I don't know that Forrest would consider that a mitigating factor," I replied. "And, really, it isn't. I am the one at fault, and I'll simply have to deal with the consequences." I shrugged. "Now, enough about that. How is everything else going, these annoyances aside?"

"Fine as far as I can tell," Lisa said. "Of course there really isn't much going on this evening other than the reception. When the presentations and everything start tomorrow, that will be the test. I'm always sure I've overlooked something, but the committee is great, and everyone is working hard to make sure things run smoothly."

While Lisa and I were talking, people continued to come into the ballroom foyer. The noise level rose steadily as people chatted, and the room grew more and more crowded.

"I'm sure it will be a great conference." I checked my watch. A few minutes before seven. "I guess the doors will be opening soon."

Lisa nodded. "Donna went in to have a last check. She's a stickler for the schedule, so I don't have to worry about complaints that the reception started late. You know how librarians are about their free food."

We shared a laugh over that. We both knew all the attendees would be on tight expense budgets, and any meal they could get for free was all to the good. Institutional travel budgets had been cut way back in recent years, and most librarians were lucky to receive funding to attend one professional meeting a year.

The ballroom doors opened promptly at seven, as Lisa predicted. People began flowing inside. Lisa and I held back for a moment to let the crowd spread out before we entered.

The catering staff had set up five stations around the room where attendees could line up to fill their plates, and there were three bar stations as well. The vendors exhibiting at the meeting contributed to the expenses for this reception, and I spotted a couple of the sales representatives I had met since taking over the interim director job.

Lisa excused herself to circulate through the crowd. I knew she wanted to make sure the attendees were happy with the food and drink on offer. I joined the line at one of the food stations, picked up a plate, napkin, and plastic fork, and surveyed the options on the table. There were several kinds of hors d'oeuvres, and I loaded my plate with enough to sate my appetite for the next hour or so. Next I went to one of the cash bars and bought myself an expensive glass of diet soda. I found a spot next to the wall with a table in front of it, set down my drink, and prepared to nosh.

I polished off about half the plateful before I heard a voice call my name above the muted roar of conversation in the ballroom. I glanced around in an effort to spot the person trying to hail me, and after a moment there emerged through the crowd two women, one short with white blond hair, the other of average height with brown curls streaked with blond highlights.

I set down my plate, wiped my hands quickly, then stepped forward to enfold Marisue Pickard and Randi Grant in a hug. After a moment I released them and stepped back. Marisue, the shorter of the two and as rake thin as ever, wore a severely tailored navy skirt and jacket, relieved only by a crisp white blouse. This look was a far cry from the casual hippie style she had favored in graduate school. Randi, taller and plumper than Marisue, sported more relaxed attire, a peasant-style skirt and blouse, a large-beaded necklace, and numerous bracelets on each wrist.

"It's wonderful to see you both," I said. "I'm surprised I didn't see you earlier, though, at the welcome. Still, I'm just glad you're here."

Marisue and Randi exchanged a glance and laughed. "We've been to enough of those *welcome to our fair city* things," Randi said airily. "Frankly, I was more interested in a nap after we drove nearly eight hours to get here."

"I don't blame you." I patted her arm. "I hate driving long distances these days."

Marisue snorted. "Don't let her kid you, Charlie. I did all the driving. When she wasn't snacking or talking, she was dozing in the passenger seat."

Randi tossed her head. "Not my fault if you're so obsessive about driving that you won't let anyone else behind the wheel."

I laughed. "I see you two haven't changed that much, after all. Still bickering just like you used to in grad school."

"If you can't give your best friend a hard time, then you'd have to take it out on some unsuspecting person instead, right?" Marisue grinned.

"Right," Randi said. "Besides, she's a tough broad. She can take it."

"I'd say you are both pretty tough broads," I said.

They both laughed, then Marisue said, "Sorry to change the subject, but we overheard a few people talking a little while ago. They were saying something about two men getting into a brawl earlier this afternoon. Know anything about that?" She and Randi watched me closely.

I felt my face redden. "Come off it, you two. You know perfectly well it was me and Gavin." I managed a laugh.

Randi shot me an impish grin. "Sorry, kiddo, we couldn't resist roasting you a little. Tell me, did you blast him a good one?"

"You're even more bloodthirsty than I remember." I shook my head. "I hit him hard enough for him to go down on his bum, I suppose. I don't think I really hurt him, though."

"Probably more damage to his dignity than anything." Marisue nodded. "With him that's worse than physical pain."

"I'm glad you did it, whatever the reason," Randi said. "I can't tell you how many times I wanted to do it when I worked with him. But of course I couldn't—couldn't afford to lose my job, and he wasn't worth that."

"Same here," Marisue said. "I don't think I've ever known anyone so self-involved, and so impressed with his own so-called *intellect*."

"Why he's not six feet under pushing up daisies already, I don't know." Randi sniffed. "If anybody was ever asking to be murdered, it's Gavin Fong."

EIGHT

I felt a sudden, brief chill at Randi's jesting words. Surely no one would actually *murder* Gavin Fong. I didn't want to go through all that again.

Marisue snorted with laughter. "The police would never be able to solve it. Too many suspects."

Randi nodded. "Yeah, way too many. Every single person who ever went to school with him or worked with him."

"I grant you he's a colossal annoyance most of the time," I said. "But what has he done that would make someone see killing him as a solution?"

Marisue shot Randi a pointed glance. "Tell you what, you fill Charlie in while I go get us some wine. If I'm going to talk about Gavin, I need fortification." With that, she turned to make her way through the crowd toward one of the bar stations.

Randi eyed the nearly empty glass of diet soda I picked up. "Sure you don't want something stronger yourself?"

"No, I'm fine with this. I have to drive home. I'm not staying in the hotel, and I presume you two are." I downed the rest of my drink and set the glass down on the table.

"We are," Randi said. "We're sharing a room the way we always do. I have to say, this is a lovely old hotel. Dripping with Southern charm that makes this California girl feel like she ought to be seeing Scarlett O'Hara come sweeping around the corner just any little ole minute now." She grinned when I winced at her attempt at a Southern accent on those last few words.

"Stick to being a California girl, all right?" I smiled at her. "Now, what all are you supposed to be telling me about Gavin?"

Randi scowled. "Did you know that both Marisue and I coauthored journal articles with him?" After I nodded, she continued. "I say *coauthored*, but Marisue and I each did most of the research for, and the writing of, our respective articles. Since we worked with Gavin at the time we did the research—in separate institutions, that is, me first in Colorado and then her later in Kansas—he decided that his name ought to go on the articles, too. Because we had to submit them to him before we could send them to the journal, and he edited them to improve them. Substantially enough that his name ought to be included."

The bitterness in her tone didn't surprise me. Gavin had obviously hijacked their work in each instance in order to give himself a free publication credit. I wondered if all the other articles and chapters on his résumé came about the same way.

"Why would you have to submit them to him first?" I asked.

"Said it was his responsibility as the head of the department to make sure anything published by one of his staff members was quality work." Randi snorted. "Pure invention on his part. There was no such regulation in place. He simply wanted to horn in on someone else's work and get a free credit out of it."

"Didn't you try to protest?" I couldn't believe Randi hadn't raised a stink about it. She was not the *suffer-in-silence* type.

"I tried to," Randi said. "Our director at the time, however, thought the sun rose and set out of Gavin's derriere, unfortunately for the rest of us. She refused to believe me. When she left abruptly after Gavin was there about sixteen months, a new director came in, and she didn't like him at all."

"What about Marisue? I'm sure you told her about this and warned her before she had to work with him."

"I did," Randi said. "But guess where my former director ended up? She couldn't wait to get Gavin there, and poor Marisue found herself in the same situation as me."

Marisue reappeared with two glasses of wine, one red, one white. She handed the red to Randi.

"Got the picture?" Marisue asked after a sip of wine.

I nodded. "Can't say I'm surprised by Gavin's behavior. I remember back in grad school, when we were assigned group projects, anyone who got stuck with him in the group complained that he did very little."

"Enough to get by, that was all," Marisue said. "He was in a group with me for one project. He did the absolute minimum, but he was the first to criticize anyone else's work."

"What I can't figure out," Randi said, "is why he thinks the world owes him a living? Why does he get a free ride while the rest of us have to work?"

"I can't answer that," Marisue replied. "He's managed to get away with it for years, though."

"He's applied for my job," I said. "I'm acting as interim while they search for a director. I don't understand how he's gotten to the level of library director with his last two or three jobs."

Randi shrugged. "You got me. I guess because he looks good on paper, and he probably interviews well." She emptied her wineglass.

"I think I know whom he uses as his references," Marisue said. "They're former supervisors of his who were either too naive or too stupid to see through him. He's like a virus. He creeps in and takes over before you know just how awful he is."

"Are you part of the search committee for your job?" Randi asked.

I nodded. "Yes, and I've already told the college president I can't recommend Gavin for the position. For one thing, he changes jobs about every three years, and has done so for a long time."

Randi cackled with laughter. "Not by his choice, I'll bet. Two years in, I'm sure a sensible person has seen through him and urges him to move along, and that person will say anything to a prospective employer to get rid of him."

"Exactly." Marisue glanced at her watch. "Charlie, sorry for us to run off right now, but we promised to meet a friend from South Carolina for dinner tonight."

"Of course," I said. "I'm ready to get out of here anyway. We're still on for dinner tomorrow evening, right?"

"We sure are." Randi gave me a quick hug. "We'll talk about things a lot more pleasant than that parasite."

After a hug with Marisue, I watched them make their way through the crowd. I had heard enough from them to be even firmer in my resolve that Gavin Fong wouldn't get within an inch of the job at Athena. I could only hope the rest of the search committee would agree with me.

If the meeting with Forrest Wyatt tomorrow morning didn't get me in trouble, that is.

Bothered by that thought, I began to ease my way toward the ballroom doors. I'd had enough of crowds and loud conversations.

I paused in the ballroom foyer to get my bearings. Where had I parked? In the lot behind the hotel, I remembered, and I headed for the rear exit. After a few feet, I stopped when an idea struck me. I was already on the town square, and Helen Louise's place wasn't that far around the square. Though I had nibbled enough cocktail party–type food to keep me from going hungry, I could make room for a piece of one of her elegant and delicious desserts. Plus, if the place weren't too crowded, I could snatch a few minutes' conversation with the woman I loved.

Accordingly, I turned and headed toward the front of the hotel. Out on the sidewalk, the evening was cool, the air pleasant after the close confines of a crowded ballroom. The walk to Helen Louise's bistro took only about three minutes. I paused at the front window and peered in. The place looked about three-quarters full. Busy, then, but not swamped. I opened the door and went inside.

Helen Louise stood at the cash register, chatting to a young couple as she checked them out. When she finished, she glanced my way. Her lovely face made my heart turn over, especially when she smiled the way she was smiling now. I made my way through the tables to the register, and she came around the counter to greet me with a brief hug and a warm kiss.

"This is a sweet surprise." She took my arm and led me to the table in the corner near the register that she kept reserved for special guests. She seated herself to my left after a swift glance around to see whether she was needed. Evidently satisfied that she could take a few minutes away from work, she turned back to me with that beautiful smile.

"I was done with the conference reception at the hotel." I reached for her right hand with my left and clasped it. "I couldn't be this nearby and not come to see you."

"And perhaps have a little dessert?" Helen Louise laughed and winked at me.

I grinned. "Well, the thought *did* cross my mind, I must admit."

"I think there *might* be a slice of the chocolate tart I made this afternoon with your name on it." Helen Louise released my hand and stood. "How about coffee to go with it? Fresh decaf?"

"Sounds wonderful," I said. "No wonder I love you. You spoil me terribly."

She bent to give me a quick kiss before heading to the kitchen. She soon returned bearing a tray with two servings of the tart, as well as two cups of coffee. She served the tart and coffee, then placed the tray on the other side of the table as she seated herself.

"Tell me what you think," she said and picked up her fork.

I had a bite of the tart, and I think I gave a little moan, it was so tasty. After I finished with that bite, I said, "Heavenly, as always. No one makes any kind of chocolate dessert the way you do."

"Thank you, love." Helen Louise ate a bite herself, chewed, and then nodded. "Yes, I think this is pretty good. I've done better, but this is good."

"You're far too modest, sweetheart. I don't see how it could be any better," I told her before I forked another, larger bite into my mouth.

We soon finished our servings of the tart, and then we chatted over the coffee. I told her about the incident earlier in the afternoon with Gavin Fong.

"You couldn't help yourself, love. I know that, but I hope it's not going to cause you trouble. This guy sounds like the type who would sue over the tiniest thing." Helen Louise, though she hadn't practiced law in well over a decade, never lost the lawyer's way of looking at things. "Have you talked to Sean about any of this yet?"

"No, not yet." I stared into my nearly empty coffee cup. "I haven't told you the worst. I had a call from Forrest Wyatt's office earlier, asking me to meet with him first thing in the morning."

"I think you'd better talk to Sean about this before you go to that meeting, just in case." Helen Louise frowned. "I may be making more of this than I should, but it's best to be prepared."

"You're right," I said. Suddenly that chocolate tart felt sour in my stomach. I drained my coffee. I glanced toward the window, where a face outside caught my attention. Gavin Fong was staring at me, but the moment he saw that I was looking back, he took off down the street.

I thought about mentioning it to Helen Louise, but decided after quick reflection there was no point. It was nothing more than coincidence.

"I'll call Sean when I get home," I said. "Though I have to tell you I don't look forward to confessing this to him."

"I know he's inclined to fuss a bit where you're concerned." Helen Louise smiled. "But he's your son, and he cares about you."

"I know. I just don't want to feel like the teenager getting fussed at by his father, and that's the way I feel sometimes." I grinned. "I have to say, though, that I like the idea I can still surprise him, shake up his notions about what his old man gets up to."

Helen Louise laughed. She glanced toward the door as the bell on it chimed. Seven people came in, and she turned back to me with a wry smile as she stood.

"Looks like my break is over, love. We're shorthanded tonight because one of my help fell today and sprained his ankle."

"No need to apologize. I know how busy you are. Call me later when you get home." I pushed my chair back and stood. We exchanged one last quick kiss before I made my way to the door.

I headed back toward the hotel, my emotions a mix of joy and annoyance. Joy from having spent even a few short minutes with Helen Louise, and annoyance at myself for letting my temper get the better of me with Gavin this afternoon. Perhaps I hadn't taken the situation seriously enough. I knew Sean would probably read me the riot act. He worried enough in the past over my *exploits*, as he called them, in solving murders.

Instead of going through the hotel to get to the parking lot at the back, I cut down an alley that ran alongside the building. The lighting wasn't good, but I could see just enough to make my way through.

As I neared the corner of the building at the back, I paused. Had I heard someone behind me? Were those footfalls?

I turned to look, then the world went dark.

NINE

||||||||||||||||||||||||||

I felt a hand on my shoulder and opened my eyes to find a face
close to mine.

"Hey, man, go sleep it off somewhere else. If you don't get
movin' soon, I'm going to have to call Athena PD. You don't
wanna spend the night in a cell, do you?"

I realized I was lying on the ground, and I pushed myself up
into a sitting position. I glared at the man in a security guard's
uniform.

"I'm not drunk. Someone hit me and knocked me down."

He stood there gaping at me. "I didn't see no one."

I got myself upright and stood looking down at him. "I don't
care whether you saw anyone. I was attacked." I rubbed the back
of my head. I remembered footsteps hurrying away right after I
hit the ground. I must have blacked out, but only for a few seconds, I thought.

"If you say so," the security guard said.

My tone was curt to the point of offensiveness when I replied. "I do say so. You can move along. I don't need your help." *Not that you helped much*, I added silently.

He shrugged. "Well, if you ain't hurt, then I guess I'll let you be." He turned and walked away.

Thankful to be rid of him, I dusted off my suit the best I could. I realized my hands had scrapes and a couple of small cuts, probably from putting them out to break the fall onto the surface of the parking lot.

I winced when I turned my head. My right shoulder was going to be stiff by morning. I think it must have taken the brunt of the impact and saved me from getting an even worse blow to the head. My head was pretty clear, and I didn't feel nauseated. No urge to vomit, either. No concussion, then, I hoped.

Mostly what I felt was anger. I felt sure I knew who was responsible for this. Gavin Fong had followed me when I left Helen Louise's place, and he saw his chance at revenge when I turned down the dark alley rather than making my way through the hotel.

I debated whether to go to the ER at the Athena Medical Center but decided against it. I was a little shaken up, but otherwise I was okay. When I got home I would tell Stewart and Haskell about the incident, and I knew Stewart would keep an eye on me, bless him, and make sure I was all right. He had come to be like the younger brother my parents never gave me.

As soon as I reached home, I would put an ice pack on the place where Gavin struck me. I needed to keep any swelling to a minimum. I made it to my car and drove home.

When I walked into the kitchen I found Stewart and Haskell at the table playing canasta. Diesel came to me immediately for attention. He told me, in indignant meows and warbles, how unhappy he was at being left behind. I bent slightly to rub his head, and I groaned. My shoulder was not happy.

"Charlie, what the heck happened to you? Have you been in another fight?" Stewart laid his cards on the table and jumped up to examine me. "Look at you. Your hands are scraped, and you've got dirt on one side of your face."

"Not a fight." I grimaced. "Well, a one-sided one. I was attacked a little while ago in the parking lot at the Farrington House."

"Did you see who did it?" Haskell went immediately into cop mode while Stewart led me to the sink to wash my hands with antibacterial soap. Diesel followed, still complaining, though in more muted tones. Dante danced around, barking occasionally.

"No." I winced as the soap made contact with the cuts in my hands. "But I'm pretty sure I know who was responsible." I explained about seeing Gavin Fong peering in the window at Helen Louise's bistro. "It was shortly after that when I left to go to my car. I'm sure it was him."

"Do you still have your wallet? Cell phone?"

I felt like an idiot. I hadn't thought about that. I remembered feeling my wallet in my pocket, however, when I fished my keys out. "I have my wallet. I'll have to check for my phone when Stewart finishes with my hands."

"In a moment." Stewart rinsed my hands under the warm water, then dried them with paper towels. He patted my jacket pocket where he knew I usually kept my phone. "It's there."

"So not robbery," Haskell said. "Then I reckon it probably was that guy, trying to get back at you. How are you feeling? Any symptoms of concussion?"

"No, I feel all right, only bruised on my right shoulder, and my hands of course. Oh, and I've got a bump on the head." I smiled at Stewart. "Would you mind making me an ice pack for it?"

"I'm on it," Stewart said. "You sit right down there and take it easy."

"Thanks." I did as he told me. Now that I was home, and my immediate needs were being addressed so efficiently, I felt able to relax. "It was a cowardly thing to do, to hit me from behind so that I couldn't defend myself, but I almost can't blame the jerk. I never should have punched him today."

"Maybe so." Haskell frowned. "But he shouldn't get away with it. If only you had seen him, you could press charges."

I shrugged, and my shoulder twinged. "I didn't see him, so there's nothing more I can do. I will do my best to avoid him the rest of the conference, I promise you." Lisa Krause would have to find someone to take my place for the panel discussion on Saturday. The less contact I had with Gavin the better.

Stewart handed me a plastic bag with ice wrapped in a towel. I held it to the bump on my head. The coolness soon began to soothe the ache.

"There were no witnesses?" Haskell seemed determined not to let it go.

"No, I don't think so. A security guard found me on the ground, but he thought I was drunk. When I told him what happened, he said he hadn't seen anyone besides me."

"I guess that's that, then," Haskell said. "The main thing is you weren't badly hurt."

"As far as we can tell," Stewart said. "I'm going to keep an eye on you, Charlie, to make sure you don't have a concussion." He grinned and batted his eyelashes at me. "Just a warning, so that when I creep into your bedroom at two a.m. and wake you up, you know why."

I couldn't help but laugh at that. I didn't relish the idea of being awakened during the night, but I knew arguing with him would not achieve anything.

"I appreciate your concern," I said. "Not a word about this to anyone else yet, if you please. I will tell the family, but when I'm ready to. Are we clear on this?"

Both men nodded, Dante barked, and Diesel meowed loudly. "I guess that covers everyone." I shared a laugh with Stewart and Haskell before getting slowly out of my chair, keeping the bag of ice in place at the back of my head. "I think I'll go upstairs and lie down for a while, if you don't mind."

"Fine, but I'm coming with you to make sure you get up the stairs all right." Stewart's tone brooked no argument.

He kept a hand on my free arm as we moved out into the hall and up the stairs. Diesel ran ahead. Haskell held Dante back in the kitchen. The last thing I needed was to take a tumble because the poodle got under my feet.

In my bedroom, Stewart helped me ease my jacket off and then my dress shirt. He pulled down the neck of my tee shirt to examine the sore shoulder. "Looks like it will be nicely colored by the morning. Let me get you another ice pack for it. I'll be right back."

He was out the door before I could say anything. I managed to get my shoes off by pushing them off my feet and letting them fall where they might. I went into the bathroom to take some aspirin, then came back to sit on the side of the bed, ice pack against my head, until Stewart returned. In the meantime, Diesel watched me anxiously, head-butting my free arm a few times. I spoke to him and assured him I would be okay.

When Stewart returned with the second ice pack, he hovered nearby while I took off my pants, then helped me position myself in bed with the two ice packs. Diesel stretched out on the bed next to me and continued to watch.

"I'll be back in a little while to check on you, maybe refresh those ice packs if you need me to." Stewart turned off the overhead light and switched on the reading lamp by the window. He came back to stand by the bed.

"Thank you. You're an excellent nurse." On impulse I added, "I'm really thankful you are part of my family."

Stewart smiled down at me. He squeezed my unhurt shoulder for a moment. "I'm thankful, too. Any time you need me, I will always be here for you," he said softly. Then he slipped out of the room.

Diesel yawned beside me, and he soon fell asleep. I felt a little drowsy, thanks to the aspirin, but the cold spots at my head and my shoulder reminded me that I still ached. My hands hurt a bit as well.

It could have been a lot worse, I told myself. I wondered what Gavin had used to hit me. I didn't think it was his hand, or hands. He wasn't the martial arts type, as far as I knew. Whatever he used, he hit hard, but not hard enough to kill.

Had he meant to do more than knock me out? I didn't know why that thought hadn't occurred to me before. I felt a little sick to my stomach as I considered the possibility.

Had he been trying to kill me? Did he really hate me *that* much?

Or did he want my job badly enough to commit murder for it?

TEN

||||||||||||||||

Stewart woke me twice during the night, and each time I came awake quickly. The second time I got up and took more aspirin, then went back to bed and fell promptly asleep. When I woke the third time, the bedside clock told me it was nearly seven. Diesel was gone from the room, and I suspected he was downstairs in the kitchen with Azalea.

I tested the back of my head. Sore, but not as painful as I expected. My shoulder had stiffened, but a hot shower ought to help that. My hands remained sore, and I needed to clean the cuts again and dab them with some antibiotic ointment.

In the shower, while I let the hot water hit my stiff shoulder, I thought about the attack. I had a gut feeling Gavin was responsible, but I had no way to prove it. Maybe he owed me that much, since I knocked him off his feet twice in twenty-five years.

I had talked to Helen Louise last night, the first time Stewart woke me. It was around ten o'clock then, and I knew she ought to be home and getting ready for bed. I didn't keep her on the phone long because I knew how tired she was after a full day at the bistro. I also didn't tell her about the incident with Gavin. I didn't think anyone else would tell her about it before I had a chance to, and I didn't want her lying awake, worrying, when she needed rest. I would tell her about it when we were face-to-face so that she could see that I was okay.

Twenty minutes later, showered, shaved, and dressed for the conference, I went downstairs. To my surprise I found my son at the table, eating a hearty breakfast. Diesel greeted me first. Sean waved a fork in greeting. I could see he was busy chewing.

I greeted Azalea in the meantime, and she poured coffee for me while I took my accustomed place at the table. When Sean could speak properly, he said, "Morning, Dad. What's this I hear about you getting in fights yesterday?"

I had a sip of coffee before I replied. "Is that why you're here this morning, instead of at home with your wife? Did you come to lecture me?"

That sounded more hostile than I intended, but Sean paid no mind.

"Alex had to leave for Jackson early this morning for a trial, and I needed to talk to you." He grinned. "And somehow I figured Azalea might have a few extra crumbs to feed me."

Azalea set my plate of scrambled eggs, bacon, and grits on the table, along with a smaller plate of biscuits. She regarded Sean with an indulgent smile. "Always like to see a man eating a hearty meal, Mr. Sean. No trouble cracking a couple extra eggs for you and throwing a few more slices of bacon on the skillet."

"And I thank you most heartily in return, Azalea. There's nothing to compare with your breakfast anywhere." Sean sighed.

"Those biscuits are so light and fluffy it's a wonder they're not floating off the table."

Azalea shook her head at his fanciful description, but I could tell she was pleased. Sean didn't exaggerate by much. Azalea's *were* the lightest biscuits I'd ever had, and I had eaten way too many to count in my fifty-plus years.

"Now, Dad, about these fights." Sean fixed me with a stern gaze, and I suppressed a sigh. Sometimes he was a little too lawyer-y for me, especially first thing in the morning.

"Yes, son, what do you want to know? I'm ready for my cross-examination." I forked some scrambled eggs into my mouth and bit off some bacon to go with them.

"First, how are you feeling this morning? Do you need to go to the doctor?"

"No, I'm fine," I said. "Sore in places, and my hands hurt a bit, but nothing serious. Stewart took excellent care of me. I suppose I have him to thank for telling you about what happened last night."

Sean nodded. "He told me about it right off this morning when I got here. He and Haskell were heading to the gym. Don't get mad at him for telling me before you did, okay? He and Haskell were talking about it when they came out the door, and naturally I asked what had happened. He told me."

"I wasn't going to be angry with Stewart," I said. "Would you like to hear my version?"

"Naturally." Sean waved his fork at me again and then resumed eating.

In between mouthfuls of my breakfast and sips of coffee, I gave my son a quick rundown of yesterday's events, from the afternoon encounter with Gavin Fong to the later attack by an unknown assailant.

"You're pretty sure it was this guy Fong, even though you didn't see the person who hit you?" Sean put his fork down, his plate now empty.

"I'm sure," I said. "I can't imagine anyone else who'd want to attack me like that. Can you?"

"Other than a few murderers that you've helped finger," Sean said, "and they're all accounted for, I can't think of anyone else, besides possibly a friend or family member of one of them."

"Even if I hadn't seen Gavin outside Helen Louise's place shortly before it happened, I'd still say he was the one."

Sean nodded. "Reasonable, though it wouldn't stand up in court."

"I know," I said. "And I'm not going to be foolish enough to press charges. I have other things to worry about, like this meeting with Forrest Wyatt at eight thirty."

"It's ten after eight now, Dad," Sean said. "You'd better get going."

"I lost track of the time." I pushed back from the table. "Azalea, I can't take Diesel with me today. Will you mind staying with him until I come home around two or two thirty?"

"Mr. Cat and me'll be just fine. You go on and do what you need to do," Azalea said.

I noticed that Diesel had been keeping a close watch on Azalea while I ate. I had no doubt she was slipping him bits of bacon when I wasn't looking. When I first brought him home she wouldn't have anything to do with him, but over time he managed to win her over.

"Thank you," I said. "If I'm held up for any reason, I'll let you know."

"I need to get to the office myself," Sean said. "Can I drive you to campus?"

"Thanks, but I need my car. I have to get over to the Far-rington House for the conference after the meeting." I gave Diesel a couple of good-bye rubs and admonished him to be a good boy for Azalea. He gave me a couple sad meows in return because he realized he wasn't coming with me.

During the short drive to campus, I allowed myself to think about the upcoming meeting. I had kept it resolutely at the back of my mind. The whole situation embarrassed me, and I didn't look forward to having to stand in the president's office and hear about the effect on the good name of the school, and how disap-pointed Forrest was, and so on. I was disappointed in myself, and I decided the best thing I could do would be to resign as interim and go back to being the part-time rare book cataloger and archi-vist if I was allowed.

I found a parking spot close to the administration building, and I presented myself to the president's administrative assistant at eight twenty-seven. Moments later, I was shown into the small conference room nearby. I had expected to find the president and the college general counsel, because of course the lawyers would have to be involved. Instead, I found the members of the search committee for the library director job seated around the table.

Forrest rose from his seat at the head of the table. "Good morning, Charlie. I'm glad you could join us at such short notice. Please, take a seat."

I nodded and found an empty spot near the other end of the table. *This is going to be worse than I imagined*, I thought. *The whole committee is here, and I've got to explain myself to all of them*. I suppressed a sigh, rested my hands in my lap, and waited for the unpleasantness to start.

Forrest remained standing at the head of the table. "Charlie, the rest of the committee and I met this morning without you. I know that's unusual, but I'm sure you will understand why in a moment."

I know why, I thought dismally. I wanted to climb under the table.

"Frankly, I think we are all disappointed in the caliber of the persons applying for the position of library director," Forrest said.

I wanted to cringe even more when I heard the first few words of that sentence. I was so focused on them, in fact, that I hardly heard the rest of it.

"We've considered the matter carefully, and the committee— again, without you—has come to a decision. I know you have told me at least twice that you are not interested in the position permanently, but the committee and I are asking you to reconsider. We feel that the leadership you have shown—not to mention the letters of support we have received from library staff at all levels singing your praises—is what our library needs.

"We know that it is more usual in academic libraries for the director to have a PhD or at least a second master's degree, but we think in your case neither of these is important. You have the administrative and leadership skills we value, and we sincerely hope you will consider taking on the task."

I sat there, stunned. I probably looked like a goggle-eyed fish, but I was having trouble taking it all in.

I wasn't here to address a complaint against me by Gavin Fong. Instead, they wanted me to be the director of the library.

"You don't have to give us an answer right away," Forrest said. "I know this perhaps comes as a surprise to you, but if you have any interest in the position permanently, we hope you will say *yes*."

Now they all stared at me, waiting for a response.

ELEVEN

||||||||||||||||||||||||||||||||||||||||||

I have been known to make decisions a little too impulsively. My gut instinct at the moment told me to tell Forrest Wyatt and the search committee "yes." I needed to be completely certain, however, that I wanted the job and was prepared to take on the responsibilities it entailed. I had grown quite comfortable with my semiretired life, working only part-time and volunteering at the public library. I loved working with the rare book collection, and I enjoyed my time at the public library. I would have to give those things up if I were going to work full-time as the college library director.

They were awaiting my response. I drew a deep breath, let it slowly out, and then spoke. "I am immensely flattered, not only by this offer, but also by your faith in me. I have been thinking about applying for the job, I must admit, but there are a few things I need to give deep consideration to before I can commit myself either way." I paused for another breath. "Would it be acceptable if

I made my decision over the weekend and communicated it to you on Monday morning?"

"Certainly, Charlie." Forrest Wyatt scanned the room, but evidently none of the search committee objected. "Monday will be fine. In the meantime, I have asked Penny Sisson, the head of human resources, to talk to you immediately after we break up this meeting. She will explain the salary offer and the benefits and answer any questions you might have. You need to have that information before you finalize your decision."

"Thank you, President Wyatt, and thank you all." I rose to my feet as everyone else stood and began to file out of the room.

Once the last committee member was out of the room, Penny Sisson entered, smiling broadly. "I'm so excited, Charlie. I hope you will decide to take the job." She pulled out the chair next to mine, placed some folders on the table, and began to give me the details of salary and benefits. Still in a bit of a daze, I did my best to follow along and absorb the important facts.

Forty-five minutes later I found a parking spot in the lot behind the Farrington House. Penny Sisson had been thorough—so thorough, in fact, that I struggled to remember much of what she told me. One fact persisted in my memory, however. The salary the college was offering was considerably more than I had ever earned in the public library system in Houston, even as a branch manager of many years' service. I was comfortably off, thanks to my pension and to my aunt Dottie, who had left me her house and a considerable amount of money. I didn't *need* a salary at that level, but there were a number of things I could do with the extra money. Important things like saving money for my grandchildren to go to college, and so on.

I realized at least five minutes had passed since I switched off the ignition. The inside of the car had grown warmer. I got out, locked the car, and then headed for the back entrance. I had to remember to keep an eye out for Gavin Fong today. I didn't want to encounter him—although a small, and I did mean *small*, part of me wanted to tell him I'd been offered the job just to see his reaction.

I wouldn't do it, of course. If he found out, he might attack me again, and the next time I might end up hurt a lot worse.

As I made my way to the front of the hotel and the meeting rooms, I kept a careful watch. At the registration table I picked up my name badge, the obligatory canvas tote bag, and a conference program. Having left my printouts on my desk at the library, I scanned the latter to see what sessions might tempt me. I checked my watch. The ten o'clock programs were about to start. There was a presentation on effective management of electronic resources that sounded promising. I stuck the program in my bag and hurried off to find the meeting room.

Ninety minutes later I emerged from a stimulating, informative session, and made my way to the nearest men's room. After I finished there, I headed into the hallway and scanned the milling crowd. There was a break until the luncheon at noon—the luncheon for which Gavin Fong was the keynote speaker. I was tempted to ditch it and find my lunch elsewhere, because I had no desire to listen to Gavin opine on anything. Lisa Krause needed my support, however, and I had to make a good showing since the college library was ostensibly the host of the conference.

There was no sign of Gavin anywhere in the crowd. After a few minutes of wandering closer to the ballroom foyer, I found Marisue and Randi in conversation with a woman who looked vaguely familiar. I walked up to them in time to hear Randi say, "Why, Maxine, that's ridiculous."

Maxine. She was the woman who approached Gavin yesterday right after I knocked him down.

"That's what I told him," Maxine replied, "but you know he never listens to anyone's advice. There's no telling what may happen in there. He's his own worst enemy."

Marisue noticed me. "Hi, Charlie. How are you? Have you met Maxine Muller? She's the associate library director for public services at the college where she and Gavin Fong work." She quirked one eyebrow, and I took the signal to mean I should be careful what I said about Gavin.

"I'm doing fine. Hope you're both doing well. Nice to meet you, Ms. Muller. I hope you're all enjoying yourselves so far."

Maxine Muller hadn't really looked at me until I spoke directly to her, but when she did, her face paled, and she took a step backward. "You're the man who attacked Gavin yesterday."

"We had an altercation, yes." I didn't like the word *attack* in reference to my striking him, since he tried to hit me first. "I regret that it happened, and I hope you will convey that message to Gavin for me."

She nodded, then abruptly turned and walked away. Randi and Marisue exchanged what I would have called a *knowing glance.* Randi nodded.

"Is she in love with Gavin?" I asked, because I knew that was exactly what they were thinking.

Marisue shrugged. "Possibly, though I can't imagine why."

"Because she's probably the type that always falls for an idiot like Gavin." Randi shook her head. "How he finds them, I don't know. Or I guess they find him."

"No accounting for taste." I smiled. "I couldn't help overhear that last bit of your conversation with her as I approached. What were you talking about, if you don't mind my asking?"

"Why should we mind?" Randi asked. "You're going to find out in a little while anyway."

Marisue explained. "Maxine told us the gist of Gavin's keynote speech for the luncheon. Apparently he's going to spend forty-five minutes telling us how we are all shortly to become obsolete."

I groaned. "Not that crap again. I'm so sick of hearing how we're no longer needed because everyone can find what they need online without our help."

"You know it's crap, and we know it's crap." Randi looked angry. "Students don't know the first thing about research these days, and even many of the faculty can't figure out how to navigate an online journal or a database."

"But the problem is, so many of them don't think they need us." Marisue appeared unruffled. "Many of them don't even realize that they can only access research materials on the Internet because the library licenses them and pays for them on their behalf."

"I know," Randi said. "I had a tenured professor, a man who certainly ought to know better, tell me the library was unnecessary because he could get what he wanted online. He and the others like him don't have a clue about licensing."

"I'm sure you set him straight on that point." I grinned at her.

"You'd better believe I did," Randi said. "That and a few other things as well, like the fact that his hand had no business on my knee or any other part of my body."

Marisue, who had been looking past Randi toward the ballroom doors, said, "They're letting people in now. Let's go find a table near the back. I want to be able to get out quickly if there's a riot." She walked off, and Randi and I followed.

I vaguely remembered Lisa Krause telling me that I was expected to sit at the speaker's table for the keynote speech today. Under the circumstances, I thought it best that I forget she ever told me. I chose a seat at a back table between Marisue and Randi. We had a good view of the dais at the other side of the ballroom. This was more than close enough to Gavin for me.

The tables had already been set with the salad course, glasses of iced tea, and dessert, a slice of raspberry cheesecake. Our table soon filled, as did the ballroom, and we chatted as we ate our salads. Before long the waitstaff came by, handing out plates of the usual grilled banquet chicken breast, along with spears of asparagus with hollandaise sauce, and roasted red potatoes.

The food was better than that of many such banquets I had attended over the years. I would have to call Donna Evans, the catering manager, later and tell her so.

As the waitstaff were clearing away our plates and beginning to serve coffee, there was activity on the dais. A tall, distinguished-looking, gray-haired man I didn't recognize stepped up to the microphone.

"Ladies and gentlemen, if I could have your attention, please." He paused for a moment, then repeated himself. The chatter died away, and he smiled. "My name is Harlan Crais." He went on to mention his affiliation with a midsize university in Tennessee and his current position there. "It is my pleasure today to introduce our keynote speaker, Dr. Gavin Fong." He rattled off some of Gavin's achievements, then welcomed Gavin to the podium.

Gavin stood at the podium for at least ten or fifteen seconds without speaking as he surveyed the audience. I couldn't see his expression clearly, but somehow I knew it was supercilious. Then he began his speech.

"Ladies and gentlemen, I am here today to tell you that our profession is dying. In five years, maybe less, we will all be out of work. The academic library is dying, strangled by shrinking budgets, greedy publishers, and staff who are poorly trained to cope with today's ever-changing technologies. Library schools have become diploma mills, turning out graduates who might just as well be working at fast-food restaurants for all the intellectual stimulation they are receiving in so-called graduate school. Master's and doctoral degrees are nothing more than a waste of time and resources. We would all be better served by taking different career paths."

A wave of sound moved around the room as the audience reacted to these incendiary words. *The sheer hypocrisy of the man.* I was incensed with him myself. He had the nerve, the colossal gall, to stand up in front of all these people and spout tripe like that after he had applied for the director's job here at Athena. If I'd been close enough to throw something at him, I just might have at that moment.

While Gavin waited, smiling, for the noise to recede, he glanced down at the podium. He frowned, then turned to look over at a table nearby. He mimed drinking from a glass, and within seconds Lisa Krause popped up to hurry toward the podium. She held up a bottle, and Gavin leaned down to retrieve it. He didn't acknowledge her in any way that I could see, and Lisa returned to her seat.

By now the noise had abated for the most part, and Gavin turned up the bottle and drank from it. He set it down somewhere, then opened his mouth to speak.

No words came out. He appeared to be struggling to breathe all of a sudden. He clutched at his throat, and the microphone magnified the gagging sounds so that everyone could hear them. I watched in horror as he disappeared behind the podium. Moments later a woman started screaming.

TWELVE

I stared at Chief Deputy Kanesha Berry, not sure I had heard her correctly. Then the import of her question sank in.

"And exactly *how* did I manage to get the poison into his bottle?" I shook my head. "No, not me. I wasn't anywhere *near* him or his bottle this morning.

"Besides," I continued, "what motive did I have to kill him? I'll admit I loathed the man, but I sure didn't kill him." I had to pause for breath.

Kanesha held up a hand. "Personally, I don't think you did it, but as a matter of routine, I had to ask. Now, I have a witness who claims you attacked Mr. Fong in public yesterday. Is this true?"

"I hit him, yes, but I didn't *attack* him. He swung at me three times—and missed, incidentally—before I hit back." I had to keep my temper under control, especially in front of Kanesha. "Look, let me give you the background on all this. It will take a few minutes."

Kanesha nodded. "Go ahead. Might as well hear it all now."

"I first met Gavin Fong in graduate school in Texas, a little over twenty-five years ago." From there I went on to tell Kanesha why I had disliked him then, and I told her about the incident involving my late wife. "Fast-forward to the present, and this conference. Also, the search for a permanent library director at Athena College. Gavin e-mailed me, basically demanding that I support his application for the job, or else he would tell President Wyatt about that incident back in grad school."

Kanesha reached for a pad and pen and began to jot down some notes. Next I told her about the incident between Gavin and me yesterday. I hesitated, however, to tell her about the attack on me last night. It could be construed as a motive for getting back at Gavin by poisoning him.

Best to tell her everything, I decided after a moment. "There's one other thing. Last night someone waylaid me in that alley beside the Farrington House. I was walking through the alley to the parking lot after stopping in to see Helen Louise. Someone struck me from behind and knocked me out for a moment."

"Did you get a look at your assailant?" Kanesha asked, her eyes narrowed.

"No, but I had seen Gavin Fong peering in the window at Helen Louise's place not long before I left. I'm pretty sure he followed me back to the Farrington House and attacked me."

"How badly were you hurt?"

I shrugged. "Not badly, really. Scraped hands, a bump on the head, and a bruised shoulder. No concussion, thankfully. I guess I have a hard head."

Kanesha snorted. "I'll say you do."

I decided not to take offense at that. I knew I had tried her patience on numerous occasions with my stubbornness.

"You went home right afterward?" she asked.

"Yes. Stewart and Haskell were there when I got home, and Stewart kept a check on me during the night to make sure I was all right. I stayed home until I had to leave this morning for a meeting on campus. From there I went straight to the hotel for the conference. I did not see Gavin until we went into the ballroom for the luncheon. I was at a table near the doors with two librarians I know, and he was all the way across the ballroom. Never went near him before he collapsed and died." After a pause I added, "And I didn't go near him after that, either."

By now I had a headache, and I desperately needed a bathroom. I wondered how much longer she intended to keep me here. I did have a question for her, though, and I wondered if she would answer it.

"He died very quickly, from what I could tell, after drinking from that bottle, because he seemed fine up till then," I said. "What do you think it was? Cyanide?"

Kanesha stared at me for probably ten seconds before she responded. "Possibly, but we won't know until the appropriate tests have been done."

I wondered how easily available cyanide was these days. Did they still use it in rat poison? If so, how much rat poison would you have to put in a bottle of water for a lethal dose? And wouldn't it taste funny? I would have to ask Stewart these questions later. As a chemist, he ought to know.

Another question popped into my mind. "Are you going to close down the conference?"

"No. The ballroom is going to be off-limits for a while, but we will want to be able to question everyone. Best to keep them busy with the rest of the program while we investigate."

"Good." I was about to ask whether she was done with me, at least for now, so I could find a bathroom. She forestalled me with another question.

"Do you know anyone—besides yourself, that is—who had any personal animosity toward the deceased?"

I wanted to laugh, but I didn't think Kanesha would find it appropriate. "I think it might be easier to find someone who *didn't*. He rubbed almost everyone the wrong way, as far as I know."

Kanesha wrote in her notebook. "Let me rephrase the question. Do you know anyone who had motive to kill the deceased?"

"No, not really," I said. "Until this week I hadn't seen the man, or heard from him, since grad school. I know various friends of mine from those days worked with him over the years, and they might have shared things about him in letters or e-mails. I don't recall anything serious enough to make a person want to kill Gavin, however."

"Are any of these friends who worked with him attending this conference?" Kanesha held her pen ready to write.

"Actually, there are two. Marisue Pickard and Randi Grant." I would have to let them know I had to give their names to Kanesha. "There may be other people at the conference who worked with him. There is one woman who actually seemed to like him. Maxine Muller, I think the name is." She was the one who probably told Kanesha that I attacked Gavin.

Kanesha nodded. "I've talked with Ms. Muller. Anybody else?"

I thought for a moment. "Yes, a young man, probably late twenties, early thirties, bald, with earrings and tattooed forearms. He'll be hard to miss. His name is Bob Coben, I believe. He works at the same college that Gavin did currently." I frowned. That didn't sound quite right, but I figured Kanesha would understand what I meant.

"The deceased had received anonymous death threats, according to Ms. Muller," Kanesha said. "Both in e-mails and through the regular mail. Ms. Muller said the deceased believed the threats came from a man. This Mr. Coben is a possibility."

I shrugged. "I guess so. There are other men who probably had reason to hate Gavin. Finding them shouldn't be that hard."

"Another thing Ms. Muller revealed is that the deceased had applied for several jobs recently, but he didn't get any of them. He seemed to think he'd been blackballed."

"That's entirely possible," I replied. "Gavin had evidently done it to others, so it was poetic justice if it happened to him."

"You said the deceased applied for your job." Kanesha regarded me intently. "Was he a serious candidate for it? Could someone have wanted him out of the way in order to get the job for himself? Or herself?"

"He had no chance at the job, I'm pretty sure." I might as well tell her. "In fact, the job has already been offered to someone. This morning, to me."

"I see," Kanesha replied. "Are congratulations in order?"

"I haven't made up my mind yet," I said. "I promised I would let them know on Monday morning."

Kanesha shot me an amused glance. "I have to say I hope you'll take it. With a full-time job you'll be too busy to get involved in any more murder investigations."

"That would suit me fine," I said, trying not to feel nettled by her remark. "Do you have any more questions?"

"Not for the moment," Kanesha said. "I know where to find you."

I nodded and rose. Once I stepped out of the small meeting room the hotel had assigned to Kanesha, I took a moment to get my bearings. Then I made a beeline for the men's room. After that, I went to the gift shop to purchase a bottle of water and some aspirin.

With my immediate needs taken care of, I found a spot in a corner of the hotel lobby to sit and think for a few minutes. I checked my watch—a quarter past three p.m. After I downed a couple of aspirin, I sipped at the water and thought about the past several hours. The picture of Gavin Fong's last moments, before he fell out of sight on the dais, lingered in my mind. I shuddered. I loathed the man, certainly, but I hadn't wished him dead.

Someone had, however. I wondered what Gavin had done to make a person angry enough to believe that killing him was the only solution. That Gavin had to be erased, as it were.

Dimly I became aware of a conversation nearby. When I looked to see who was talking, I recognized the two men. One of them was the young man I had mentioned to Kanesha, Bob Coben. There was no mistaking the bald head, earrings, and tattooed arms. From where I sat I had a clear view of him on a sofa about six feet away. The man with Coben was the one who had introduced Gavin Fong at the luncheon today. What was his name? I thought for a moment. Harlan Crais, that was it.

"Why are you so certain he was responsible?" Crais asked. "Frankly, I'm finding the whole thing rather hard to believe."

"You knew him, Harlan. You worked with him for what, three or four years?" Coben sounded impatient. "You can't tell me he didn't really chap your hide the way he did everyone else's."

Crais shrugged. "Yes, I worked with him, but that was several years ago. I hadn't had anything to do with him since. He didn't bother me, and I didn't bother him."

Coben snorted. "Yeah, right. Then how come I overheard him

telling his little toady Maxine that he kept you from getting that job in Tennessee?"

"That's ridiculous." Crais waved that away. "Gavin didn't have that kind of power. He couldn't stop me from getting that job. As a matter of fact, they offered it to me, but I turned them down."

"Seriously? *You* turned *them* down?" Coben shook his head. "Man, that was a good job. Dean of libraries, wasn't it? Why would you turn that down?"

Crais shrugged. "I just did, that's all. It wasn't the right job for me."

From what I could see, Coben didn't believe the older man. I frowned as I tried to remember what Crais had said about himself before he introduced Gavin. He was head of collection development at his current library, I thought.

"In my case," Coben said, "I *wanted* the job, but I found out through somebody I know at that library that Gavin had basically told the director I'm too immature for the responsibility the job entailed." Suddenly he slammed a fist into the sofa cushion beside him. "I could have killed him for that alone."

THIRTEEN

IIIIIIIIIIIIIIIIIIIIIIIIIIIIIIIIIIIIIIIIIII

The violence of Bob Coben's tone startled me, as did his action in striking the sofa cushion.

Harlan Crais appeared uneasy. "You'd better not talk like that." He glanced around, and I shifted my gaze to my feet. When Crais spoke again, he lowered his voice so that I could barely hear him. "You don't know who could be listening."

I leaned back in my chair, eyes shut, and rested my head. I wanted the two men to think I wasn't paying any attention to their conversation.

"So what?" Coben said, his tone defiant. "I didn't kill him, Harlan, and you'd better not be going around telling people I did."

"Don't be an ass," Crais snapped back. "I'm not going to tell anyone anything. If you get into any trouble over this, it will be your own fault."

I opened my eyelids a fraction, in time to see Coben jump to his feet. He stared down at Crais, who shrank back against the sofa. "I'll keep *my* nose clean," Coben said. "You'd better be worrying about your own." He turned and walked swiftly away.

I closed my eyes a moment, in case Harlan Crais chanced to look my way. Then I opened them, yawned, and sat up. Crais was on his feet. He didn't appear to notice me. Instead he seemed absorbed by his thoughts as he wandered away, hitching his canvas bag up on his shoulder.

You do not want to get involved in another murder investigation, I told myself.

But, my self argued back, *you just overheard things that could be useful to Kanesha. You have to tell her what you heard.*

I sighed. At the moment I felt too tired to make the effort, but before long I knew I would either call or e-mail Kanesha to share the fruits of my eavesdropping. I didn't care for feeling like a tattletale, but needs must when the devil drives, as the old saying went.

Bob Coben had come up to me after the incident with Gavin yesterday, I remembered, and offered to serve as a witness if Gavin tried to make a fuss or sue me. Evidently he had personal reasons for loathing Gavin—no surprise there—but I didn't want to see him in trouble if he hadn't killed Gavin. He had said he didn't, but naturally the killer would lie about it.

I decided I would e-mail Kanesha when I got home. My dinner with Marisue and Randi was scheduled for tonight, and I planned to take them to Helen Louise's place. I wanted to get out of my suit and into more comfortable clothes before I came back to the hotel to escort them to the bistro.

After a quick glance at the conference program, I decided I might as well go home now. None of the last group of panels that started at three forty-five interested me. I had no great need to go back to the office on a Friday afternoon. Melba would have called or texted me if anything important had cropped up.

On the brief drive home I tried to force my mind away from the subject of murder. I had no doubt Marisue and Randi would want to talk about nothing else tonight. Instead, I tried to concentrate on the job offer I'd received this morning.

Being considered competent for the job was a boost to the ego. Part of me felt elated simply to be asked. Another part—and perhaps the larger part—dreaded the thought of going back into the nine-to-five world. I hadn't worked full-time for nearly five years before I stepped in as interim director. I had come to relish the time I had as a semi-retiree, time to piddle around, reading, napping, volunteering, and so on. That would go away if I agreed to take the job.

When I pulled my car into the garage, I had yet to come to any firm conclusion. I knew I had to let my subconscious stew over it for a while longer before I was ready to make up my mind.

Diesel met me right inside the kitchen door. His loud chorus of trills and warbles made for a happy welcome home. Unlike some felines, Diesel rarely sat with his back to me to let me feel the cold of his displeasure over being abandoned. He was usually too happy to see me after even a brief absence to indulge in such a ploy.

"You home early, Mr. Charlie." Azalea sniffed. "Wasn't expecting you for another hour or more. You feeling all right?"

"Other than being tired after a long week, I feel fine." I decided not to tell Azalea about the murder right now. "Since we're eating out tonight, why don't you go on home early?"

"I think I will." Azalea untied her apron, folded it, and retrieved her purse from the kitchen cabinet that was its second home. She tucked the apron in her purse, then turned to me to give me a brief list of dishes in the freezer and the fridge that she prepared for the weekend.

"Thank you." I smiled. "We certainly won't go hungry."

She nodded, the barest hint of a smile hovering around her lips, then she departed through the kitchen door.

"Come on, boy," I said. "Let's go upstairs so I can change out of these clothes."

Diesel kept up a running commentary throughout our progress from kitchen to bedroom. I felt sure he was telling me all about his day with Azalea. When we reached the bedroom, the meowing and trilling stopped, and he hopped on the bed to stretch out. He watched while I stripped out of the suit and slipped into a pair of comfortable shorts and an old tee shirt. I decided to stretch out on the bed for a few minutes, and before long I drifted into sleep beside the napping cat.

After a nap troubled by odd dreams, I woke in time to freshen up and dress for dinner. The dreams faded quickly from my memory, though I still had a vague feeling of disquiet from them. Dinner with friends at Helen Louise's place would help me shake off that feeling. I put Diesel into his harness, loaded him in the car, and set off once more for the Farrington House.

Marisue and Randi awaited us in the lobby, I was pleased to see. Marisue had always been a stickler for punctuality, a quality I appreciated. Randi tended to be a dawdler when Marisue wasn't around to chivvy her along. I doubted she had changed much since our grad school days.

Diesel went right up to them, and they both made a fuss over him. I explained that he was welcome at the place where we would dine. "In fact, the owner is my girlfriend." I used the term a bit self-consciously. "She's a Paris-trained chef, and I promise you the food and wine will be, as she would say, *magnifique*."

"Sounds marvelous," Randi said. "I'm delighted that we'll have *two* handsome gentlemen with us at dinner." She stroked Diesel's head.

"Surely having a cat in the restaurant violates the local health code." Marisue frowned. "It doesn't bother me, though. I have two cats and a dog back home."

"Technically, it is a violation," I said, "but Helen Louise simply tells people that if they have a problem with it, they can go eat elsewhere. Besides," I grinned, "the health inspector is addicted to her *pain au chocolat*. If he writes her up, his supply line gets cut off."

Marisue laughed heartily, and Randi giggled.

"Shall we go, ladies?" I gestured toward the front door. Diesel and I led the way, and I held the door for them.

The evening was pleasantly cool, and the sun still had about a half hour to go before it set. I pointed out a couple of landmarks during our walk to the bistro, including our local independent bookstore, the Athenaeum. "Drop in if you have a chance," I said. "It's a great place."

Randi groaned. "If I do I know I'll come out with a bag full of books, and I ran out of shelf space at home ages ago."

"That's never stopped you before," Marisue said with a chuckle. "Me, either. I think that would be a good place to visit after lunch tomorrow."

By now we had reached the bistro, and I opened the door. "You're such a gentleman, Charlie." Marisue chuckled as she entered. "I'm not used to it these days."

Helen Louise was not in evidence when I showed Randi and

Marisue to my usual table. Diesel looked around expectantly, and I told him, "She must be in the kitchen." He warbled in response.

Randi appeared startled, then she laughed. "You were talking to the cat, weren't you?"

I felt a bit sheepish. "Yes, it's a habit I got into early on with him. I swear, most of the time he understands what I say to him."

"I'm not surprised," Marisue said. "He's a smart kitty."

Diesel meowed, and both women chuckled.

"Ah, here's Helen Louise." I saw her coming from around the counter toward us. I greeted her with a peck on the cheek, and then I performed the introductions. After that was done, Helen Louise was able to give Diesel the attention he craved.

Once my guests and I were seated, and the cat was out of the way beside my chair, Helen Louise said, "I'm delighted Charlie brought you here, and I trust that you will have a memorable meal. For an appetizer, I can offer a *pâté de campagne*, or country pâté, and for the main course, *Poulet Provençal*. That is braised chicken with tomatoes and olives. The wine I suggest is a white Bergerac."

Randi's expression turned rapturous, and Marisue's eyes glazed over. The latter said, "That sounds truly *magnifique*, as Charlie told us it would be."

Helen Louise offered them a mischievous smile. "I hope you will feel the same after you've tasted it all. I'll be back in a moment with your wine and the appetizer."

Marisue, Randi, and I chatted about the bistro, and I told them some of Helen Louise's history, how she had gone to law school to please her parents, practiced for a few years, then chucked it all to live in Paris and learn everything she could about French cuisine.

95

"Good for her," Marisue said. "Takes a lot of guts to ditch a career like that to follow your dream."

Helen Louise returned to the table in time to hear the last few words. She quirked an eyebrow at me as she efficiently set before us the pâté, bread, and a bottle of the Bergerac. She deftly opened the wine, poured a taste in each glass, and waited. Marisue and Randi each gave an enthusiastic thumbs-up after testing the wine, and Helen Louise poured more.

There was little conversation as my friends and I helped ourselves to the tasty appetizer, along with the freshly made bread. I figured that, at the rate Marisue and Randi were sipping at their wine, we would easily get through a couple of bottles by the end of our meal. I was delighted to see them enjoying themselves so much.

One of Helen Louise's staff came to clear away the empty plates and gave us another bread basket. Marisue topped off our glasses with the rest of the wine, and I asked the server, Henry, for another bottle. Henry nodded and smiled pleasantly at my guests.

"He's adorable," Randi said after Henry walked away. "Young enough to be my son, but adorable nevertheless." She sighed.

"They're all old enough to be our children these days." Marisue's tart tone amused me.

"No harm in looking," Randi said.

"No," Marisue replied. "Just don't try to sample."

Randi giggled at that, and I couldn't help but laugh.

Soon Henry came back with our main course, the braised chicken with tomatoes and olives. He also set a saucer of boiled chicken down by my plate. "Diesel's treat," I explained to my friends.

While we savored the delicious dish, we avoided talk of Gavin Fong. I figured that the subject would come up over coffee and dessert. Near the end of the meal, however, Randi glanced across the room toward the door. She stiffened for a moment, then poked Marisue's arm.

"Look who just walked in," Randi said.

Harlan Crais stepped toward the counter, and Marisue and Randi exchanged glances.

Marisue leaned toward me and said in an undertone, "I wouldn't be surprised if he turns out to be Gavin's killer."

FOURTEEN

||||||||||||||||||||||||||||||||||||||||||||||||||||||

"What do you know about him?" I hadn't realized my two friends were acquainted with Harlan Crais.

Marisue's gaze slid sideways toward Randi. "Better ask her. She knows much more about him than I do."

To my surprise, Randi's face reddened, and she shot Marisue an angry look. "I wish you'd forget I ever told you about that."

"About *what*?" I felt a paw on my thigh. Diesel stared at me and meowed to let me know he was still near starvation. I showed him the empty saucer that had earlier held his boiled chicken. "You've eaten it all." He meowed again. "No, that's all." He stared at me another moment, then stretched out by my chair.

I found my dinner companions regarding me with amusement. "Sorry," I muttered. "Now, what is all this about Randi and Harlan Crais?" I watched the object of our curiosity at the counter. He paid, received a bag, and then exited the bistro while we discussed him.

Randi grimaced in the direction of the man's departing back. "I might as well tell you, Charlie, because Miss Louella Parsons over here will. I had a brief fling with him when we worked together in Colorado."

"Was that at the same time you worked with Gavin?" I asked.

Randi nodded. "Yes, and he found out about it and made a bit of a stink with our boss, the dean of libraries."

"Harlan was married at the time," Marisue said.

"I didn't know that, you understand." Randi glared at Marisue, then switched her focus to me. "I was new, you see, and on the rebound from a relationship that ended when I decided to move to Colorado. Harlan was hired at the same time, and he hadn't told anybody about *Mrs.* Crais. Especially not me," she added in a bitter tone.

"Gavin was jealous," Randi continued. "For some reason, he decided I was exactly what he wanted, and he bugged the crap out of me. I couldn't stand him, but I tried to be polite about it. Then, when the thing with Harlan started, Gavin really got unpleasant."

"Sorry you had to go through that. I know it must have been awkward working with the two of them," I said. "What about Crais and Gavin, though? I can see why Gavin was angry with Crais, but why did Crais hate Gavin so much Marisue thinks he could have killed him?"

"That came later," Marisue said. "This is where my part of the tale comes in." She had a sip of wine. "Mercy, this is delicious. Well, fast-forward about three years, and I was in Kansas. Gavin was hired as head of public services—a position that I applied for, mind you, but got passed over for, but that's another sorry tale. So, Gavin was there about three months when our as-

99

sociate dean for technical services retired. Harlan applied for the position, and he actually interviewed for it. I thought he would have been the better choice of the two who interviewed, but somehow Gavin managed to convince the dean that Harlan wasn't suitable."

"Harlan was still in Colorado," Randi said. "He had recently divorced his wife, and he wanted to move on. He's also ambitious, and he wanted to move up as well. That job in Kansas would have been his stepping-stone to become dean of libraries eventually."

"Gavin, though, blackballed him, basically," Marisue said. "I don't know why the dean put so much faith in Gavin's opinion, but she did. So, it was a setback for Harlan's career. Big setback."

"He was stuck in Colorado after that for several years, until he finally managed to get his current job, wherever it is," Randi said. "He knew Gavin was the reason he didn't get the job in Kansas, and he has hated him ever since."

"Interesting," I said. Harlan Crais ostensibly had a motive—revenge—for murdering Gavin Fong. Poison, however, was more often a woman's choice for killing. At least, that was the way it was in all the classic detective stories I had read.

Marisue frowned. "What I don't understand is why Harlan was the one to introduce Gavin today. I can't imagine that he volunteered to do it. I wouldn't think he'd want to be in the same room with Gavin, let alone introduce him as a keynote speaker. Something is definitely odd about that whole setup."

I decided I would talk to Lisa Krause about this. As chair of the local arrangements committee, she might know how Crais got picked to introduce Gavin Fong. I had several questions to pose to Lisa. For one thing, I was curious about the bottle of water, ostensibly the vehicle for the poison that Gavin swallowed. I remembered her telling me that he insisted on a particular brand of bottled water. The killer probably knew that, I reasoned.

The big question—besides the identity of the murderer—was, how did the poison get into the water bottle? I hadn't really had time to think about it, but now the question teased at my brain.

My mind went off on a tangent, and for the moment I completely forgot my duties as host of this small dinner party. Randi reclaimed my attention by rapping on the table.

"Charlie, come back, come back, from wherever you are," she chanted.

"Sorry," I said, wrenched back to the here and now. "Woolgathering."

"Already trying to solve Gavin's murder, no doubt." Marisue winked at me.

"One can't help but wonder," I replied.

Our server, Henry, came back to the table to clear away, and then returned shortly with coffee and dessert. The bistro had people waiting for tables, and Helen Louise had little time to come over and chat. Marisue and Randi expressed delight over the always popular *gâteau au chocolat*—my particular favorite among the numerous gourmet treats Helen Louise offered.

I would have liked to linger a bit more over coffee and dessert—not to mention the gossip—but I was conscious of diners no doubt impatient to sample the food and wine themselves. Once my guests had finished, I left a generous tip for Henry and went to pay the check. Diesel came with me while Marisue and Randi visited the ladies' room.

I had no opportunity to see Helen Louise again. She seemed to be on a continuous circuit of counter to kitchen and back again. I managed to wave and mime a kiss and received a quick smile in return.

Marisue and Randi found me outside with Diesel. The temperature had dropped several degrees while we dined, and the air had a slight chill to it. We walked back to the hotel, and along the way I ventured an observation and a question.

"You two both obviously know more about Gavin's life and career since graduate school than I do, so I wonder if you can think of anyone else at this conference who might have seized the chance to wreak revenge."

We paused in front of the hotel while I waited for one of them to answer. Marisue and Randi looked at each other. Finally, Marisue turned back to me and spoke.

"There are two women we are acquainted with who are here, and they both worked with Gavin at some point. We don't know either of them well, so we can't say whether they might have had anything against Gavin."

Randi continued. "Nancy Dunlap and Cathleen Matera. They both worked with him in California or Colorado at different places. I think they may work together now, somewhere in Louisiana."

"Cathleen Matera." The name rang a bell, and I tried to remember when I had heard it. Then I remembered. "I met her yesterday, after the incident with Gavin. She came up to me afterward and said she would be a witness for me if he tried to make a fuss."

"When you run into her again, you might mention you know us," Marisue said. "You might get her to talk to you about Gavin."

I nodded. "I will. I'll be on the lookout for Nancy Dunlap as well. Is there anyone else?"

Randi frowned. "I know I saw another familiar face. A man's.

Now, what is his name?" She thought for a moment. "Marisue, what's the name of that guy from South Carolina, the one who writes science fiction under a pseudonym?"

"Mitch Handler," Marisue said after a moment's hesitation. "I think he writes as Berger Mitchell. Does that sound right?"

"Yes, that's him," Randi said. "Average height, salt-and-pepper hair, glasses, on the quiet side. I heard something happened between him and Gavin, but I don't know what. I'll try to remember who told me about it."

"Don't look at me," Marisue said. "I've read some of his stuff. He's good. Other than that, I don't know anything about him."

"These are some good leads," I said. "Well, I won't keep you any longer, ladies. I'm so glad we had time to visit tonight. I know I'll see you both again before the conference is over."

"Of course. Thank you for that divine meal." Marisue gave me a hug, and Randi followed suit. She thanked me also, then both women bade Diesel and me good night.

I watched them enter the hotel lobby, then realized foolishly that I would have to follow them in, unless I wanted to go back down the alley beside the hotel to get to my car. I wasn't superstitious, generally, but after my last experience with that alley, I didn't feel like walking through it again just yet.

I pushed open the door, and Diesel entered ahead of me. The hotel staff had seen me here with him in the past, so I didn't expect one of them to raise a fuss when we were simply walking through to get to the parking lot.

We encountered two guests who looked askance at us, however. I started to pass them by, but then I remembered where I had seen one of them. She was the woman who had come up to Gavin after I knocked him down. What was her name? Maxine Muller.

I hesitated for a moment, thinking I might say something to her. As I turned, I heard her speak in an urgent whisper to her companion, an older woman with brown hair liberally streaked with white.

"That's him, Sylvia. He's the one who killed Gavin."

I did stop then, and I turned to confront them, even though Diesel tugged at the leash. He knew we were headed for the car, and he was ready to go home.

They were scurrying away. I started to call out to them, but my cell phone rang. I would have to find the two women and try to talk to them tomorrow.

I pulled out my cell phone. Lisa Krause's name popped up on the screen.

"Hi, Lisa, what's up?"

I heard a sob, then a deep breath before she spoke.

"Charlie, I've got to talk to you as soon as possible. I think they're going to arrest me for murder."

FIFTEEN

||||||||||||||||||||||||||||||||||||||

"Where are you now, Lisa?" I asked. The poor thing sounded terrified.

"I'm about to leave the sheriff's department. They're going to bring me back to the Farrington House." She sobbed again, then collected herself. "Can you meet me there? I hate to impose, but I really need to talk to you."

"I'm already at the hotel. Diesel and I will wait for you in the lobby. Don't worry, now, I'm sure we can get this sorted out."

"Thank you." She ended the call.

I put away my cell phone and looked down at my cat. "Well, boy, I guess we're not going home for a while yet. Come on, let's go sit over there out of the way until Lisa gets here."

Diesel resisted for a moment and pulled against the leash when I tried to lead him toward the lobby sitting area. He meowed in protest, but after a stern look and a "stop that" from me, he gave in and followed me to a small sofa. The moment I seated myself he jumped up and lay his head and the upper half of his body across my lap. The rest of him extended to the other arm of the sofa, and his tail thumped against the upholstery.

I worried for a moment about the cat hair that would no doubt get left behind, but then I figured that, over time, there had probably been far worse things on this sofa. The sheriff's department was nearby, so Lisa ought to be here soon.

While we waited, I stroked Diesel's back to keep him happy. He purred in response, and I knew he would be satisfied for a little while. My thoughts turned to the encounter with Maxine Muller and her friend, Sylvia. I supposed it didn't take a great leap of imagination on her part for Ms. Muller to connect me with Gavin's murder after she saw me knock him down. I didn't kill him, though, and I would try to get that point across if I could get her to talk to me. As someone who had seemed friendly to Gavin, she could be helpful in identifying persons with motives far stronger than mine to get rid of the man.

Lisa Krause walked into the lobby and made a beeline for me the moment she spotted us on the sofa.

"Oh, Charlie," she said, her breath catching in a sob. "I feel like I'm going crazy. You've got to help me."

"I will. I promise." I gently moved Diesel aside so I could stand up. He chirped in protest and climbed down from the sofa to rub against Lisa's legs. "We can't talk about it in the lobby, though. Aren't you staying here during the conference?" At her nod, I suggested we go to her room, and we headed for the elevator.

In her fifth-floor room, I checked out her view of the town square before I settled into a low-backed chair. Diesel stretched out beside me, while Lisa sat on the edge of the queen-sized bed. She appeared calmer now in this quiet space.

"Okay, tell me what's been happening with you."

Lisa nodded. "It all started because I was the one who handed Gavin Fong that bottle of water he drank from right before he collapsed." She shuddered. "That was awful. I don't think I'll ever forget the shocked expression he had right after drinking from that bottle. At first I was so stunned by it all that I didn't think clearly. It wasn't until someone at my table asked me about the bottle that it dawned on me that whatever killed him was inside it."

"You couldn't have known there was poison in the bottle," I said. "If, indeed, that turns out to be the case."

"No, I couldn't have," Lisa said. "But the fact is, I handed it to him. I brought the bottle to the table. Actually I brought a couple of them because he, Gavin, I mean, insisted that he had to have them. He refused to drink the hotel water."

"There were two bottles. That's interesting. Where did they come from?" I asked.

"From his suite," Lisa said. "I arranged to have two dozen there for him during the conference. I figured that ought to be enough water for anyone for three days. Any that were left over he could take home with him, and I told him that."

"How many were left when you went to get the two that you brought to the table?"

Lisa gave me a blank stare. "I'm not sure." She thought for a moment, then shrugged. "There are a dozen bottles in each shrink-wrapped package. One package was still intact. The other one was open, of course, and I think maybe five bottles were left after I took two. Could that be important?"

"I don't know," I said. "It might be. They're going to have to figure out when someone had the opportunity to put the poison in the bottle. Did you happen to look at the caps? Perhaps notice if one had been opened already?"

"No, why would I?" Lisa said. "They were still with the others in the shrink-wrap, and I simply pulled them out. I wouldn't have had any reason to examine them closely."

"You wouldn't," I said. "The killer had to count on the fact that no one was looking closely at the caps, I suppose, unless there was another way of getting the poison into the bottles." I frowned. "It seems a chancy thing to do, frankly. A lot of people would check to make sure the seal was unbroken before they would remove the cap. I usually do."

"I guess." Lisa frowned. "If I'm in a hurry I don't pay much attention to things like that. From now on, though, I darn sure will."

"Probably a good idea," I said. "Now, about the sheriff's department. Why do you think they might arrest you? I think if they seriously intended to, you wouldn't be here. You'd still be at the sheriff's department."

"They kept me down there for four hours. I thought I would go crazy because they kept asking me the same questions over and over." She shot me a dark look. "That friend of yours, the chief deputy, nearly scared the life out of me. She looks at you like you're about to be taken to the gas chamber if you don't answer her questions."

I had certainly experienced that same look from Kanesha, and, while intense, it wasn't as scary to me as Lisa claimed it was for her.

"What seemed to be the focus of the questions?"

"First, they asked me how well I knew the deceased. I told them I didn't know him. I'd maybe seen him at a couple of SALA meetings, but that was it." Lisa paused for a breath. "Then it was all about the stupid bottle of water. I had to go over, and over, and over, every blinking thing I knew about the bottles."

"I think they're trying to zero in on opportunity," I said. "To my mind, that's the critical question. When did the killer have the opportunity to add the poison?" I thought for a moment. "I suppose there's a chance that the poison was delivered some other way, but his collapse only seconds after drinking from the bottle seems to preclude that. They have to take a hard look at you, naturally, because of opportunity. They can figure out the motive later."

"Because I retrieved the bottles from his suite and had them in my possession." Lisa nodded. "I guess I was too upset earlier to think clearly about that."

I remembered that she had mentioned bringing two bottles to the luncheon. I asked her about that.

"He finished one of them a few minutes before he was going to speak," Lisa said. "He ducked out to the restroom for a minute, and when he got back, it was almost time for him to go up on the dais."

"I wonder why he didn't take the bottle with him then." That puzzled me, because it would have been the obvious thing to do. Yet he hadn't done it.

Lisa snorted. "Knowing him, he left it deliberately so he could snap his fingers and make me bring it to him. He did other things like that to show that he had to be waited on."

I shook my head. "Sad, but that does sound like something he would do. Now, another question. The tables were set for eight people, so who was at your table, besides you and Gavin?"

"Let me think a moment." Lisa peered at a spot over and behind my head. "Well, there was Maxine Muller. She was always hanging around him. She was like a puppy trailing after him. I've known her slightly for several years. Then of course there was the man who introduced him. Harlan Crais." She paused. "The rest were the current president of SALA and the other main officers, the vice president, the treasurer, and the secretary." She rattled off their names, and I didn't recognize a single one. They weren't any of the people Marisue and Randi named to me earlier.

"Discounting you and Gavin, then," I said, "there were six other people at the table who could feasibly have tampered with the bottle." I didn't feel I could share with Lisa what Marisue and Randi told me earlier about Harlan Crais. Though I might share it with Kanesha Berry, I wasn't going to pass it along idly to another librarian.

"That's true." Lisa's expression brightened. "Harlan Crais sat on one side of Gavin, and Maxine on the other. They were both closer to the bottle than I was."

"Did you tell the deputy that?"

"Yes, she had me draw her a diagram," Lisa said. "It took me a few minutes to remember who was where because the deputy had me pretty rattled by that point."

"Either of them is far more likely to have done it than you," I said. "Kanesha knows that already, I have no doubt. They both worked with Gavin more closely, and for a longer period of time, than you did the past few days."

"I don't know how they stood him for more than two days running." Lisa snorted. "He was the most obnoxious waste of time I've ever dealt with."

"Once she digs into his past, no doubt she'll find a lot of people who wanted revenge on him for things he did," I said. "The question is, which of them would go as far as murder. But Harlan Crais and Maxine Muller were at that table. Did you see either of them handling a water bottle?"

"The deputy asked me that, too," Lisa replied. "But I didn't. I had to leave the table a couple of times to visit the restroom myself, and I was probably gone three or four minutes each time. Either one of them could have done something while I was gone."

"Maybe one of the SALA officers saw something," I said. "Although how the killer got the poison into the bottle is a mystery in itself. Sitting there, opening the bottle, and dropping something in it would attract attention." I shook my head. "It just seems too risky to do it then."

"I certainly wouldn't have the nerve to try it," Lisa said. "Someone would see me for sure."

"Kanesha will also try to find out whether anyone visited Gavin's room," I said. "It's certainly possible a visitor had the opportunity, or that the killer managed to get into the room when Gavin was out of it."

"Or it could have happened during the party," Lisa said.

SIXTEEN

||||||||||||||||||||||||||||||||||||||||

"Party? What party?" This was the first I had heard about it.

"Sorry, I forgot you didn't know about it." Lisa frowned. "Gavin hosted a party in his suite last night. Not a big one, only about a dozen people maybe. I wouldn't have known about it myself until later, except that I happened to be passing the front desk, and one of the managers called me over about eight last night. She wanted me to approve the charges Gavin had made to the room, since they exceeded the limit we had given the hotel."

"Did Gavin order a lot of food and drink, expecting SALA to pay for it?" I was appalled by the idea. Unprofessional and downright rude behavior, not to mention totally selfish, in my opinion.

"He certainly did." Lisa's tone grew heated as she continued. "I couldn't believe the colossal nerve of the guy. It put me in a difficult position, because Gavin evidently told the front desk I had given permission. They had already delivered the food and drink by the time the manager called me over to sign for the charges. I had to go ahead and sign. I tried calling the SALA treasurer, but she didn't respond to my call or text. I found out this morning she was out to dinner and had left her cell phone in her room."

"Have you told her about it since?" I asked.

"First thing this morning, she called me back," Lisa replied. "She was livid, too, but she didn't blame me. She was furious with Gavin and said she would see that he reimbursed SALA for the unauthorized expense." Lisa threw up her hands. "But of course now SALA is stuck with the bill."

"Yes, I'm afraid you'll have to eat the expense," I said. "What a jerk to do something like that. Did you confront him about it last night?"

"I went to his suite to talk to him about it, but he refused to discuss it. Said it was the least SALA could do, since he was a featured speaker. It was one of his perks, he said."

"Unbelievable." I sighed. "You really had a lot to put up with, having to deal with that kind of behavior."

"Yes, I did, but I didn't kill him over it." Lisa looked defiant.

"No, I didn't say you had," I replied. "But did you tell Kanesha about this?"

Lisa's defiant expression faded rapidly to be replaced by a sheepish one. "No, I didn't."

"You should have told her," I said, "even though your part in it is probably irrelevant to the murder. She should have all the facts if she's going to figure the whole thing out."

"I know, you've told me that before." Lisa glanced away for a moment.

I knew we were both recalling the recent events involving the murder of my predecessor as interim director. Lisa had been a part of the investigation in a small way and had, at the time, not been completely forthcoming to the sheriff's department. I thought she would have learned her lesson with that, but evidently not.

"So you will tell her?" I asked.

Lisa nodded. "I will."

"Good," I said. "Now, you were in Gavin's suite. For how long?"

"Maybe ten minutes at the most," Lisa replied. "I saw there was no point in trying to talk to him about it, and I gave up and left."

"Did you have time to notice who all was there?" I asked.

"I suppose," Lisa said. "I know Maxine was there, and she seemed to be chatting with another woman. I think I heard the name Sylvia." She paused for a moment. "That guy with the bald head, the earrings, and the tattoos was there. He's hard to miss. I wouldn't have the guts to walk around in short sleeves the way he does, not with that ink all the way down to his wrists."

"He is pretty memorable," I said. "Anybody else?"

"Right when I was leaving, two women came in. I think you know them. Marisue and Randi. I can't remember their last names at the moment, but they're always together at these conferences."

"I do know them," I said. "In fact, I had dinner with them tonight. They never mentioned Gavin's party, though." I found that odd. Why wouldn't they have told me about it?

"Then there was Harlan Crais. I noticed him, because he was standing in the corner, nursing a beer, and staring at Gavin. There were a couple of other people, but I didn't know them. I will probably recognize them when I see them again, and if I do, I'll try to get their names. Would you like me to do that?"

I nodded. "That would be helpful, and I'm sure you'll give them to Kanesha as well. Tell me, where were the bottles of water that Gavin had to have?"

"On a shelf underneath the bar," Lisa replied. "Anyone could have found them there and tampered with one, I guess."

"Yes, and my bet is that is when it happened. The killer would be less likely to attract attention. I assume everyone served themselves?"

"Yes, from what I could see," Lisa said. "The party was a bit raucous, too. There was music playing, and people were trying to talk over it. I don't think anyone would have thought twice about a person spending a minute or two behind the bar."

"That will be Kanesha's job," I said. "She'll have to figure out who all was there and ask them what they might have seen."

"I didn't go near the bar the few minutes I was there," Lisa said. "At least I'm in the clear on that."

"Yes," I said. "I think there were other people who had as good a chance to tamper with the water as you, and they had more motive. Or so I would guess."

"Thank you, Charlie," Lisa said. "You've made me feel a lot less scared and miserable. You're so good at that. Sensible and kind. I wish you could stay on as director at work. That's what everyone really wants, you know."

"I'm very flattered by that," I said. As much as I would have liked to tell her the job was mine if I wanted it, I couldn't. If I decided to accept the offer, Lisa would have to find out when the rest of the library staff did.

I pushed myself out of the chair, and Diesel yawned and stretched. "Time for us to head home. I don't know about you, but I'm pretty wiped out from the day."

Lisa laughed. "Definitely. Thanks again, Charlie. Good night, Diesel." She showed us out, and I heard the dead bolt click when she shut the door behind us.

"I don't know about you, boy," I said as we walked toward the elevator, "but I'm ready to get home and go to bed." Diesel meowed in agreement.

The moment we stepped into the kitchen, Diesel bolted for the utility room. He didn't even wait for me to undo his harness. I felt guilty at keeping him out so late. I checked the front of the fridge but didn't find any messages stuck there, nor were there any notes left on the table. I went on upstairs. Diesel would follow when he finished his business.

My brain felt jammed with too much information, too many impressions, from the day. My thoughts had been preoccupied with Gavin Fong's murder, but now, in the quiet of my home, I started thinking about Laura and Frank and the decision they had to make. It was too late now to call to talk to Laura, to find out whether they *had* made their decision. I knew, though, she would have let me know by now if they had.

Thoughts of Laura and Frank led in turn to the decision that I had to make by Monday morning. I kept going back and forth, from *no* one minute to *yes* the next. That was ridiculous, I thought. Surely a man my age ought to know his own mind better at this stage in life.

But I didn't. My emotions were too wrapped up, I realized, in the outcome of my children's decision. Until I knew what Laura and Frank were going to do, I wouldn't be able to make up my own mind completely.

That thought brought a small measure of relief to my overtired brain. Diesel ambled into the bedroom and hopped up on the bed beside me. I removed his harness, and he rubbed his head against my arm. Then he stretched out on his side of the bed, his head on the pillow.

I followed his example and soon, despite my state of mind, drifted into sleep.

When Diesel and I walked into the kitchen the next morning, we found Stewart and Haskell finishing breakfast. Haskell wore his uniform, while Stewart was in pajamas. Dante bounced forward, barking to greet Diesel. The cat meowed, and when he headed for the utility room, Dante trotted alongside him.

After an exchange of greetings, I said to Haskell, "You're on duty today?"

He nodded. "Got called in because of the homicide at the Farrington House yesterday."

Stewart set down his coffee cup. "What do *you* know about this murder, Charlie? I figure you must know something about it. Were you there when it happened?"

I poured coffee for myself while I answered. "Yes, I was there. Near the ballroom doors and well away from the action." I took my usual seat at the table and sipped at my coffee.

"Did you know the victim?" Stewart asked.

I nodded. "Yes, I did. The guy I told you about, the one I knocked down the other day."

Haskell checked his watch. "Sorry, got to get going. Have to meet Kanesha for a briefing in about fifteen minutes." He rose from the table, and so did Stewart.

"I'll be back in a minute, Charlie." Stewart followed Haskell into the hall, and a minute or so later I heard the front door open and close.

Stewart walked back into the kitchen. "So, this guy you didn't like was killed."

I nodded. "I admit I loathed him, but I'm sorry he died like that."

"I'm sorry you had to sit there and see it happen," Stewart said. "I'm sure it wasn't pleasant."

"No, it wasn't," I said. "I'm thankful, though, that I wasn't anywhere near to see, well, you know."

Stewart nodded. "That part would have been ugly."

"I'm figuring it was cyanide," I said. "But I can't figure out how someone would have gotten hold of it. It's a regulated substance, isn't it?"

"Yes, it certainly is," Stewart said. "A person can't simply walk into the neighborhood drugstore and ask for it over the counter. There are chemical supply houses—that's how we obtain the cyanide we use in the labs at work. But an ordinary person can't order it." He got up from the table to refill his coffee. "The killer could have stolen it from a lab, I suppose, but that wouldn't be easy."

"Is there any other way you can think of?" I asked.

"Yeah," he replied. "Online."

SEVENTEEN

||||||||||||||||||||||||||||||||||||||||||||||||||||||||

I nearly dropped my coffee cup at Stewart's answer. "Online? You mean you can order *poison* over the Internet?"

"Not in this country," Stewart said as he resumed his seat at the table. "You know that people buy drugs from overseas online, right?" When I nodded, he continued. "Well, there are disreputable firms in other parts of the world that sell chemicals illegally, too, without regulation."

"Good heavens." I felt slightly nauseated.

"Pretty frightening, I know," Stewart said. "Another way to get it would be from a college chemistry lab, although it would be a really slipshod lab if they let dangerous chemicals get taken."

"Do you have it in the chemistry labs at Athena?" I asked.

"Yes," Stewart said. "We keep careful control over it as we do all our chemicals, and access to them is limited."

"That's good to know," I said. "Still, the killer got hold of it somehow."

"Do you know for sure that the killer used cyanide?" Stewart asked.

"No." I felt sheepish when I continued. "I'm basing it solely on how quickly it happened, how he behaved before he fell out of sight, and on reading many mysteries over the years that had cyanide as the murder weapon."

Stewart chuckled. "I know it's not funny, but hearing you say that makes me think of Agatha Christie."

"Exactly," I said. "She worked in a hospital dispensary and became quite knowledgeable about poisons."

"I think I read that somewhere," Stewart said. "Tell me what you saw."

I related the scene as I recalled it, and Stewart nodded when I finished. "That sounds like cyanide poisoning," he said. "Tasteless, soluble in water, and he probably drank so fast he had no idea what he'd swallowed."

How vulnerable we are. That thought gave me the shivers.

"The toxicology report could take several weeks, even longer," Stewart said. "In the meantime, cyanide seems likely to me."

"I think figuring out *when* the killer got the poison into the water bottle is the key to solving it," I said. "Once Kanesha knows that, she can probably isolate the suspects and figure out who did it and why."

"Plus find out where they got the cyanide in the first place," Stewart added. "I'm curious about that part."

I nodded. "Me, too. I think I know when the killer had the best opportunity to poison the bottle." I told Stewart about the party Gavin hosted in his suite. "That must be when it was done."

"Probably," Stewart said. "But wasn't the killer taking a risk that someone else might have gotten hold of that bottle instead?"

"I hadn't thought of that," I said. "Depends on when during the party it was done, I suppose. Gavin wouldn't have wanted to share his particular favorite brand of water with anyone else, and I'll bet the others at the party knew that. I'll have to ask Lisa if she remembers whether there was other water available."

"The other thing that strikes me is the fact that this guy drank from the poisoned bottle during the luncheon. If the killer poisoned the water in the suite, he or she had no way of knowing exactly when the victim would actually drink it and die."

"That's true," I said. "Well, Kanesha will have to figure all that out, if she can."

I got up to refill my coffee, and I suddenly heard a ruckus coming from the direction of the stairs. Stewart and I looked at each other and grinned. Diesel and Dante were playing one of their favorite games, running up and down the stairs, taking turns chasing each other. Dante barked occasionally, and Diesel meowed loudly. The game usually lasted about five minutes, by which time they had expended enough energy and were ready to rest for another round later. The early stage of the game wasn't noisy. The longer they went at it, however, the louder and faster they got.

Stewart and I waited for about a minute, and the two racers came trotting into the kitchen, breathing hard.

Stewart glanced at his watch. "Time for me to get ready for the gym. Come on, Dante." The dog trotted over to him, panting, and Stewart scooped him up. "We'll see you later, guys." Dante licked Stewart's face as the two exited the room.

Diesel stretched out on the floor by my chair and started grooming himself. I prepared a small bowl of cereal and popped two pieces of bread into the toaster. Once I finished my cereal and toast, I contemplated another couple of pieces of toast, but decided on an apple instead. Every once in a while I made a healthier choice.

My thoughts turned to Laura and Frank. I badly wanted to call Laura to find out what was going on. Had they made a decision yet? Was there still a chance they might choose to stay in Athena?

I knew I shouldn't call. Laura knew I'd be stewing over this, anxious to know the outcome. She would talk to me as soon as she and Frank were ready to share their decision. I had to be content to wait. Patience, in matters like this, was never my strong suit.

I forced my mind to the conference schedule. I had that panel on cataloging to do. Would someone step in to take Gavin's place? I wondered. I also speculated, somewhat uneasily, how technical the other librarians on the panel would get. With the change from the old Anglo-American Cataloguing Rules, known fondly to catalogers as AACR2, to the newer standard, Resource Description and Access, known as RDA, the world of cataloging had changed. Though I was familiar with RDA and some of the important changes, I didn't have a complete grasp of it by any means. I didn't want to appear ignorant if the others started spouting rule numbers that meant nothing to me.

Too late to worry about that now. I would have to wing it and hope not to come off looking like a complete fool. Given everything else going on in my life right now, this panel was a minor thing.

That realization made me feel better. I put my dishes in the dishwasher, made sure the coffeepot was off, and then Diesel and I headed upstairs. I needed to get ready to face the outside world.

Half an hour later I was prepared to leave the house, dressed in a suit but without the tie. Five days a week were enough with a tie around my neck, I decided. Most of the men I had seen at the conference yesterday weren't wearing them, and I might as well go with the trend.

Before I went to the Farrington House, however, I had to deliver Diesel to Melba Gilley's house. She had volunteered to take care of him today so that I wouldn't have to leave him at home with only Dante for company. Both cat and dog tended to make mischief when left without human supervision, and I didn't care to come home and find every shoe I owned dragged out of my closet and left with teeth and claw marks. Lesson learned.

I chatted with Melba a moment while Diesel disappeared quickly into the house. He had been here before, and I had no doubt he headed straight to Melba's sofa. I passed over the harness and leash in case she wanted to run an errand while she babysat.

The conference started at nine this morning, and I made it to the hotel about ten minutes before nine. I paused in the lobby to scan the program. Nothing in the nine o'clock session appealed to me, and my panel started at half past ten. *Might as well visit the vendor exhibits.*

Because the SALA conference was a relatively small meeting, the exhibits occupied only half the ballroom. I remembered the exhibitors' hall at the Texas Library Association Annual Meetings, held in convention centers, and the vast space it covered. I could easily make my way around these exhibits in under an hour unless I stopped to chat with vendors at each booth. I did want to speak with salespeople from our chief subscription agent and introduce myself. In case I decided to accept the director's job, I knew I shouldn't pass up an opportunity to acquaint myself with these people.

I quickly found the booth I sought and introduced myself to one of the salespeople, a curly-headed young woman whose name tag read *Carol Seiler.* We soon discovered that we had mutual librarian friends in Texas and chatted away. She introduced me to several of her coworkers, and we discussed some of the particulars of the Athena College account.

While we talked I became aware of two women, both strangers who appeared to be in their late seventies, at least. They stood nearby, perhaps seven or eight feet away, staring at me. I glanced sideways several times and saw them whispering to each other, and twice one of the women pointed in my direction. I realized I had lost the thread of the conversation with Carol and her coworkers and made an effort to ignore the women.

Why were they staring and pointing at me? I wondered while I listened to Carol's remarks about a new product. Different visitors to the booth claimed the other salespeople's attention, but Carol continued her conversation with me. I made an effort to listen and comment intelligently, but at the back of my mind I was stewing over the behavior of those two women.

When I allowed myself a quick sideways glance in their direction, I saw that they were no longer nearby. I wanted to turn around and look for them, but I couldn't be that rude. Carol, however, noticed my distraction.

"Is everything all right?" she asked. "Something seems to be bothering you."

I hesitated before I answered. "Well, actually, there is. Did you happen to notice those two women who hovered nearby for a few minutes? They seemed to be staring and pointing at me, and I don't know why."

Carol shook her head. "No, sorry, I didn't notice them. Perhaps they were waiting to speak with you but didn't want to interrupt."

I shrugged. "Well, if that's the case, I suppose they'll track me down at some point." I thanked her for her time, and she gave me her business card. I tucked it into my jacket pocket, wished her a good day, and wandered down the row to survey the other booths.

At the end of the row I paused at the exhibitor's table and picked up a brochure that touted their databases, all designed for general academic libraries. I asked a few questions, received a free thumb drive and a couple more brochures, then rounded the corner to go down the next aisle.

I ran right into the two women who only a little while ago had been watching me and whispering to each other. "Sorry," I said with a brief smile. "I wasn't looking where I was going."

One of the women uttered a muted shriek and stepped back, while the other stared at me with avid interest. I would have sworn she licked her lips before she said, "If you're the one who killed that obnoxious Gavin Fong, I'd like to shake your hand."

EIGHTEEN

||||||||||||||||||||||||||||||||||||||||||||||||

For a moment I was too taken aback to do anything other than stare blankly at the two women. Then the bizarre nature of the situation struck my often quirky sense of humor, and I was hard put not to laugh.

Instead I said, "Ma'am, I'd be happy to shake your hand, but it would be under false pretenses. I didn't kill Gavin Fong."

The woman who shrieked a moment ago eyed me with suspicion. When she spoke, her voice came out in a hoarse whisper, and I had to strain to hear her. "Are you sure? I could have sworn someone told me you were the man who beat him up Thursday and nearly put him in the hospital."

The woman who had offered to shake my hand glared at her companion. "What idiot told you that, Ada Lou? You saw that jerk Fong at the luncheon yesterday. Did he *look* like he'd been beaten up anywhere near bad enough to be in the hospital?"

"Well, no, Virginia, I guess not." Ada Lou looked confused.

"Of course not," Virginia snapped. "We were sitting a couple of tables away from him, and he didn't look like—or move like— a man who'd been beaten, did he?"

"I already said he didn't, Virginia," Ada Lou said. "I wish you wouldn't keep on at me like that. My eyesight is better than yours. I could see that table a lot better than you, in fact. I was looking straight at him most of the time, and that man who was sitting next to him. You're the one who complained that there was a real big head in the way when you tried to look."

"Well, there was a big head," Virginia said. "You were sitting right there. Surely you could see a head that big for yourself, if your eyesight is as good as you keep saying it is."

By now several people had paused to eavesdrop on this peculiar conversation, and I was ready to move on before it became even more bizarre. While Virginia and Ada Lou continued to bicker, apparently having forgotten about me, I sidled away. I was curious about why Virginia hated Gavin Fong enough to want to shake my hand, but for the moment, I decided, finding that out could wait. I could always track them down later. In a group this size it shouldn't be that hard.

Perhaps my encounter with Virginia and Ada Lou had made me abnormally sensitive, but as I continued to make my way through the exhibits and speak occasionally to vendors, I felt the weight of numerous gazes directed my way. Was I imagining this, or were the starers all thinking I killed Gavin Fong?

I probably had Maxine Muller to thank for this, I decided. I recalled that she had accused me of murder to Kanesha Berry. She must have been busy spreading the word at the conference. I grew increasingly uncomfortable in the exhibit hall and decided I'd had enough.

I walked out of the ballroom into the foyer and found a secluded spot behind a pillar near a wall. A check of my watch informed me that I had twenty minutes before my panel started. I debated whether to abandon it and head home for the rest of the day. I knew Lisa Krause would be disappointed in me, not to mention angry, for doing so, and I told myself I had to tough it out.

Being the center of attention had never appealed to me, although a few times I had done stupid things that briefly put me right in the limelight. The two times I knocked down Gavin Fong were prime examples. I wouldn't describe myself as self-effacing, exactly, but neither did I seek out attention for the sake of being noticed and puffing up my ego. I preferred getting on with my life without most of the world around me paying any attention.

Oh, stop feeling sorry for yourself. This will all pass over as soon as Kanesha solves the case, and all these people will forget who you are. I could almost hear my late wife, Jackie, and my aunt Dottie telling me that in unison.

Still, I continued to feel a bit nervous. After a brief visit to the restroom I made my way to the room where my panel on cataloging would start in about five minutes. The previous session ended at ten fifteen, but people lingered near the front of the room. I went around the chairs on one side of the room and reached the front. A young man took away the name cards on the table and replaced them with those of the members of the cataloging panel.

I felt a slight jolt when I spotted one with Gavin Fong's name on it. Evidently the young man didn't realize Fong wouldn't be attending. I wondered whether I should remove it but decided that I would let someone else do it if they wanted to. Even without a name card I knew Gavin's presence would probably be felt. Given the incendiary tenor of the opening remarks to his keynote speech yesterday, I felt reasonably sure he would have expressed opinions on cataloging that would have angered the audience today. Had he lived long enough to finish his remarks at the luncheon, he likely would have faced a roomful of angry librarians.

As I waited for the other members of the panel to make themselves known, I speculated whether Gavin's attitude toward his profession could have anything to do with his murder. I didn't take it seriously as a motive, but it could be a contributing factor, of a sort. Maybe when I got home later this afternoon I would do a little digging, check out some of Gavin's publications, to find out whether he had expressed these provocative opinions in professional journals.

I emerged from my woolgathering and looked at my watch. The panel should have started seven minutes ago. I also noticed that the room was nearly empty. I counted three other people besides myself.

What was going on? Where were the other members of the panel?

Moments later a harassed-looking Lisa Krause hurried into the room. Her expression forewarned me of bad news.

"What's going on?" I asked. "Am I in the wrong room for the cataloging panel?"

Lisa shook her head. "No, this is the room." She hesitated, then plunged into speech. "I'm sorry, Charlie, the other panel members all canceled. I only found out about this a few minutes ago, or I would have let you know sooner."

"They *all* canceled? Why?" I thought I knew why, but I wanted to hear what Lisa had to say. My head started to ache as my earlier feelings of self-consciousness resurfaced.

"They all suddenly came down with really upset stomachs."

Lisa glowered. "Of all the ridiculously lame excuses I've ever heard, this one is the lamest."

"Don't worry about it," I said. "I wasn't particularly looking forward to it myself." After a brief pause, I continued in a rueful tone. "I'm pretty sure I'm the cause of those upset stomachs."

"Oh, Charlie." Lisa reached out and squeezed my upper arm, her expression one of sympathy. "They don't know you like I do, or they would never behave in such a ludicrous way. Frankly I'm surprised they're not all avoiding *me*. After all," she added bitterly, "I'm the one who gave the bottle of poisoned water to Gavin Fong."

"But you weren't the one who knocked him down in front of a lot of people." I shrugged. "By now I'm sure every single one of the people at this conference knows who I am and what I did." I told Lisa about my run-in with Virginia and Ada Lou. She rolled her eyes at the mention of their names.

"I know them. They're retired, have been for probably ten years or more, but I've seen them at every SALA meeting I've attended. I think they both get weirder every year. I'm sorry you had to deal with them."

I chuckled. "I'll admit it was disconcerting at the time, but now I can laugh about it. A little, anyway."

"Good," Lisa said. "Since you no longer have a panel to do, are you going to hang around for the rest of the day?"

"Am I going to tough it out, you mean?" I nodded. "Unless people start screaming and running away from me like I'm Frankenstein's monster, I'll hang around. I'd like to see more of some friends who are here, and there are some interesting sessions this afternoon."

Lisa patted my arm. "I hope you won't run into any more idiots. Well, I've got to go." She glanced at her watch. "Heck, I was supposed to meet someone five minutes ago." She turned and sped from the room.

I noticed that the two people still remaining in the room watched Lisa hurry out. They put their heads together to talk, and I had a feeling they were talking about Lisa. Maybe people were taking more notice of her than she realized.

I walked toward the man and woman. "Sorry, but evidently the panel is canceled. The rest of the speakers are all under the weather." I gave them a pleasant smile and left the room without waiting for a response.

Back in the foyer of the ballroom I debated whether to return to the exhibits and wander around for a while. I didn't feel like attending any of the sessions going on right now. I didn't even bother to consult the program because I knew I would be unable to focus on the speakers. I felt too restless, and I didn't want to sit in a room on an uncomfortable chair for an hour or so and fidget.

I went to the gift shop in the lobby and paid too much for a diet soda and a small bag of salted peanuts. I found a spot in the hotel lobby, a chair that faced the windows, and made myself comfortable. While I nibbled on peanuts and drank my diet soda, I watched the activity on the square and let my thoughts roam.

While I had some interest in the solving of Gavin Fong's murder, I had two other matters that continued to stew in my subconscious. What would Laura and Frank do? I couldn't help but think that their decision could affect my own decision about the full-time director's job at the college library.

I promised Forrest Wyatt and the others, however, that I would give them my decision on Monday morning. I had no idea when Laura and Frank would make theirs. If I had to give an answer about the job before I knew what my children were going to do, I would be deciding without all the facts, in a way.

These thoughts made me realize that if Laura and Frank by some small miracle remained in Athena I really didn't want to take on the full-time job. I wanted to be able to spend time with my grandchild. *Grandchildren*, I corrected myself. Sean and Alexandra were having a baby, too, and in my preoccupation over Laura's potential move, I had lost sight of the fact that, even if she and Frank relocated to Virginia, I'd still have one grandchild in Athena. I needed to consider that, too.

Suddenly I felt too restless to sit any longer. I got up, discarded my empty soda can and the peanut bag, and headed to the front door of the hotel. I needed fresh air, and I would also soon be ready for lunch, despite my snack. As long as I was this close, I might as well have lunch at Helen Louise's bistro.

The sun warmed my face, but it was not unpleasantly hot. A light breeze made for a pleasant walk around the square. I nodded a few times at people I knew and stopped once to chat briefly with a neighbor who lived three houses down from mine.

The conversation finished, I resumed my walk toward the bistro. My cell phone rang, and I pulled it out. Lisa Krause's name came up. I was tempted to let it go to voice mail, but I knew I couldn't do that to Lisa.

"Oh, Charlie, where are you?" Lisa broke into speech right away, not even giving me time to say hello. She didn't wait for an answer to her question, either. "Wherever you are, I need you right away. I think somebody poisoned her, just like Gavin."

NINETEEN

||||||||||||||||||||||||||||||||||||||||||||||||||||

Lisa started sobbing, and I almost had to yell over the phone to get her attention. Passersby stared at me, and one woman made as if to approach me. I held up my hand and smiled to let her know I was okay.

"Lisa, you've got to calm down enough to tell me where you are," I said. "I can't help you if I don't know where you are."

I heard her draw a shaky breath. "Sorry, Charlie, you're right." She sniffled. "I'm at the hotel. Room 602. Can you come?"

I had already turned in the direction of the hotel and started walking back. "Yes, I'm on the way. Who is it you're talking about? Are you sure she's dead?"

Lisa sobbed again into the phone, but she caught hold of herself right away. "Maxine Muller. She's dead. She looks so awful I can't stand to look at her."

"Have you called 911 yet?" I started moving faster, and my calves ached from the strain. I wasn't used to this pace.

"No," Lisa said. "I was so scared I called the first person I thought of. I guess I'd better call them now."

"Yes, and then notify the front desk. I'm on the way." I shut off my phone and stuck it back in my pocket. By now I was only about thirty yards from the hotel. I kept up the pace, despite the pain in my legs, and I almost ran into the front door of the hotel.

I made it through to the elevator without knocking anyone over, and I muttered under my breath while the agonizingly slow elevator doors opened to admit me. The elevator stopped twice on the way up. The moment the doors opened wide enough on the sixth floor I hurried out and looked for the sign that indicated the locations of the rooms by number.

Maxine Muller's room lay almost at the end of the corridor to my right. I could see Lisa sitting on the floor in the hallway. She glanced up as I approached, then struggled to her feet. She fell into my arms when I reached her, and I patted her back awkwardly when she started crying.

"I know this is a horrible shock for you," I said in gentle tones, "but I need you to get yourself together. The police ought to be here any moment, and the hotel manager, too. You did call, didn't you?"

Lisa pulled away and fumbled in her bag. She extracted a tissue and nodded as she dabbed at her eyes.

"Good," I said. The door stood open, and I resisted the temptation to go inside. "You're absolutely certain that she's gone?"

"Yes," Lisa said. "She's dead."

"Before everyone else gets here, let me ask you a question or two."

Lisa nodded.

"What were you doing here? Were you meeting her here?" I

remembered that she left me earlier in the meeting room, saying she was supposed to meet someone and was late.

"No, we were supposed to meet downstairs," Lisa said. "She's going to be—*was* going to be—chair of the local arrangements committee for next year's meeting, and we were going to go over a few things. But she didn't show up. I thought I'd missed her because I was late."

"Surely she could have waited five minutes or so," I said.

"That's what I thought." Lisa frowned. "I tried calling her, but it went to voice mail. I left a message and waited a few minutes, but she didn't call back. Then I sent her a text message and told her I'd catch up with her later."

"Did she respond to either message?"

Lisa nodded. "She texted me a couple of minutes after I texted her and said to come up to her room in ten minutes. She had to talk to someone first, but then she'd be ready for our meeting." She paused for a deep breath. "I waited like she asked me to, even though I was getting really irritated over the delay because I have so many things to check on today. But I came on up. Her door wasn't closed completely. I knocked and waited. I didn't hear any response, but I figured she might be in the bathroom. I pushed the door open and called out to her." She shuddered.

"What happened next?" I glanced down the hall. I'd heard the elevator doors open, and several people stepped out and headed toward us.

"I s-s-saw her feet and legs sticking out between the beds," Lisa said. That was all she had time for, because the hotel manager, along with a couple of police officers and another hotel staff member, had reached us now.

The hotel manager barely acknowledged us. He brushed past Lisa into the room, and one of the policemen and the other hotel staffer went right behind him. The other police officer motioned for Lisa and me to step aside, and he drew us a few feet down the hall.

Now began the routine I had come to know better than I ever wanted to. The officer, who looked vaguely familiar, spoke gently to Lisa, having identified her as the 911 caller. He appeared to know who I was already, and I tried to remember when and where I might have met him.

The hotel manager stumbled out of the victim's room, his face pale and his mouth twisted in a grimace. He looked at me, and his eyes narrowed. "I might have known *you'd* be involved in this somehow."

I didn't appreciate the man's attitude. I tried to keep my tone even as I responded. "I wasn't the one who found the body. I'm here only because Ms. Krause, who did find it, called me and asked for me to come. She was naturally quite upset."

The manager's gaze softened as he observed Lisa in conversation with the police officer. "Sorry," he muttered. "This is all too much. First that man dying right in the middle of a luncheon, and now this."

The other policeman and the hotel staffer exited the room. He indicated he would remain outside the door until the county crime scene investigators arrived. The policeman who had been talking to Lisa had the rest of us move about ten feet down the hallway before he stopped. He started to question Lisa further, but the elevator doors pinged open, and several uniformed men and women stepped out. Some of them carried bags and equipment. After a quick word they passed us and headed down the hall.

Accompanied by three deputies, Kanesha Berry stepped out when the doors of the second elevator opened, and her gaze seemed to focus right on me. I knew she wasn't happy to see me here, but neither was I all that pleased to be here myself.

She greeted the police officer. "I'll take over from here." He nodded and left us to join the group down the hall. She directed the three men with her to keep anyone from getting close to the crime scene. Then she addressed the hotel manager.

"Mr. Hampton, I'm afraid we're going to have to take over that part of the floor until the preliminary crime scene investigation is finished. The room will have to be sealed off. Is it a room with a connecting door to another room?"

Hampton looked at his staffer, who shook his head.

"No, it's not," he said. "How long do you think all this is going to take, Deputy Berry? Our guests in this area aren't going to be happy about not having access to their rooms."

"Yes, I realize that," Kanesha replied. "We will do our best to finish what we need to do in a timely manner, but that could still take several hours. I'm sure people will understand."

Hampton nodded. "Of course."

"Please wait here until I've had a chance to examine the scene. Then I'll need to talk to all of you." Kanesha walked on down the hall, and I watched as she entered the victim's room.

We waited in silence for nearly twenty minutes before Kanesha emerged from the room. She paused in the hall to have a brief conversation with another officer, then she rejoined us.

"Thank you for waiting. Mr. Hampton, I need a space to use while we are conducting the investigation. What do you have available?"

The manager and his staffer consulted for a moment. "One of our conference meeting rooms on the second floor is open. I believe it will serve your purpose."

"Good. Can you take us there now, please?" Kanesha nodded to me and Lisa. "I'd like you both to come with me, Ms. Krause,

Mr. Harris." She motioned for one of her men to join us. I wondered why Haskell Bates wasn't with her. He was one of her senior deputies.

"Certainly, Deputy Berry," I said. We followed her and the others to the elevators. The deputy brought up the rear.

No one spoke again until we stepped inside the conference room. Kanesha moved immediately to the head of the large table inside. "Would you gentlemen mind waiting at the other end of the room while I talk to Ms. Krause?" Kanesha indicated a chair to Lisa while Hampton, his associate, and I did as Kanesha requested. The deputy remained with Kanesha, standing off to the side behind Lisa.

The room, I estimated, would comfortably fit thirty people—space for half of them at the table, and the other half in chairs around the walls. A good size, but not so large that I couldn't hear Kanesha's conversation with Lisa.

Kanesha took her through the same questions I asked Lisa earlier, and Lisa responded with the same answers.

Then Kanesha went further than I'd had time to do. "How well did you know the deceased? Ms. Muller?"

"Not all that well," Lisa said. "I mean, I knew her as a colleague from another library. We served on a couple of committees together in the past five years, but we weren't friends. Only acquaintances."

"So your only contact with her was on a professional basis?" Kanesha asked.

"Yes," Lisa said. "Exactly."

"Tell me more about the subject of the meeting you were supposed to have with her."

"Okay." Lisa nodded. "I was the chair of the local arrangements committee for the meeting this year, and Maxine was going to be chair for next year's meeting. She was on the program committee for this meeting, and I think she was on it for last year's meeting, too." Lisa paused for a moment, then nodded. "Yes, she was. Anyway, she volunteered to be in charge of local arrangements for next year, and I told her I would meet with her during this meeting to go over some of the things I'd learned."

"That seems clear enough," Kanesha said. "Ms. Muller was a friend of Gavin Fong's. She spoke to me about him yesterday. Did she happen to tell you anything about him? Or anything she might have known or suspected about his death?"

"No, I don't think so," Lisa said. "Really, we hadn't time to talk much. At the luncheon yesterday she spent most of her time talking to Gavin Fong." She paused for a moment. "Maybe I shouldn't say this, because it probably doesn't mean anything, but I did hear her say one thing that was pretty odd. I don't think she realized I could hear her."

"What did she say?" Kanesha asked when Lisa didn't continue right away.

"I'm trying to remember her exact words," Lisa replied. "I think I've got it now, though. She said, *What are you going to do if he doesn't pay you like he promised? Will you send that letter?*"

I wondered what Maxine Muller had meant. Was Gavin Fong trying to collect on a debt, and if he couldn't, was he going to write to someone about it? Perhaps a demand letter?

Kanesha frowned. "Did you hear Mr. Fong's response?"

"He just said, *Shut up, Maxine. Not now.* He gave her kind of an ugly look when he said it. She drew back in her chair, and that was the end of it, I think. At least while we were at the table," Lisa concluded.

After I thought about it a moment, I realized there was a more sinister interpretation. Was Gavin Fong blackmailing someone? And what did Maxine Muller know about it?

TWENTY

I knew already that Gavin Fong was willing to resort to blackmail—or extortion—to get what he wanted. I wasn't really surprised that he might have been blackmailing other people. I supposed there could have been a less criminal interpretation put on Maxine Muller's questions to him, but Gavin had been murdered.

Blackmail was a powerful motive for murder.

Kanesha said, "Neither Mr. Fong nor Ms. Muller mentioned a name in connection with these questions?"

"Not that I heard," Lisa said. "I'd been talking to my neighbor to the left just before that. Maxine was on my right. I had turned to say something to Maxine when I heard her ask Gavin those questions."

"Let's go back to your discovery of the victim for a moment," Kanesha said. "When you arrived on the sixth floor, did you see anyone else?"

Lisa frowned. "I don't think so." She paused. "No, wait a minute. Yes, I did, toward the other end of the hallway. I didn't see a person, though. I saw one of those housekeeping carts a few doors down from the elevator."

"About what time would you say you reached the sixth floor?" Kanesha asked.

"It was a minute or two before I called Charlie," Lisa said. "I'm not really sure of the exact time."

"Can you check your phone to see what time you made the call to Mr. Harris?"

"Of course, how stupid of me." Lisa fumbled in her purse and, after a moment, pulled out her phone. She tapped the screen several times. "I made the call at ten fifty-seven. So I guess I arrived on the sixth floor about ten fifty-five."

Kanesha made a note of it on her pad. "All right then, Ms. Krause. You can go. I might have more questions later."

Lisa dropped her phone back in her bag and rose quickly from the table. "Thank you, Deputy Berry. I'm happy to help in any way." She looked toward me, and I nodded and smiled. Then she hurried out of the room.

I wished I could follow her. I knew Kanesha was annoyed that I was involved in this.

"Mr. Harris, I'd like to talk with you next. Please join me." Kanesha indicated the chair Lisa had vacated.

I did as she asked and kept my expression as bland as possible when I faced her.

Kanesha's gaze flicked to the other end of the room where Hampton and his assistant still sat, then back to me.

Was she trying to tell me something? I decided maybe she was warning me to be careful what I said. Maybe she didn't want

Hampton and his associate to know that she and I knew each other well.

Kanesha's chilly tone when she asked me the first question told me I could be right.

"What were you doing on the sixth floor with Ms. Krause?"

"She called me in a panic. I couldn't ignore her plea for help, because I don't think she was calm enough to think clearly. I told her to call 911 and then the front desk, and that I would be with her in a couple of minutes."

"Where were you at the time you received the call?"

"I'd left the hotel a few minutes before Lisa called me," I said. "I was on the way to the bistro, Helen Louise Brady's place, and I was nearly there."

"You turned back immediately?"

I nodded. "As I said, she sounded pretty shaky."

"Can you verify the time of that phone call?" Kanesha asked.

I pulled out my phone and checked the list of calls. "Yes, ten fifty-seven. The call lasted almost a minute."

"How long after that was it before you reached Ms. Krause on the sixth floor?"

"No more than five minutes," I said. "Probably no more than three, three and a half."

"Did you see anyone on the sixth floor when you arrived there?"

"No, only Lisa." I frowned as I recalled what Lisa said about the housekeeping cart. I hadn't noticed one, and I told Kanesha that.

"Could it have been there and you simply overlooked it?" Kanesha asked, her pen poised to write down my answer.

"I suppose so," I said, "but I don't think I did. I had to check the sign to see which way to go to get to the room, and I probably looked both ways down the hall."

"But you can't be absolutely certain?"

I wondered why Kanesha was pressing this particular point.

"No, I can't be absolutely certain," I said.

"When you arrived at the room and found Ms. Krause, what happened then?"

I gave Kanesha the details she wanted, and then she took me through it all again.

When I finished, Kanesha fixed me with her laser stare. "Did you at any time look into the room? Or go into the room?"

"No, I neither looked nor went into the room," I said. "I didn't want to risk contaminating the scene any further."

"Wise of you," Kanesha said in a low tone. "For once."

I inclined my head slightly. "I thought so."

Kanesha dropped her pen on the pad. "I think that's all for now, Mr. Harris. If I have further questions, I'll be in touch."

"I'm always happy to answer your questions, Deputy Berry." I rose from the table, nodded in the direction of Hampton and his associate, and exited the room.

Once the door closed behind me, I leaned against the wall near it for a moment. I ought to be used to this situation by now, given the events of the past two years, but I definitely wasn't. Adrenaline had brought me this far. Now, however, I felt the inevitable letdown, and my head throbbed.

The first thing I needed was water, and I headed for the closest restroom. There was a water fountain outside it. I drank enough to keep a camel going for a week in the desert, and then I used the restroom.

By the time I came out into the hall again, my headache had begun to recede. I checked the time and was not surprised to see that it was nearly twelve thirty. That diet soda and bag of peanuts had been almost two hours ago, and I was hungry for both food and caffeine.

I considered the bistro but decided I would have lunch here in the hotel restaurant. A hamburger and a salad—though I would have preferred french fries—should suffice, along with a couple of glasses of iced tea. I found the stairs, walked down to the ground floor, and made my way to the restaurant. I found it not as crowded as I thought it might be—certainly not as crowded as Helen Louise's place always was on Saturdays around lunchtime.

The hostess greeted me and led me toward a table. On the way, I spotted Marisue and Randi. They waved and motioned for me to join them. I steered the hostess in their direction, and she left me there with a menu.

"Good afternoon, Charlie," Marisue said. "We were hoping we'd run into you today."

"Have you heard the latest?" Randi's eyes were alight with curiosity.

"Good afternoon." I opened my menu and laid it flat on the table. "What's the latest you've heard?" I was curious whether news of Maxine Muller's murder had started making the rounds.

"Some poor woman was strangled to death in her room," Randi said in an undertone.

I didn't bother to correct her about the method of murder. "Who told you that?"

"You don't seem surprised by the news," Marisue said. "Did you already know about this?"

There was no point in prevaricating. "Yes, I did." I figured I might as well share a few of the main details, aside from the way the poor woman died.

"Poor Lisa," Marisue said, and Randi echoed her. "How awful." Marisue looked a bit ashen.

"Who was murdered?" Randi asked.

"Maxine Muller," I replied.

The irrepressible Randi didn't seem much bothered by the thought of Lisa's ordeal or by Ms. Muller's unfortunate demise. "The person who killed poor Maxine had to be the same one who poisoned Gavin, don't you think?"

"It seems pretty likely," I said. "You didn't answer my question. Who told you about the murder?"

"The maid who was cleaning our room," Randi said. "We popped upstairs for a moment before coming down here, and she was in our room. She almost jumped out of her skin when we walked in. The poor thing was terrified."

"When we asked her why, she told us that a woman had been found strangled in her room on the sixth floor," Marisue said. "We didn't know until now, though, that poor Maxine was the victim."

"Maxine must have known something about Gavin's murder." Randi exchanged a glance with Marisue.

"I would think that's certainly possible," Marisue said. "But we have an expert right here. What do *you* think, Charlie? You've had a lot of experience with this kind of thing, haven't you?"

"Unfortunately, more than I would care to admit to anyone besides friends of long standing," I said. "I think Maxine is connected, and the killer obviously felt Maxine had to be got out of the way for some reason. I sure wish we knew what that reason was."

"I didn't really know her that well," Lisa said. "I'd see her at these meetings and usually at ALA. We served on an ALA committee together twice, I think."

"Same with me," Marisue said. "I do know that she had a thing for Gavin Fong, and that I found extremely strange. I can't imagine why a sane woman would be attracted to that narcissistic creep."

Randi giggled. "Maxine was odd. I always thought so. Most of the time she carried a knitting bag around with her. She was always knitting sweaters for her dogs."

"I'd forgotten about that." Marisue grimaced. "She gave me a couple once because I made the mistake of telling her I had a Yorkie, too. They were dreadfully twee. I donated them to the local animal shelter when I got home."

I found the image of Maxine knitting dog sweaters sweet, but also rather sad for some reason. I hoped there would be someone to give her dogs a good home. I hated to think of orphaned pets. There was never any way to explain to them why their human was never coming back.

Randi could have read my mind. Her face clouded. "I didn't think about her poor little orphaned fur babies. I hope someone will take them and give them a good home." For a moment I thought she was going to cry, she looked so sad.

Even Marisue appeared moved by the plight of Maxine's dogs. Before we turned maudlin, I decided I'd better change the subject. I wanted to bring up blackmail as a motive, but I needed to be careful doing it. I couldn't share with Marisue and Randi the bit of conversation Lisa overheard at the luncheon.

I couldn't think of a graceful way to do it, so I dove right in. "I've been thinking about that story you told me at dinner last night. The one involving Harlan Crais."

"What about it?" Marisue asked.

"About Gavin blackballing Crais to keep him from getting a job."

"It was nasty," Randi said, "and you couldn't really blame Harlan for hating Gavin the way he did."

"No, I suppose not," I said. "Look, here's what I'm wondering. If Gavin was willing to blackball someone, what are the chances he would threaten to do it, but tell his victim he wouldn't if he got paid enough not to?"

TWENTY-ONE

||||||||||||||||||||||||||||||||||||||||||||||||||||||||||||||

I glanced from one to the other and back again as I tried to gauge their reactions to my question. Both Marisue and Randi seemed to freeze for a moment, then they shared what I interpreted as an uneasy glance.

Marisue responded first. "With Gavin, anything low and underhanded was always a possibility, I suppose."

"Yes, he could have done something like that," Randi said. "I wouldn't put it past him."

I sensed that they both knew something but were reluctant to tell me what it was. "We've already talked about the fact that I have experience with a murder investigation, haven't we?"

They both nodded. "What's your point?" Marisue asked.

"My point is this," I said. "If you know something that could have a bearing on the case, then you really need to share it with the investigating officer. I can assure you, from personal experience, that Chief Deputy Berry is an intelligent, seasoned investigator. She's tough but fair."

I sat back and waited for them to mull over my words. Our server came to the table with a glass of water for me, introduced himself, and then asked if we were ready to place our orders. I waited for Marisue and Randi to give theirs, then I told the young man what I wanted, the All-American Cheeseburger and salad, with unsweetened iced tea, no lemon, to drink. I loved their sweet tea, but it had way too much sugar in it.

Once the server finished writing down our orders, collected the menus, and moved away, I looked at Marisue and Randi and waited for them to respond to what I had said right before the server came to the table.

Randi fiddled with her spoon and avoided meeting my gaze. Marisue stared at something over my shoulder. I waited, however, and didn't prompt them to speak.

Finally Randi broke the silence. She glanced quickly at Marisue and away again as she spoke. "The thing is, Charlie, we don't know anything for sure. I mean, we have no proof of it. It's more like an educated guess."

"That's a start," I said.

"A couple of years ago, we heard that Gavin bought a new car," Randi said. "A BMW, one that sells for well over a hundred thousand dollars."

I almost spit out the water I'd sipped the moment before. How on earth could a librarian afford a car that expensive?

He could if he was blackmailing someone or, in fact, several people.

I set my water glass down and swallowed the mouthful of water. "That is highly suspicious, don't you think?"

Marisue shrugged. "He could have inherited the money, because he evidently paid cash for it. At least, that's what we heard through the grapevine."

"Yes, that's possible," I said.

"But from what we heard, Gavin never mentioned a death in the family or ever boasted of having rich relatives," Randi said. "He was the type who would, though, if he had some."

"Yes, that would have been entirely in character," I said. "Unless he'd been saving for years in order to buy a car like that."

"He was good at getting other people to pay for things," Marisue said. "If you ever went out to eat with him, he always managed to leave his wallet at home or at the office and never had money to pay his share. He'd say he would pay you back, but that never happened."

"That's one way to save money," I said.

Marisue shared a grim smile. "Anyone who worked with him learned not to go out to eat with him after the first couple of times, though. So that trick didn't work for long."

"He always wanted to go to expensive restaurants, too," Randi said. "No fast food or a diner for him."

"I suppose, then, he *could* have saved the money," I said. "I think it's something Deputy Berry will want to investigate, though, in case the money actually came from blackmail."

"Do we have to tell her?" Randi asked. "Can't you do it for us?"

"I can tell her," I said. "But she will probably want to talk to you about it. If she asks me where I got the information, I will have to tell her."

"All right, then," Marisue said. "I suppose we'll have to do it ourselves."

The server brought the grilled chicken salads Marisue and

Randi had ordered and informed me that my food would be out soon. I nodded and smiled, but waited until the young man was out of the way before I continued.

"There's another part of this," I said. "I know you might balk at it, but I have to ask."

Both women looked up from their salads and frowned at me. "Ask what?" Randi said at the same time Marisue said, "Balk at what?"

"If Gavin was blackmailing people and getting money from them, and you both agree with me that is a distinct possibility," I said, "then I have to ask you if you have any ideas about whom he might have been blackmailing."

Marisue put down the fork she had been about to stab into her salad. "I can't give you a specific name, and I don't think Randi can, either." Her gaze slid sideways to her friend and then refocused on me. Randi shook her head in agreement with Marisue.

"But," Randi drew out the word, "I'd say the most obvious targets for blackmail would be people who had worked with Gavin who were trying to move up and out to higher-paying jobs."

"People like Harlan Crais, for example," I said.

Both women nodded.

"Do you think he would have limited himself to people he worked with, or might he have tried his hand at targets outside his own workplace?"

"He could have, I suppose," Randi replied.

Marisue leaned back in her chair and folded her arms over her chest. "Correct me if I'm wrong, but I think what you're getting at here is whether Gavin went around collecting gossip, looking for anything he could make a profit from."

I wondered about Marisue's defensive body language and

whether it was an unconscious reaction. Had she been one of Gavin's victims? I hadn't considered the possibility that either of my friends here could be a viable suspect in Gavin's death. And, by extension, Maxine Muller's.

"Yes, that's what I'm getting at." I noted that Randi didn't seem bothered by either my question or Marisue's response. *Interesting, but even the best of friends don't share* everything, I told myself.

I suspected they knew more than they were willing to share with me, and I wondered if I could get more out of both of them if I managed somehow to talk to them one-on-one. I'd have to give it a try if I could think of a way to separate them.

"Where Gavin is concerned, anything sleazy is possible," Randi said.

Marisue nodded, picked up her fork, and began to eat.

"I will mention that possibility to Deputy Berry," I said. "She can take it from there if she has to dig deeper into Gavin's activities."

The server brought my cheeseburger and salad, and for the next few minutes I focused on eating my lunch. Neither Marisue nor Randi spoke, other than to say how good their salads were. I decided to let the silence build and waited to see what, if anything, they chose to say.

I thought about the nature of Maxine Muller's role in Gavin's alleged blackmail activities. Based on what Lisa Krause overheard at the luncheon yesterday, I was willing to bet that Maxine knew something. The question was, how much did she know?

That led to another thought. Was she murdered because she was a partner in the scheme? Or did she know just enough to spook the killer into taking her out as a precautionary move?

Then a truly terrifying thought struck me. How much cyanide—

or whatever poison was used—did the killer still have? I hadn't considered this. I was sure Kanesha had considered it, though.

Maybe the killer had finished, once both Gavin and Maxine were dead. I could only pray that this was so and that more deaths wouldn't follow. Talk about a nightmare scenario. My lunch suddenly soured in my stomach. I put down the last bit of cheeseburger and pushed my plate aside.

My expression must have alerted Randi that something was wrong. "Are you okay, Charlie? You look a little green. Is it heartburn?" She grabbed her purse and started rummaging through it. "I have some antacids in here somewhere."

"No, not heartburn. I suddenly felt full, that's all." I gave what I hoped was a convincing smile. "I'm trying to be more careful about how much I eat." I certainly couldn't tell them the truth about what I was thinking. I didn't want to terrify them and start a panic.

Randi eyed me as if she didn't believe me, but she set her purse back down and resumed eating. Marisue didn't appear to be all that concerned, and that was okay.

"Would you be offended if I pulled out my cell phone and sent a text?" I asked. "Ordinarily I try not to do things like that during meals, but I thought I would go ahead and let Deputy Berry know I need to talk to her."

"You truly are a Southern gentleman." Marisue smiled, and Randi nodded. "Hardly anyone bothers to ask these days. I don't mind. Do you?" She glanced at Randi.

"No, certainly not," Randi said. "Not after Charlie asked so nicely."

"Thank you for the compliment," I said, "and the permission. I won't take long."

My message to Kanesha was simple. *Have potentially useful information. When can we talk?*

I set the phone on the table. I had no idea how long it might be before Kanesha responded. She had to be under tremendous pressure to find the killer, and she might not be in the mood to talk to me. Although, to be fair to myself, I didn't think I'd ever wasted her time when I had what I considered pertinent information to share.

The server arrived to hand us dessert menus and to clear away our plates and used utensils. I put my menu aside immediately, tempted though I was. Marisue and Randi, however, did not demur. The server returned to take their dessert orders, and I listened with envy as they each ordered the double-chocolate brownie, served hot with a scoop of cinnamon vanilla ice cream. I felt my resistance weakening as the server glanced at me.

"Okay, I know I'll regret this later, but I'll have one as well." So much for my willpower. I handed the server my menu, and he departed. I grinned at Randi and Marisue. "It's all your fault, naturally. I ordered dessert just to be sociable."

Marisue laughed. "Think of it as a party, and you have to have something sweet and chocolaty at a party."

Randi nodded. "Of course you do."

The word *party* reminded me about the party Marisue and Randi had attended in Gavin's suite the night before he died. I was still curious why they hadn't mentioned it to me at dinner last night. I decided to ask them point-blank.

"Speaking of parties," I said. "How come you didn't mention Gavin's party to me last night? I heard you both were there."

They both tensed for a brief moment, then relaxed. Marisue shrugged. "It wasn't that big a deal, frankly. We only put in an appearance to be polite."

Randi wouldn't meet my gaze when I turned to her. I looked back at Marisue.

"Why would you even bother to show up? I thought you both loathed Gavin so much you wouldn't want to be in the same room with him."

"Free liquor, what else?" Marisue said. "What the hell difference does it make to you, Charlie, whether we attended that lame party? You know librarians rarely turn down the chance of free food and alcohol."

Stung by her tone, I waited a moment before I replied to make sure I didn't snap back at her. "Because I'm pretty sure whoever killed Gavin and Maxine Muller was at that party. Either of you could have seen something without realizing it that could help Deputy Berry solve the murders."

"I doubt it." Marisue shrugged. "I told you we weren't there long."

Randi shot her a quick glance, then focused again on her lap, from what I could see.

I didn't know why, but I had the strongest feeling that Marisue was lying to me. Why? What was she trying to hide?

TWENTY-TWO

As I regarded the palpable tension in both Marisue and Randi, I realized that, despite our close friendship back in library school, over the years we had grown further and further apart. So much so that I really didn't know them as well as I thought I did. When you don't have regular contact with friends, even the best of friends, you don't see how their lives have changed, how their opinions may have altered, and what might motivate them to do things you never would have believed they could do.

Like kill someone.

I told myself I was overreacting, simply because Marisue and Randi seemed not to want to confide in me. I couldn't really believe that either one of them, or the two of them in concert, killed two people.

But I couldn't be sure.

In the same way, they couldn't be sure of me, either. Not because they thought I killed Gavin Fong and Maxine Muller, I reckoned, but because of my involvement in murder investigations over the past several years. They might be leery of telling me anything they didn't want Kanesha to know.

If they weren't implicated in the two murders, however, why should they be reluctant to tell me—and Kanesha, of course—about what happened at the party?

I realized I had let the silence last too long, and Marisue and Randi now looked even more uncomfortable. I forced a smile.

My phone buzzed to let me know a text had arrived. "Pardon me." I picked up the phone to read the message. From Kanesha, as I expected.

E-mail me please. No time to talk f2f right now.

The *f2f* stumped me for a moment, then I realized she meant *face-to-face.* I texted back *Ok, will do as soon as I can,* and set the phone back on the table.

My thoughts had strayed from my earlier panic over the thought of more cyanide running loose. My fear was legitimate, because the killer could have plenty more of the deadly substance, especially if it came from overseas. I wondered just how much you could order.

If the killer had stolen it from a chemistry lab, however, the chances were that the amount was very small indeed so as not to arouse suspicion. Although, as Stewart told me, a well-run lab would know that even a minute amount had been taken.

Our server arrived with our desserts, and they turned out to be sinfully delicious. Our mutual enjoyment of the brownies and ice cream seemed to have erased the awkwardness that had sprung up over my questions about the party. I decided to let the subject drop for the moment and waited to see if either Marisue or Randi mentioned it.

Randi finished hers before Marisue and I were barely halfway through ours. "That was lovely." She put down her spoon and patted her lips with her napkin. "Although I swear I could eat another one."

"Yes, it's wonderful," Marisue said. "But one is more than enough. We should probably have split one between us, the brownies are so big." She pushed her dessert plate away with about a third left.

Randi eyed it, and Marisue noticed. She picked up her plate and set it in front of Randi. "Go ahead." She shook her head as Randi quickly finished the remains.

Marisue turned her gaze to me. "If you must know, Charlie, we went to Gavin's party because we were afraid not to."

I nearly dropped my spoon. "Afraid not to? Why on earth?"

"Because he could be vindictive if you didn't do what he wanted." Randi stacked Marisue's empty plate on top of her own.

"What were you afraid he might do to you?" I savored the last bite of brownie while I waited for an answer.

"Write nasty anonymous letters to our directors, for one thing, telling them who knows what," Marisue said. "He was capable of anything underhanded. My boss would probably ask me about it, but I don't seriously think she'd believe the crap Gavin would invent. It would be horribly embarrassing, though, to have to deal with it."

"It was easier just to go to the stupid party. Let Gavin see us there and gloat because he knew he'd forced us into it." Randi picked up her water glass, and I noticed that her hand shook slightly as she raised it to her mouth and drank.

"All it cost us was a couple hours of our time." Marisue's tone was bitter. "And a few ounces of pride."

"I'm sorry," I said, although I knew how inadequate that was. "I have to ask you this, and I hope you'll forgive me, but had Gavin ever written such a letter about either of you? Or about anyone you know?"

"Not about me," Randi said.

Marisue shook her head. "Me, either, but you already know about Harlan Crais." She paused for a moment. "You might talk to Maxine's friend, Sylvia O'Callaghan, though. If she'll talk to you, that is."

Given Ms. O'Callaghan's reaction to me previously, I figured I'd have a hard time getting close enough to her even to explain what I wanted to talk to her about. Still, I'd have to try.

I didn't share these thoughts with Marisue and Randi, however. Instead I asked, "Can you tell me who else was at the party?" I picked up my phone, selected an app I often used to make notes of things I needed to remember, and waited.

"I suppose so," Randi said, though she sounded uncertain. "I guess you'll find out anyway in the long run."

"Besides Randi and me," Marisue said when Randi failed to continue, "the others were Harlan Crais, that young man with the tattoos, Bob Something-or-Other, Maxine and her friend Sylvia, Cathleen Matera, and Nancy Dunlap."

"And Mitch Handler," Randi added. "He's so quiet, you probably forgot about him."

"Yes, he was there, too," Marisue said.

"Anyone else happen to come in while you were there?" I wondered if they remembered Lisa Krause.

They were both quiet for a moment, then Marisue said, "Yes, Lisa Krause. She wasn't there for long, though."

"Thanks." I finished typing in the last name and closed the app. Now that I had the list I wondered exactly what I was going to do with it. I wanted to talk to each of them, but how should I go about it?

I knew that Kanesha wouldn't appreciate what she might legitimately consider meddling on my part, but I could always use the

excuse that the college library was the official host for the meeting. As director of the host library, therefore, I should make an effort to talk to people and get feedback on the conference.

One of my paternal grandmother's sayings popped into my head. *That's your tale. I'm sitting on mine.* My grandmother, bless her, had little patience for prevarication of any kind. No doubt my conscience dredged up that bit of folk wisdom, but despite that, I would go ahead with my plan if I could.

Marisue checked her watch. "If we want to make that session on liaison services in small academic libraries, we'd better scoot. It starts in about eight minutes."

"Oh, gosh, yes, that's one I really don't want to miss a minute of." Randi grabbed her purse and started digging in it.

I caught the attention of our server, and he came over to the table. He had the separate checks ready, and he presented each of them. Randi and Marisue charged theirs to their rooms, and I had enough cash to cover mine, along with a healthy tip.

"I think I'll come with you," I said as the three of us rose from the table. "That session sounds interesting."

"Fine." Marisue strode toward the dining room door, and Randi and I followed.

When we reached the meeting room for the session we wanted to hear, Marisue and Randi found seats near the middle of the room at the end of an aisle. I found an aisle seat several rows back. I had sensed that both women were ready to get away from me for a while, and I decided not to make more of a nuisance of myself than I needed to at the moment.

I got out my program and turned to the pages where the afternoon sessions were listed. I scanned through to see if there were any others that might interest me. Nothing stood out as particularly

exciting, though there was a session on the licensing of electronic resources that was a possibility. After the afternoon sessions ended, there were no further events for the day. Programming resumed tomorrow morning, Sunday, and ran until noon, when there was a final lunch session with another keynote speaker.

Everyone had a free evening tonight. I wondered idly what they would find to do. Those who chose to venture out of the hotel had a number of excellent choices with nearby restaurants, and there were a couple of bars within walking distance.

One of the presenters called for attention, and then she began to introduce herself and the other two presenters, another woman and a man. I paid little attention to what she said, because I'd had an idea and was running through the possibilities in my mind.

The scheme was audacious, and I was nervous even thinking of it. I could imagine what Kanesha would say, but if it helped toward a solution of the double homicides, then most likely she would be willing to overlook the part I planned to play in it. I would have to do some fast work to get everything in place, but I had persons I could count on to make it work.

The more I thought about the logistics, the more nervous I became. I pulled out my phone, opened the note-taking app, and started tapping away.

Could I get this together in the next six hours or so? I hoped so, and I would have to count on the fact that Kanesha didn't know about it in time to stop it.

I was going to have a party in honor of the memories of Gavin Fong and Maxine Muller, and my guests would be everyone who attended Gavin's party on Thursday night. I figured getting them all together in one place again could yield interesting results.

Results that might lead to the arrest of a double murderer.

TWENTY-THREE

I was so caught up in my fantasy of playing Hercule Poirot, bringing all the suspects together in the drawing room for the big reve-
lation scene, that I hadn't really paid attention to one crucial point
that finally forced its way to the forefront of my consciousness.

Well, make that two crucial points.

First, one of the people in my house would be someone who
had already killed twice. Someone who might still have cyanide
in his or her possession.

Second, that person could easily decide to kill again, and who
would be the most likely choice to play the victim?

Hercule Poirot, that's who—otherwise known as Charlie
Harris.

Sobered by these thoughts, I rapidly lost enthusiasm for my
grandiose idea.

Perhaps if Kanesha and one or two deputies were on hand,

that would greatly lessen the chance that the killer would strike again.

I brightened momentarily at that idea, but I realized Kanesha would never go for it. Too dangerous, she would say, and I couldn't disagree.

So much for my big idea. I deleted the notes I'd made on the app and decided I might as well listen to the presentation going on at the front of the midsize room.

There were about forty people in a room that probably held roughly sixty, I estimated. I checked my program to see who the presenters were and what institutions they represented. I almost dropped my program when I read the names.

The one man among the three was none other than Mitch Handler, the librarian-writer Marisue and Randi had told me about earlier. Now that I finally focused on the presenters, I realized I had met one of the women two days ago. Cathleen Matera, who was talking now, had come up to me after the incident with Gavin on Thursday. She had offered to serve as a witness for me. The other woman wasn't anyone I knew.

Cathleen Matera seemed to be nearing the end of her part of the presentation when I tuned in.

"So you can see that's how we make the program function with a group of only five reference librarians. With the help of our colleagues from technical services—four additional librarians, as I stated earlier—we manage to make sure each academic department has a contact person within the library. Now I will turn the program over to my colleague, Mitch Handler." She closed her presentation on the large screen on the wall and handed a device to Mitch Handler when he reached her. She sat, and

Handler busied himself at the podium getting his part of the presentation up on the screen.

I thought about what Cathleen Matera said moments before about each department at her institution having a contact person in the library. Turn that around, and all the librarians had contacts in various departments at their universities.

For example, a contact in the chemistry department, where one of the chemicals kept in stock could be cyanide.

The liaison librarian might even have an undergraduate degree in the sciences, perhaps even chemistry. That was not an unusual scenario. One of the reference librarians at Athena had a bachelor's degree in biology, for example. Not all librarians were English or history majors, unlike what many people thought.

I knew Kanesha was having background checks done on people, and I was pretty sure she would be focusing primarily on the guests at Gavin Fong's Thursday night party. I certainly would.

I couldn't stand it. I had to go do a bit of background checking myself. I wasn't going to be able to concentrate on any presentations until I knew for myself more about the backgrounds of the party attendees.

I sent Melba a text to let her know that I would soon be at her place to pick up Diesel. I would have the quiet I needed at home, and I was more than ready to have my feline pal by my side again. I was so used to having him with me all day, and now that I hadn't seen him in several hours, I wanted to spend time with him. Even though I knew Melba would never let any harm come to him, I still would feel better when I had Diesel in my sight again.

The main reason I liked sitting at the back of the room for occasions like a conference session was that I could get out quickly and with little fuss. I did so now and made my way downstairs and out to the parking lot behind the hotel in less than two minutes.

Melba responded to my text with a simple *OK*. When she opened her front door, Diesel stood a few inches behind her. The moment he saw me he started talking. From the slightly indignant tone, I figured I was being scolded for disappearing for such a long time. He loved Melba, but he didn't like not knowing where I was for more than a few minutes at a time, usually.

"I'm sorry, boy, but we're going home now, okay?" I reached out to pat his head, and to Melba's amusement and mine, he drew back and gave me a look loaded with disdain. He didn't turn his back on me, but he made it clear that I wasn't forgiven yet.

He did deign to follow me to the car after I thanked Melba for looking after him.

"You know it's always a pleasure." Melba grinned. "He was doing just fine until you texted me and I told him you were coming to get him. That's when he started acting all haughty and peeved."

"I'll try to make it up to him." I thanked her again and then got the cat into the car for the drive home.

All was quiet at the house. Haskell, I knew, was on duty, and Stewart's car was in the garage. Stewart and Dante were probably on the third floor in their suite, as I had come to call it.

Diesel had thawed enough by now that he let me stroke his head a couple of times. After we each made a bathroom stop, he followed me into the den. I powered up my desktop computer, because I didn't want to take the time to retrieve my laptop from my bedroom. I hung my jacket on the back of the desk chair, rolled up my sleeves, and started my searches to dig up information on my list of suspects.

I never ceased to be amazed at the amount of information you could find on people. After only a little poking around, I found Nancy Dunlap's résumé on her library's website. She had achieved the rank of full professor at her university, and I skimmed through a list of publications and professional activities until I found her degrees listed. She had earned a bachelor's degree in biology, a master's degree in library science, and a second master's degree in biology. Though biology wasn't chemistry, it was still a science, and that made Nancy Dunlap more interesting as a suspect. I checked back through her résumé to find a description of her current position, and there it was: liaison to the departments of biology and chemistry, along with mathematics. Nancy Dunlap obviously had the necessary contacts.

Next on the list to check was Cathleen Matera. I found her information on a social media website for professionals who wanted to network with one another. I supposed if I took the director's job I might consider creating a profile on it for myself, although I wasn't sure what purpose it might serve. I pushed that distracting thought aside and focused on Ms. Matera's background. English major and liaison to the departments of English, foreign languages, and fine arts. I recalled vaguely that cyanide was sometimes used in photography in the developing process, but I doubted it was used much these days because of its extreme toxicity. I left a question mark by Cathleen Matera's name and moved on to the next person.

Sylvia O'Callaghan, I discovered, had retired three years ago and did not appear to have active connections to an academic library. From what little I could glean about her, she must have been an English major. She didn't appear all that promising. Besides, I wondered if she would have murdered her friend Maxine Muller. Another question mark. Kanesha would probably find out more about her than I could.

Harlan Crais had been a history major and had a master's degree in European history, along with his master's degree in library science. His position as an upper-level library administrator didn't seem to include liaison work, but if he had been a liaison in the past, I doubted it was for a science department of any kind. Thus, no promising connections there that I could discern.

Mitch Handler, though, turned out to have a bachelor's degree in organic chemistry along with the obligatory library science degree. He also wrote science fiction. As I would have expected, his liaison duties included the typical science departments at his campus.

Bob Coben, the final person on my list, had what was to me the most interesting background. He had been a music major—his instrument was apparently the oboe—with a minor in biology. Not a combination I would have expected to find. Still, it did give him a bit of a connection, though his liaison duties included the music department, fine arts, and biology at his school.

I was pretty sure I remembered both Marisue's and Randi's backgrounds, but I checked to make sure. Both had been English majors in college, and Marisue came to library school right after college, as I had done. Randi, I knew, had worked for about seven years as a secretary before deciding she wanted to be a librarian. I left question marks by both their names, though I strongly doubted either of them had committed two murders.

I had been so absorbed in my research that I had neglected Diesel, and I became aware of a large paw on my thigh. Claws dug into my leg ever so slightly, and I looked down at him, amused by his innocent expression.

"Yes, I know I've neglected you terribly today. Come on, let's sit on the sofa together, okay?"

Diesel understood the word *sofa*. He climbed onto it right away and waited for me to take my place. Once I was seated, he stretched out, his head and front legs in my lap. I talked to him for a couple of minutes and combined words with suitable physical gestures that soon had him purring loudly.

Once Diesel yawned and appeared to go to sleep, I allowed my thoughts to return to the information I had learned about the librarians who had attended Gavin's party.

The source of the cyanide—keeping in mind that I didn't know for sure that cyanide was the murder weapon—was key to the solution. Any of these eight people could have ordered cyanide over the Internet, obviously. But if several of them had sources closer to hand, it was possible they had obtained the cyanide that way.

I realized, of course, that I was spending a lot of time on this—time that no doubt could have been better spent focusing on the major life decision I had looming before me. But I didn't want to think about that decision right now, or about the decision facing my daughter and son-in-law. It was easier to let myself be distracted by the double murder, even if all my speculation and information gathering turned out to be useless. Kanesha possessed the actual facts in the case—as far as they were known at the moment, that is. I didn't.

Kanesha. I promised to e-mail her with the information I had received earlier from Marisue and Randi about Gavin's expensive car and my idea that he could have been blackmailing people to get the money for it. There was the information about the party to share as well, although I hoped Lisa Krause would tell Kanesha about that. I needed to get back to the computer to take care of it. I didn't like composing e-mails of any great length on my phone. It was simply too tedious.

The cat resting partly on my lap and partly on the sofa deterred me for a few moments longer. I eased Diesel off my lap, got up from the sofa, and let him stretch out. He opened his eyes, yawned, and then closed his eyes again. He seemed content to let me leave him there.

At the computer I opened my home e-mail, and a few minutes later I sent Kanesha a message containing the information I had promised to send her. Whether she would find it helpful, I didn't know, but at least she had it.

My cell phone rang, and I picked it up to see who was calling. Laura.

My heart started racing. Was she calling to tell me they'd made a decision about Virginia?

TWENTY-FOUR

||||||||||||||||||||||||||||||||||||||||||||||||||||||||||||||||||||

My hand trembled so badly I almost dropped the phone on the floor. I managed to tighten my hold on it, though, and tapped the icon to answer the call.

"Hello, sweetheart, how are you?" I was thankful my voice didn't waver.

"Hi, Dad," Laura said. "I'm a little tired, as usual, but otherwise okay. How has the conference been going?"

I hesitated. I didn't want to give my daughter any reason to worry, because she had more than enough to occupy her mind right now. "It's been okay, a few hiccups. I'll tell you all about it later." I hoped she wouldn't press me for details. I would tell her about the murders another time.

"Better you than me." Laura giggled. "I don't care much for meetings like that, especially these days."

"No, I suppose not," I said.

"I know you've been wondering about this big decision we're

having to make," Laura said. "We haven't made it yet, although I think Frank is really leaning toward accepting the job."

My heart sank. I tried to form words but couldn't.

Laura continued without apparently noticing my lack of comment. "He's told his department chair about the offer, though, and she's invited us to dinner tomorrow night. I know she's not happy about losing him, so I'm pretty sure she wants to try to talk him out of it. She asked him not to make a final decision until after dinner tomorrow night."

Now I was able to speak. "Do you think she has a chance of changing his mind?" I hoped the woman would be able to come up with enough money and perks to keep Frank and Laura in Athena.

"I don't really know, Dad. He knows I'm concerned about leaving so soon after the baby is born, but we're both aware of the advantages of the new job."

"I want what's best for you, you know that," I said. "But I'm going to be praying that the department chair manages to find some incentives to keep Frank here."

Laura sighed. "Me, too, Dad. We probably won't see you until sometime after we've had that dinner tomorrow night, but I'll let you know what happens."

"All right, sweetheart," I said. "Try not to worry. I know you and Frank will make the best choice for all three of you."

"Thanks," Laura said. "I've got to go, but I'll call you tomorrow."

I put down the phone and stared blankly at the computer screen. I hated this feeling of suspension—waiting for the worst to happen, even though there was a chance it wouldn't. I wanted to know *now*, to end this tension one way or the other, but I knew it wasn't possible.

I also wished I could make up my mind about my own future. Did I really want to work full-time again? With two grandchildren soon to be born, did I want to be tied down to the nine-to-five routine five days a week? Then I thought about how much I had been enjoying—for the most part—the work I was doing as the interim director. I would miss that if I didn't take the job.

There was also the question of my relationship with Helen Louise. We both were comfortable with things the way they currently were. She loved her business, despite the huge demands it made on her time and energy. We spent time together when we could, and we both tacitly agreed that marriage at present wasn't a huge priority. Though I know we both wished we had more time together, I didn't expect Helen Louise to give up a business she had worked so hard to make successful in order to marry me.

Everything would work out for the best. I had to believe that. I had to trust that we would all make the best decisions we could, and then we would go forward. I felt like a superannuated Pollyanna thinking that, but optimism was always a better choice.

My phone buzzed to notify me that I had received a text message. From Kanesha, it read simply, *Got the e-mail. Interesting. Thx.* Nothing more. I sighed and set the phone down again. I really wished I could sit down with Kanesha and find out more about the progress she was making. The longer it took to identify the killer, the more worried I was that someone else might die.

My phone buzzed again. Perhaps Kanesha wanted to talk to me.

No, this text was from Lisa Krause. *Charlie, where are u? Been hoping to run into u. Need to talk about tonight.*

I frowned. What about tonight? I wasn't sure what she meant. I texted back that I was at home and told her to call me. I hated long text message exchanges because my big fingers didn't handle the small keyboard all that well. I couldn't do the two-thumb typing that so many young people did with such ease.

Lisa called two minutes later. "Hi, Lisa, what about tonight?"

"Don't tell me you've forgotten about the post-reception party in my suite at the hotel, Charlie." Lisa sounded exasperated and tired.

Oops. Lisa had told me about that last week, but it had slipped my mind until now. "Oh, that," I said, trying to sound halfway knowledgeable. "What about it?"

"I wanted to get your okay on the budget for the drinks and the food. Dessert-type things, you know, like mini-cheesecakes and things like that. I was going to go out and get the stuff myself, but there wasn't time, so I arranged for the hotel to do it. And that costs more, of course, but I'm hoping you won't think it's too much, since the library is paying for it."

"How much are we talking about?" I asked. As overseer of the library budget, I had to keep a tight rein on costs for everything.

Lisa named a figure, and although I winced inwardly, I told her it would be okay. The amount wasn't that much more than the original figure I'd signed off on, and I would sort it out next week when we had all the bills for the conference expenses in hand.

"That's okay," I said. "We need to make sure that's it, however. No more wiggle room in the budget after that."

"I understand," Lisa said. "Now, I've told people that they can come as early as seven thirty, though I expect we won't see many until after eight. Most of them will head out for dinner after the reception from five thirty to six thirty."

"How many people are you figuring on turning up?" I asked.

"Fewer than fifty," Lisa said. "Frankly, I'd be surprised if as many as twenty show up. By the time most of them finish with dinner, they'll probably be headed to a bar or to bed."

"If you really don't think all that many people will show up," I said, "I might bring Diesel with me. What do you think?"

"That would be great," Lisa said. "I've had quite a few people ask me about him. You don't think it would be too much for him, do you? I wouldn't want him to be frightened or upset."

"If there are a lot more people than you expect," I said, "I will bring him home. He did fine at the retirement party last month, though, and there were about thirty people at that." One of our senior librarians had retired after forty years at Athena, and her one special request was to have Diesel at her going-away party. Diesel had seemed to enjoy all the attention.

"That's fine," Lisa said. "I won't tell people that he's going to be there in order to keep the numbers down, how's that?"

"Good plan." My idea about having a party with all of Gavin's party guests in attendance forced its way back into my consciousness. Should I simply wait and see if any of them turned up? Or should I make an effort to get them there? I figured Randi and Marisue would come if I asked them, but I didn't know about the others.

"Thanks, Charlie. I'd better get going," Lisa said. "Can you and Diesel be there by seven thirty?"

"Yes," I said. "Look, Lisa, can you do me a favor?"

"Sure, what is it?"

"If you happen to see any of the people who were at Gavin's party on Thursday, could you tell them how much you would like them to come to your suite tonight? Don't sound too effusive, but see if you can get them to show up."

Lisa didn't respond right away. Finally she said, "I guess I can do that. What exactly are you up to, though? I have to tell you, you're making me nervous."

"I'd like to talk to them," I said. "Nothing more. Maybe having them in a party situation again will stimulate their memories, and we could learn something that's pertinent to the murder investigation. You never know."

"I hope you know what you're doing," Lisa said. "All right, I'll make sure to talk to any of them that I happen to see. Now I've really got to go."

I put my phone down feeling both excited and apprehensive. I hoped I hadn't set up a possible disaster. Perhaps I should make Kanesha aware of my little plan. I'd have to think about that. I would have to be particularly vigilant, and I'd definitely have to keep a close watch on Diesel. That shouldn't be too hard, because he would probably stick close to me in a group like that. If he showed any signs of stress from the gathering, I would of course take him home right away.

Probably I'd be lucky if even half of the people on my short list showed up tonight. The lure of more food and drink at someone else's expense might suffice, if some of them were on tight travel budgets. They might rather save their per diem and pocket it, rather than spend it on a restaurant if they could get enough to fill them up at the two parties tonight. I remembered times when I attended conferences outside of Houston when I'd had to stretch my travel allowance as much as I could in order to avoid dipping into my own pockets. Particularly in the days when I had two young children who seemed to outgrow their clothes and shoes every couple of months.

My phone rang, and I saw that Helen Louise was the caller. She must be taking her midafternoon break, I reckoned. The time was a few minutes past three thirty.

"Hello, love, how are you?" I asked.

"I'm doing fine, love." Helen Louise sounded tired, but she rarely ever would say that, at least during the workday. "We've had a really good day today so far. I must say, all your librarian colleagues seem to have made the bistro their favorite place to eat. Business has boomed since the conference started."

"I'm not surprised," I said. "The food of course is fabulous, and your prices are reasonable. They can afford to eat good meals and not worry about running their expenses up."

Helen Louise chuckled. "All I have to say is *bless them*. Hungry librarians are a good thing." She paused for a moment. When she continued, her tone was more serious. "What time do you think you might be through with the conference today? Or tomorrow? I know you said it runs through noon tomorrow."

"Yes, it does," I said. "I've got to be at a reception the library is having for attendees at the hotel from seven thirty to probably around nine or nine thirty. What's up?"

"I want to talk to you about something," she said. "I'm just wondering when will be the best time for us to sit down and talk when neither of us is distracted."

"When is best for you?" I asked. "I'll make my schedule work around yours as much as possible."

"Thank you for that, sweetheart," Helen Louise said. "I don't want to impinge on what you need to do for the conference, though. I don't think I'll feel up to it tonight after we close, and I don't imagine you'll feel like talking then, either. So how about tomorrow afternoon sometime? Before Sunday evening dinner?"

"That should be fine," I said. My curiosity about what she wanted to discuss was growing every second. Several possibilities danced around in my mind, but the one that made me terrified was the thought of illness. I knew she'd been to see her doctor the previous week for a routine checkup, and so far she hadn't shared the results of that with me. I prayed I wasn't going to hear devastating news about her health. "Can you give me any idea about what this is you want to discuss?"

She probably heard the note of fear in my voice. "Don't worry, sweetie, I promise you it's nothing terrible or scary." She hesitated a moment. "I guess I might as well tell you now, so you can be thinking about it when you have time. I'm considering turning over the running of the bistro to Debbie and Henry and stepping back, taking more time off."

TWENTY-FIVE

I was too surprised by Helen Louise's announcement to respond right away.

"Charlie, are you still there?" Helen Louise asked.

"Yes, sorry," I said. "What brought this about?" At the back of my mind I was still worried that she was ill and wasn't telling me.

"I know what you're thinking, and I promise you I'm not sick," Helen Louise said. "But I have to face the fact that I'm not thirty-five anymore, and I need to slow down a bit. Otherwise I will wear myself completely out before I'm sixty. And that's not nearly as far away as it ought to be." She paused for a breath. "As much as I love what I do, I need more time off than what I have now."

"I can understand that," I said. "I've been thinking about that myself."

"I know, love," she said. "You've got this big decision to make, and I don't want to add to the stress. But I also thought I should tell you this now instead of waiting until later."

"I'm glad you told me now," I said. "This definitely affects my decision about the job at the library. If you're not going to be working as much, I want to have the time to be able to spend with you. Not to mention time with the grandchildren who are on the way."

"Yes, they're on my mind, too," Helen Louise said. "I decided I didn't want to be working all the time while they're babies. There are too many moments in their lives I would miss."

Helen Louise had never married and had no children. I knew she loved Sean and Laura and would love their children as well. Sean and Laura loved her, too, and had already accepted her as their stepmother, even though we weren't married.

"We have a lot to talk about on Sunday," I said.

"Yes, we do," she replied. "Let's leave it at that for now. We both need time to think about all this."

"All right," I said.

We talked for a few moments longer, then said good-bye. I put my phone down and turned to Diesel. He was staring at me intently, and I knew he understood that my emotions were running high right now.

"Everything is okay, sweet boy," I told him. "Nothing for you to worry about."

He meowed, and I got up from my chair and went back to the sofa to sit with him. He crawled into my lap and rubbed his head against my chin for a moment.

"How would you like it if Helen Louise came to live with us?"

Diesel warbled loudly in response. Whether he actually understood the question, I had no idea. But even if he didn't, I think he understood the emotion behind it. I felt almost dizzy over the sudden change that was looming in my life, and I leaned back, Diesel cuddled to my chest. We sat that way for a while.

The news that Helen Louise planned to cut back on the time she spent at the bistro made my decision about taking the full-time job at the library much easier. If I had to choose between more time with family and a full-time job, I would choose family. If I needed the income from the job, I would have to consider this all more carefully. But fortunately for me, I didn't have to worry about that.

I did want to continue to work part-time at the archive, and I knew Helen Louise would still be spending part of every day at the bistro. We would have to plan out our schedules so that we worked similar hours and had our time off together whenever possible. There would be adjustments, but they would be worth it in the long run.

This significant change meant that the time was approaching when we could finally discuss marriage. For Helen Louise and me, marriage had been a little more complicated than it might have seemed at first. Helen Louise owned a house that had been in her family for several generations, and she loved it. She had grown up there and had returned to it after her parents died. I loved my house, too, even though it wasn't my childhood home. Aunt Dottie had left it to me, knowing how I felt about it, and I couldn't let the house go out of the family. I would see that as a violation of her trust in me.

So, where would we live? In this house? In Helen Louise's? That was a big decision, but thankfully one that could be put off for a while yet.

I took a deep breath. So much going on, suddenly, in my life and in my family's lives, all of it positive for the most part, but still it was a period of uncertainty. That I didn't care for much, frankly, but I would have to keep reminding myself that it would all get sorted out.

Kanesha would get the double homicide sorted out, too. I had the utmost faith in her ability to get the job done. Tenacious, astute, perceptive—she was all those things and more. I ought to stay out of her way and let her work. But the nosy part of me, and the part that always wanted to be helpful, probably would defeat my intention to stay out of the way. I had already put my nose in by asking Lisa Krause to try to get certain people to come to her suite tonight.

Diesel wiggled in my arms, and I knew that meant he was ready to change positions. He had been sitting against my chest for longer than he usually did. I realized I was hot, and no doubt he was also. He stretched out on the couch, his head touching my thigh. He then twisted on his back into one of those positions that we humans tend to think are uncomfortable but that cats consider ordinary.

I thought about changing clothes before going back to the hotel for the reception and the after-party in Lisa's suite but decided I didn't need to. I grimaced as I glanced down at the front of my shirt and the upper legs of my trousers. I would have to use one of those lint rollers, however, to de-hair myself. I was inured to the fact that I carried cat hair with me wherever I went, no matter how hard I tried to get it off my clothes. But what I had on me at the moment might have been enough to make a small kitten.

"You can rest here if you like, boy," I said to Diesel as I rose from the sofa. "I have a little chore to do." He chirped at me and closed his eyes. I left him there and went into the kitchen to find the lint roller.

After I deposited nine of those sticky roller sheets in the garbage, I figured I'd removed as much as I could. I washed my hands, and while drying them I heard my cell phone ringing faintly. I hurried toward the den to grab it before the rings stopped. Diesel opened his eyes and meowed at my sudden return.

Naturally the darn thing ceased its ringing the moment I picked it up. I tried to catch the call, but it had already gone to voice mail. I checked to see who had called and was surprised to see that it was Kanesha. I knew her message would be brief. I waited to listen to it before I returned her call.

The message consisted of six words: *Need to talk. Please call soon.*

I hit the button to call her and waited for her to pick up. "Hi, Kanesha. Sorry I didn't get to the phone fast enough just now."

"No problem," she said. "First, I wanted to thank you for the tip about the blackmail racket Fong might have been working. I had our computer guy get to work on Fong's laptop, and he managed to get in somehow and find a spreadsheet that looks suspicious. Dates, numbers, initials. Could be a record of payments. The numbers themselves aren't that big, but they add up to well over a quarter million dollars."

I nearly dropped my phone in shock. I fumbled to keep hold of it. "Good heavens," I said when I had it steady again. "He must have been doing this for quite some time."

"Maybe as far back as ten, twelve years ago," Kanesha said. "If I'm interpreting the dates correctly."

"Have you been able to identify any of the possible victims?"

"A few," she replied.

"Anyone willing to talk to you about it?" I asked, then added in a rush, "Not that I'm asking for any names, you understand. Simply curious whether you could get one of them to talk to you."

"Not so far," Kanesha said. "That's where I actually might need help from you." She paused. I knew she didn't like having to do this. "You have a knack for picking up information in these situations. Have you heard anything that could help me get anyone to talk to me?"

"Have you talked to my friends Marisue Pickard and Randi Grant?" I asked. "I know they could tell you a little."

"They're proving a bit difficult to track down," Kanesha said. "I've left messages through their room voice mail, but so far they're not responding."

"That's odd," I said. "I thought they would have come to talk to you by now." I gave her a summary of my luncheon conversation with Marisue and Randi.

When I finished, she said, "Talked to Crais, but he didn't admit to anything. I'll have to call him back in for more questions."

"You also need to talk to a young man named Bob Coben." I ran through the conversation between Coben and Crais that I'd overheard. "Coben certainly sounded threatening to me, even though he told Crais that he wouldn't actually try to kill Gavin."

"I've talked to Coben, too," Kanesha said. "Got a little more out of him than I did Crais, but still not enough to get me any closer to verifying the blackmail racket."

"Maybe now that you have my report of their conversation, you can get further with them. I'll also try to track down Marisue and Randi. They really should have talked to you already. I'm frankly puzzled."

"They're going to have to speak to me at some point," Kanesha said. "I have to talk to anyone at this conference who ever worked with Fong and the other victim, Muller."

"What names do you have so far?" I asked.

"Hang on a moment. Yeah, here they are. Nancy Dunlap, Mitch Handler, Sylvia O'Callaghan, your two friends Pickard and Grant, and of course Coben and Crais. I don't know if that's everyone, but those are the names I got from Lisa Krause. She said they were all at the party Fong had on Thursday night."

"About that party," I said. "Do you think that's when the killer planted the poisoned bottle of water?"

"That was a good opportunity, provided there were enough distractions," Kanesha said.

"Do you know yet what poison was used?" I asked.

"We won't have the toxicology report for several weeks," Kanesha replied. "But, based on the signs on both victims' bodies, the doctor who examined them thinks cyanide is the most likely answer."

"How did Maxine Muller come to ingest it?"

"The same way Fong did," Kanesha said. "Poisoned water bottle."

TWENTY-SIX

|||||||||||||||||||||||||||||||||||||||||||||||||||||||||||

"Good heavens," I said. "Was it the same brand of bottled water?"

"Yes, and I suspect it came from the stash Fong had in his suite," Kanesha said. "The lot numbers matched, but that could be coincidence."

"But you don't think it is, do you?"

"No, I don't," Kanesha said.

"I wonder how many of those bottles were poisoned," I said.

"We'll be checking the ones left in Fong's suite to find out," Kanesha said, "but we don't know yet whether anyone else has one from there."

"From what Lisa Krause told me, Gavin was not exactly the sharing type," I said. "I'd be surprised if he gave any of them away, other than maybe to Maxine Muller. I suppose she could have simply helped herself to one without his knowing about it."

"Possibly," Kanesha said. "Her death could be accidental, but for now I'm treating it as murder."

"Any leads yet on the source of the poison?" I knew I was probably trying her patience with all these questions, but I figured I might as well see how much she was willing to share with me.

"Nothing solid yet," Kanesha replied.

"I got an idea from a presentation I heard earlier today at the conference, about liaison programs in libraries," I said. "I did some digging online, looking at all the people who were at Gavin's party, trying to find out what their roles are on their respective campuses."

"Trying to find out if any one of them is a liaison to the chemistry department on their campus," Kanesha said, sounding slightly amused. "I've been looking into the same thing."

"Then I guess you won't need my list," I said in a light tone.

"No, but I appreciate the thought," she replied. "I have someone following up on those particular leads, and once I have more information I'm going to be talking to anyone who has any kind of connection with a chemistry department."

"I can imagine how anxious you must be to trace the source of the poison," I said. "Frankly I get chills whenever I think about the fact that the killer may still have more of it."

"That's why I'm trying to solve this case as quickly as possible. I don't want anyone else to die," Kanesha said. "Thanks for the additional information. I need to act on it now, though. I'll talk to you later."

I was used to abrupt ends to conversations with Kanesha. She had a tremendous task to accomplish, and I understood that. I wished there were more I could do to help. I didn't want anyone else to die, either, but that was a possibility as long as the murderer remained at large.

I realized I'd forgotten to ask Kanesha if they knew how the killer had gotten the poison in the bottles. I presumed it was done without opening the bottle. Otherwise surely a person would have noticed that the seal was broken when he opened the bottle to take a drink. I supposed that a person in a hurry—like someone in the middle of a talk in front of a large group of people—might not notice and would simply open the bottle and drink before going on with the talk. That could explain what happened with Gavin.

What about Maxine Muller, though? Would she have noticed that her bottle wasn't sealed properly? She might have been too distracted to realize it. She no doubt had a lot on her mind at the time she took that fatal sip. Another thought occurred to me, that the killer could have poisoned Maxine's bottle after she'd opened it. But that hardly seemed likely.

The killer must have managed to get the poison into the bottles without removing the twist caps. How could it be done?

Struck by a sudden idea, I hurried back to the kitchen. Diesel came with me this time, and I heard him in the utility room, scratching in his litter box, when I opened the fridge in search of a plastic drink bottle. I had a water pitcher with a filter, so I usually didn't have bottled water. I did, however, have a couple of bottles of diet soda. I pulled one out to examine.

I took the bottle to the sink and switched on the light there. I looked closely at the bottle, turned it around a few times, while I thought. My idea was that the killer could have used a syringe to penetrate the plastic and insert the cyanide. Of course that would depend on the form that the cyanide was in and whether it could be inserted in such a manner.

The bottom of the bottle was the likeliest place to do it. People didn't usually examine the bottom unless there was a leak. How could the killer then have sealed the bottle to prevent a leak and avoid having someone see that the bottle had been tampered with? Perhaps superglue would do the trick. I had a tube of that on hand, but I didn't have a syringe with which to experiment. An ice pick would work, but I decided not to try it. I didn't want to make a mess, and I invariably got that glue on my fingers whenever I used it. I put the bottle back in the fridge. My theory was likely workable, I decided. The experts would figure it out.

Diesel padded out of the utility room and meowed at me. Loudly, several times.

I knew what that meant. I followed as he turned to go back to the utility room. His dry-food bowl held only a few pieces of the crunchy bits he loved. I added more to it, then took his water bowl over to the sink, rinsed it, and filled it with fresh water.

"There now," I said. "Everything okay?"

Diesel stared up at me and meowed. He turned and walked out of the room. Mission accomplished.

I smiled and walked into the kitchen behind him. After giving Diesel water, I realized I was thirsty. I remedied that, and then I thought about the evening ahead. That in turn reminded me of what Kanesha had told me about Marisue and Randi. I was concerned that they hadn't talked to Kanesha yet. What was going on?

I pulled out my phone to send Marisue a text. *Where are you? Everything ok? Deputy Berry needs to talk to you.*

If I didn't hear back from Marisue in a few minutes, I would text Randi. I wasn't sure what I would do if neither of them texted back.

About three minutes later my phone signaled that I had received a message. From Marisue: *Leaving ER headed back to hotel. Will call soon.*

The ER? I was sure she meant the emergency room. Good grief, what on earth could have happened to them?

I didn't have to remain in suspense for long. Marisue called moments later.

"Sorry for the cryptic message, Charlie." She sounded a bit out of breath. "We'd just got into the taxi to go back to the hotel. We're both okay. Randi tripped and landed hard on her left arm while we were out on the square."

"Oh my goodness, did she break her arm?"

"Yes, but thankfully it was a clean break," Marisue said. "She's not feeling too perky at the moment, and she's half gaga on pain pills, but she'll be all right."

"Thank goodness," I said. "Well, no wonder neither of you was responding to Kanesha's messages. I guess she didn't have your cell phone numbers."

"No, she wouldn't have," Marisue replied. "Look, we're pulling up to the hotel. I've got to get Randi into her room and settled down. I think she'll probably nap for a while. As soon as I can I will call Deputy Berry, I promise."

"That's fine," I said. "In the meantime, if there's anything I can do to help you both, please let me know."

"Will do." Marisue ended the call.

Poor Randi, I thought, *breaking an arm while attending a library conference. Rotten luck.* She wouldn't feel much like talking for the rest of the day, I was sure. Hopefully Marisue would be able to answer Kanesha's questions sufficiently in the meantime.

I wondered if Randi's accident would keep Marisue from coming to the after-reception party in Lisa's suite tonight. I supposed it depended on how much assistance Randi needed. Probably the main thing she needed at the moment was rest and quiet. I'd never broken a limb, and thankfully neither had either of my children or my late wife. I didn't have any experience with looking after anyone with a broken arm.

A glance at my watch confirmed that I had time to take a nap myself before I needed to head back to the Farrington House. I decided that, since I wanted to take Diesel with me, I would take a pass on the reception at five thirty and instead have an early dinner at home before the party in Lisa's suite.

"Come on, Diesel," I said. "Let's go upstairs and rest, okay?" He looked at me and chirped. He liked taking naps with me. We headed up to my bedroom and got comfortable. I drifted off not long after.

I must have been more tired than I realized. When I woke and checked the clock, I was surprised to see I had slept for nearly two hours. I had never been one of those people who was totally with it and ready to go at the moment of awakening. It took me several minutes before I was ready to sit up and get out of bed. Diesel woke up when I did, but he sat up and stretched. Then he began grooming himself.

My brain continued to feel foggy until I had bathed my face in cold water and put my clothes back on. I had a little over an hour before I needed to leave for the party at the hotel. Time enough for dinner, at least.

Diesel padded down the stairs along with me. The kitchen was dark, and that was unusual. Stewart must have turned out the lights before he either went upstairs or left the house. I couldn't remember offhand what his and Haskell's plans were for this evening. I figured Haskell might still be on duty, thanks to the double homicide investigation.

I was hungry, but I didn't feel like taking one of Azalea's casseroles from the freezer and heating it up. Instead I decided on a couple of ham sandwiches, along with the last of the potato salad

Stewart made a couple of days ago. That bottle of diet soda I'd looked at earlier provided my beverage for the meal. No dessert tonight, since I would no doubt find things to nibble on at the party. Not to mention, my conscience reminded me, that sinful dessert I'd had at lunchtime.

After my exciting dinner I went up to brush my teeth and freshen up, then came down to get Diesel ready for the ride to the hotel. He would have to remain in his halter with the leash attached the whole time. He might find that frustrating, because I usually didn't have to keep him leashed. On this occasion, however, with a number of strangers around, I needed to be sure he remained close to me.

Nearly twenty minutes later we walked into the Farrington House from the rear entrance and made our way to the lobby. Diesel had been in the hotel before, several times in the past. The owners were animal lovers, and they welcomed guests with family pets—other than reptiles or exotics, that is. Diesel no doubt remembered the place and so far showed no signs of fear, though he was walking close by my legs.

Before we went up to Lisa's suite, I wanted to try talking with Marisue. I pulled my phone out and texted her to see if she had time to chat.

She responded almost immediately and invited me to her room.

I led Diesel to the elevator, empty at the moment, and punched the button for Marisue's floor. We soon arrived at her door, and she answered my knock so quickly she must have been standing right on the other side.

"Come in," she said. "I heard something a few minutes ago that might help solve the murders."

TWENTY-SEVEN

Marisue urged me in again when I stood there for a moment, trying to process what she had told me. "Come on, Charlie," she said. "I don't want to have this conversation with you standing out in the hall, for Pete's sake."

"Oh, right." I moved forward, and Diesel trotted in ahead of me while Marisue shut the door behind us.

"Make yourself comfortable." Marisue waved a hand in the direction of the two small armchairs her room offered. I chose the one on the right. Diesel sat at my feet and watched Marisue as she sat in the other chair. She stretched out a hand to the cat, and he rubbed his head against it. "You are so handsome, but I bet you know that."

When Diesel meowed in response, Marisue laughed, and I could see her visibly relax a little. She had seemed tense when she opened the door, but now she looked less so. Diesel often had that effect.

"Now, what is this you've heard that could solve the case?" I asked, trying not to sound impatient.

Marisue shifted her focus from Diesel to me and sat back in her chair. "I was down on the meeting room level until about ten minutes ago. You'll be happy to know I was talking to your good friend the deputy." She grinned. "My goodness, that woman can be more than a little terrifying, but I guess she'd have to be in her position."

"She has to be pretty tough," I said.

"Anyway, I finished answering her questions, and I headed back to the elevator to return here. When the doors opened, there stood the Bobbsey Twins in the middle of one of their bickering sessions. I almost let the door close to wait for the elevator to come back, but I got on anyway."

Marisue's reference to the Bobbsey Twins threw me. I knew all about Bert and Nan and Freddie and Flossie, because I'd read the books when I was a youngster. I knew she wasn't talking about them, however.

"I don't know whom you're talking about," I said.

Marisue grinned. "Sorry, I forgot you haven't been coming to these meetings for years like the rest of us. You may have seen them around, two women in their late seventies, maybe early eighties? Nobody knows exactly how old they are. Virginia and Ada Lou. They always come to these meetings together, and most of the time they bicker over the craziest things."

"Yes, I've met them," I said. "Go on. What were they bickering about when you got in the elevator with them?"

"At first, I couldn't make much sense of it," Marisue said. "Their conversations can be incredibly oblique sometimes, you know. But then I realized they were talking about Gavin and something they'd seen or overheard involving him. That's when I really started paying attention."

She paused for a moment. "I get tired simply thinking about those two. So they're talking about Gavin and an argument he was having with someone. Evidently they didn't hear much of it, and they aren't completely sure who the other party was, except that they're sure he was a man."

"Where and when did this happen?" I asked.

"I *think* maybe early on Thursday afternoon, when people first started arriving and checking into the hotel," Marisue said. "They're staying on a higher floor, I guess, because I had to get out before I could hear much more. They never even noticed when I got on or when I got off."

"Did you manage to hear anything about the subject of the argument Gavin was having with the unknown man?" This was certainly intriguing, but also annoying, since everything was rather vague. I didn't envy Kanesha the task of trying to get those two women to talk and then make sense of it all.

"The little bit I got out of it," Marisue said, "was that Gavin was angry over something the other man had done to him. Mr. X was taunting Gavin with it, and either Virginia or Ada Lou—sometimes I can't remember which of them is which—repeated that line from Shakespeare about being hoist with your own petard. What play is it from, do you remember?"

With an actress daughter who adored Shakespeare, and as an admirer of the Bard myself, I told her. "It's from *Hamlet*." I could have told her more, but I didn't want to sound like a know-it-all.

Marisue nodded. "Thanks. Anyway, one of them repeated it, and of course I'm not absolutely certain Mr. X said that to Gavin, or whether that was Ada Lou–Virginia's interpretation. Do you think it could have any bearing on the murders?"

"I don't know," I said. "But Kanesha definitely needs to hear about this, and she will of course have to talk to these two women."

"I really don't want to have to go back down there to talk to the deputy again," Marisue said. "I don't mean to sound whiny, but between dealing with Randi and her broken arm and then spending nearly an hour being grilled, I'm ready to load up on a bottle or two of my favorite wine and do some serious chilling out."

"I understand," I said. "Spending time at the ER is a draining experience for anyone. Let me text Kanesha on your behalf. At the moment I'll tell her she needs to talk to these two women and ask them about an argument they overheard. I can explain later— or rather, *you* can explain—what you overheard. Okay?"

"Sounds fine to me," Marisue said. "I could kiss you, Charlie, but I'm too tired to get out of the chair and do it." She grinned at me.

"I appreciate the thought." I smiled in return as I got my phone out to message Kanesha.

She responded quickly to thank me and to say that she would follow up with me soon. The important thing now was for her to talk to Virginia and Ada Lou. Marisue could tell her about overhearing the women's conversation later.

I nearly dropped my phone as a terrible thought occurred to me. "Marisue, do these women go around all the time, talking like that, as if nobody else is around them? Are they that oblivious to their surroundings?"

Marisue nodded. "When they really get going, I think they lose all sense of where they are and who might overhear them." Then she realized what I was getting at. "Oh my stars, the killer could have heard them gabbling away, and they would never know they had put themselves in danger." Her earlier lethargy disappeared, and now she was as on edge as I was.

"I'll text Kanesha again," I said. "Tell her it's an emergency and to call me ASAP."

"Do," Marisue said. "Those silly old bats. I hope they're okay."

Kanesha responded within seconds of my 911 text. "Yes?" she said. She never wasted time.

I explained as quickly as I could about Virginia and Ada Lou, citing Marisue as a reference. When I finished, Kanesha said, "I'll talk to them right away. I will make sure they're safe." The phone call ended.

I still felt agitated, even though I knew Kanesha would move quickly to protect the two elderly women. *As long as the killer hasn't gotten to them first.* I banished that thought. They would be all right. Kanesha would find them, find out everything they knew, and then would make sure they were safe from the killer.

My heart rate began to return to normal. Marisue, however, still looked upset.

"I should have made Virginia and Ada Lou go with me right then and there to talk to the deputy." Marisue thumped the arm of her chair with a tightly closed fist. "If anything has happened to them, I'll never forgive myself."

"Don't start that," I said. "You were tired. No surprise after the day you've had. You saw that it didn't hit me right away, either. I'm sure Kanesha will find them and make sure they come to no harm."

Diesel put a large paw on my knee, and I glanced down at him. He meowed twice, and I patted his head. "It's okay, boy, we're fine." I spoke soothingly to him for a few moments longer, and he stretched out again by my feet.

"Is he okay?" Marisue asked.

I nodded. "He is now. He picks up on it when I get agitated or upset about something. When anyone around him does, really. Calming him down always helps me to keep myself from losing it."

"How does he do around sick people?" Marisue asked. "Or, in this case, injured? I know Randi would get a kick out of seeing him for a few minutes, if she's awake."

"He would be fine with that. Actually, I've thought about getting involved in one of those therapy animal programs, because I think he would be great for that. He's really sociable most of the time."

"Why haven't you?" Marisue asked.

"Lack of time, mostly, and of course with the current job, I have even less," I said.

"That's too bad." Marisue pushed herself up and out of her chair. "Shall we go to Randi's room?"

"Are you feeling up to it?"

"No, but she's got the wine." Marisue grinned. "Come on, she's only a couple of doors away." From the nearby desk she picked up a couple of key cards, each in its own sleeve, and slipped one into the pocket of her slacks. Diesel and I followed her out of the room and to another room two doors down and across the hall. Marisue knocked lightly, waited a moment, and then inserted the key card.

I waited outside the room with Diesel while Marisue made sure Randi was awake and in a state to receive visitors. Diesel and I didn't have to wait long. Marisue came back soon and invited us in.

Subdued lighting greeted us, and I paused a moment to let my eyes adjust after the door swung shut behind us. Marisue went over to the king-sized bed and sat on a corner by the foot. I approached the bed, watching Randi's face as I did. She was obviously still a bit woozy from her pain meds. She blinked owlishly at me for a moment before she smiled.

"Hi, Charlie." She yawned. "Sorry about that. So tired. Nice to see you and your kitty." Her cast made her left arm look nearly three times its normal size, and I hoped she wasn't too uncomfortable. With the pain meds at work, she probably didn't feel much, at least. Marisue had her propped against several pillows so she could sit up and talk.

"I'm sorry about your arm," I said. "I hate to see you incapacitated like this. Is there anything I can do for you?"

"Not that I can think of." Randi yawned again. "Sorry. Can't seem to stop."

"No need to apologize," I said. "If you don't feel like talking, don't worry. We won't stay long."

Diesel meowed, and Randi smiled. With her uninjured right arm she patted the bedspread beside her. "Come on up, kitty. Come on, now, let me rub your head."

Diesel needed little urging. He understood the tone of Randi's words, if not their precise meaning. He climbed on the bed and stretched out by her side. Randi stroked his head, and I could see that doing so made her perk up a little.

"How did it happen?" I asked. "Do you remember?"

Randi grimaced. "Way it always happens with me. Flapping my gums, not watching where I was going." She fell silent after another yawn.

Marisue shook her head. "She stepped off the curb, and I guess she didn't realize it *was* the curb. She stumbled, and down she went before I could grab her."

"Not the first time." Randi's eyes closed, then opened again a moment later. "Sorry, keep wanting to sleep. Thirsty, though." She looked hopefully, I thought, at Marisue. "Wine?"

"Certainly not, not with the pain medication." Marisue got up from the bed and headed for the small nook that housed the refrigerator, coffeemaker, ice bucket, and cups. She came back with a bottle of water.

I glanced at the bottle as Marisue paused to twist off the cap. The brand name looked familiar. Then I remembered why I recognized it.

"Don't open that bottle." I reached to grab it away from Marisue.

TWENTY-EIGHT

||||||||||||||||||||||||||||||||||||||||||||||||||||||||||||||||

I had to stop Randi before she drank from the bottle. When I reached out for it, Marisue stared at me as if I had totally lost my mind.

"Don't open it." My tone was sharp, but Marisue complied with my demand. She jerked her hand away from the cap.

"What is it?" Randi demanded, now more alert than before.

"That's the same brand of water that Gavin drank." I took the bottle from Marisue's unresisting hands. "Where did you get this bottle?"

Marisue looked at me, then at Randi. "Is this the one you took from Gavin's party the other night?"

Randi nodded weakly. "Oh dear Lord, do you think it's poisoned?"

"I don't know," I said, my heart still pounding, "but I don't think we should take any chances. Is this the only one you have from Gavin's suite?" I took a couple of deep breaths to try to steady myself. Diesel meowed and moved away from Randi toward me. I reached over and rubbed his head, and we both calmed a little.

"Yes," Randi said. "Thank the Lord I hadn't tried to open it before." Her skin had an ashy cast to it, and I knew how frightened she was from a potentially narrow miss. I patted her right hand.

"You're fine now," I said. "I'm probably overreacting."

Marisue went to the bathroom and came back moments later with a cold washcloth, folded it in half, and laid it on Randi's forehead. "Thank you," Randi said.

"I need a drink." Marisue went over to the nook and poured a cup of wine and drank half of it in a gulp. "Charlie, how about you?" She refilled her cup.

"I'm fine," I said. "Is there another water bottle for Randi?"

"Yes, the expensive one the hotel provides," Marisue said. In a wry tone she added, "Worth three dollars in this case." She brought the bottle over to Randi and twisted off the cap. Randi took the bottle and drank deeply while Marisue went back for her wine.

"Better?" I asked, and Randi nodded. "Are you hungry at all? It's been a long time since lunch."

"Actually, I am hungry." Randi sounded surprised. "I don't feel like going anywhere, though. I guess it will have to be room service."

"I've already had something." Marisue went over to the desk and found the room service menu. "I'll order it for you and help you eat." She studied the menu for a moment. "They've got only a few items, an expensive steak, an expensive salmon dish, an expensive chicken dish with pasta that sounds good, and then of course they have several expensive sandwiches to choose from."

"Hamburger?" Randi asked, and Marisue nodded. "I'll have a hamburger," Randi continued. "You know how I like them."

"With fries, potato chips, or steamed vegetables?" Marisue asked.

"French fries this time," Randi said. "I think I've earned them."

I had to smile at that. After what she'd been through today, Randi should have whatever she wanted in the way of comfort food. While Marisue phoned room service, I pulled one of the armchairs nearer Randi's bed, making sure I was within an easy line of sight for her so she didn't have to strain her neck to see me. Diesel, now completely relaxed again, lay stretched out beside Randi on the bed.

"Do you feel up to talking awhile longer?" I asked.

Randi nodded. "At least until my food comes."

Marisue resumed her seat at the foot of the bed. "They said about twenty minutes. That means anywhere from ten minutes to forty-five, probably, depending on how busy they are."

"I'm not going anywhere." Randi grimaced. "What do you want to talk about, Charlie?"

"Gavin's party," I replied. "I want you to tell me whatever you can remember, both of you." I glanced in Marisue's direction, and she nodded.

"I'll start," Marisue said, "and Randi can break in when she has anything to add. We were the last to arrive, except for Lisa Krause who came in for a few minutes and then left, pretty early on." She paused for a sip of wine. "The whole thing was awkward, of course, because no one really wanted to be there, except Gavin."

"And Maxine," Randi added. "You know she stuck by Gavin like a leech most of the time, when he wasn't yelling at her to leave him alone."

Marisue shrugged. "They definitely had a weird relationship, cooing and holding hands one minute, and the next spitting at each other like a couple of cats. Sorry, Diesel." She raised her cup at him and then drained it.

"What mode were they in at the party?" I asked.

"They were hardly speaking to each other," Randi said. "In fact, most of the time we were there, Maxine never went near him. Instead she and Sylvia sat together, whispering back and forth."

"Were she and Sylvia really good friends?" I wondered whether Kanesha had found out anything useful from talking to Sylvia O'Callaghan.

"I'm not really sure," Marisue said. "I think they'd known each other a long time."

"They worked together about ten years when they were first out of library school," Randi said. "Sylvia told me that. But then one of them took another job on the other side of the country, and they didn't see each other except at the occasional convention."

That was enough about Sylvia for the moment, I thought. "How were the other people there interacting with Gavin?"

Marisue got up to refill her cup. At the rate she was hitting the wine she might soon be a bit squiffy. *Not your business.* No, it wasn't.

Marisue rejoined us. "About what you'd expect. No one was interacting with him willingly, as far as I could see. I certainly wasn't. Gavin, of course, was going around, poking at each one of us, trying to get some reaction."

Randi giggled. "Not literally poking, you understand, but if he'd had a stick, he probably would have."

Marisue rolled her eyes at her friend. "Verbal poking. He knew we were all there because we were afraid of what he might do to make our lives uncomfortable." She frowned. "It was a bit like waiting for a dangerous animal to come after you but hoping he would go after someone else instead."

"I'm sorry you had to endure that," I said. "He really was a piece of work, wasn't he?"

"You're not going to find anyone wearing black on his account, I can guarantee," Marisue said.

"No, I guess not," I replied. "What about the others? Can you give me some specifics about how they were dealing with Gavin?"

"I talked to a couple of the other women," Marisue said. "Nancy Dunlap and Cathleen Matera. They were trying to avoid talking to Gavin as much as I was. He did come over at one point and make snide remarks about Nancy being a professor now with tenure."

From my research into everyone's careers, I remembered that Nancy Dunlap had degrees in biology and was a liaison to the chemistry department at her university. Cathleen Matera had no connection to the sciences that I could recall.

"How did she react to him?" I asked.

Marisue chuckled. "Nancy brushed him off. I guess now that she's tenured, she's not too worried about what he could do to her career. She's pretty much set. When he started in on Cathleen, Nancy told him to back off. Surprised the heck out of me, but he did. I guess he figured he wasn't going to get anywhere with Cathleen as long as Nancy was there. He glowered, but then he walked away."

"Did he try getting at you?" I asked.

"Not right then. If Nancy hadn't been there, he probably would have." Marisue stared into her cup. "A little later, he caught me by myself. He did the usual things, stood too close, tried to touch my arms, you know the routine."

"Disgusting," I said.

"I finally used a few words that would have my grandmother spinning in her grave if she even suspected I knew them." Marisue smiled grimly. "That pissed him off, and he left me alone after that."

I decided not to broach the subject of blackmail with them, especially since Kanesha had that spreadsheet and would be working on deciphering it and trying to connect it with Gavin's victims. That was definitely a task better left to a professional.

"You know, there was another person who didn't seem all that bothered by Gavin and his remarks." Randi shifted in the bed, and the pillow bracing her head and shoulders slipped. "Would you mind fixing my pillow?" She looked at Marisue, but I responded first.

"Thanks, Charlie," she said. "Now, what was I saying? Oh, yes, Harlan Crais. He sat in one corner and watched most of the time. Looked to me like he was smirking. What do you think?" She directed her question at Marisue, who nodded.

"I thought so, too," she said. "Maybe he's like Nancy and has tenure. I don't know, but he didn't seem all that bothered by Gavin." She frowned. "And you know, I don't think I saw Gavin speak to him at all while we were there."

"Maybe Gavin was avoiding him then but went after him later, once we'd left," Randi said.

"Could be," Marisue replied. "Well, let's see, who was there that we haven't talked about?"

"The other two men," Randi said.

"Right, trust you to remember the men," Marisue said. "I talked to Mitch Handler for a bit, mostly about his writing. I've read most of his books and was curious about a few things. He's a nice guy, but boy, is he shy. It took a little while to get him to say more than four or five words at a time. I guess it's a good thing he's a cataloger so he doesn't have to deal with the public at work."

Mitch Handler interested me particularly, because he had a degree in organic chemistry. He served as liaison for the science departments at his institution, so he obviously had a connection to a chemistry lab. He was a dark horse, however, when it came to his connections with Gavin. They must have worked together at some point. This was another one Kanesha would have to dig further into, unless Randi and Marisue knew something more about him.

I recalled a remark Randi made during one of our conversations. I reminded her of it. "You said you'd heard something about Gavin and Mitch Handler, but at the time you couldn't recall it. Can you remember it now?"

"Did I say that?" Randi asked. "If you say so, I guess I did." She thought for a moment, then shook her head. "Sorry, my brain is too fuzzy right now. If I can recall whatever it was, I'll tell you."

That was frustrating, but I knew I couldn't push her at the moment. Maybe by the time she felt ready to talk to Kanesha, she would have dredged it up out of her memory. I glanced at Marisue, but she shook her head. "Sorry, I don't know what it was, either."

"Well, then, that leaves us with Bob Coben," I said.

Randi giggled again. "The bad boy." She licked her lips and quirked her eyebrows at me.

"What do you mean?" I asked, though I had an inkling.

"He looks like a bad boy," Randi said. "That bald head, all the tattoos, the earrings. You know, like he should come roaring in on a motorcycle, wearing a leather jacket. That kind of bad boy."

Marisue snorted with laughter. "He doesn't seem anything like that to me."

"You have your fantasies, I'll have mine," Randi retorted. "I actually talked to him for a little while before Marisue started yanking on my arm to get me to leave."

"I did not *yank* your arm," Marisue said. There was a knock on the door, and she went to answer it.

Figuring it was room service, I told Diesel to come down off the bed to sit by me. Randi wouldn't want to eat with a cat on the bed beside her, I figured.

The server brought the tray in, and Marisue cleared the nightstand on the side of the bed where Randi sat propped up. She signed the ticket for Randi, and the server left. Marisue began to prepare the food for Randi to eat, adding mayonnaise and mustard to the hamburger and opening the tiny ketchup bottle for the fries.

I knew Randi was ready to eat by the way she looked at the food tray, but I wanted to hear about Bob Coben before I left her and Marisue. I said as much, and Randi nodded.

"All right, all kidding about hot bad boys aside," Randi said, "I talked with him for a while, and he mostly wanted to talk about his plans for his career. He's a musician, did you know that?"

I nodded, and she continued. "I thought he wanted to go further into music, but he told me he was working on a master's degree in chemistry. He wants to go on for a PhD, but he has to work for a couple more years to save up the money."

A master's degree in chemistry? If Bob Coben was taking classes, then he was actively working in a lab—where he would have direct access to all kinds of chemicals, including cyanide.

TWENTY-NINE

Neither Randi nor Marisue seemed to understand the implications of what Randi told me about Bob Coben. After a moment, however, Marisue figured it out. Randi, after dropping her bombshell, had reached for a french fry. In the midst of chewing it, her mouth dropped open, and I looked away.

Randi evidently swallowed quickly, because when she spoke she did so clearly. "No, I don't believe it. Surely he wouldn't poison anyone."

"How could he expect to get away with it?" Marisue said. "Don't they have to keep careful track of any chemicals they use in their labs?"

"I'm sure they do," I said. "Look, I don't know that Bob Coben is the one who put the poison in Gavin's bottle, or in Maxine Muller's. The thing is, he had easy access to it, or at least *easier* access than anyone else in the case that I know of."

I pulled out my phone and texted Kanesha a quick message

about Bob Coben. She might already have found out about his getting a degree in chemistry, but in case she hadn't, I thought she ought to know right away.

Moments later my phone buzzed, and I thought I'd received a reply from Kanesha. Instead, the message came from Lisa Krause.

Where r u? Need u at the party.

I had lost track of time, talking with Randi and Marisue, and forgotten about the party in Lisa's suite. I checked the time on my phone. I should have been in Lisa's suite ten minutes ago.

I responded that I would be there in two minutes. I explained to Marisue and Randi that I had to leave.

"Thanks for talking with me," I said. "I know you're both exhausted."

Marisue nodded, and I noticed that she looked rather wilted now. Randi actually looked perkier, but that was probably because she was eating.

"I'll check in on you tomorrow," I said. "When were you planning to leave?"

"Not till Monday morning," Marisue said. "We both took the day off so we didn't have to rush back tomorrow."

"Good, you'll have time to rest before the drive. I'll see you tomorrow."

Diesel and I took our leave of my friends and made our way to Lisa's suite on another floor.

The door stood open, and when we entered I saw Lisa talking to a couple of women who looked vaguely familiar. That meant I had probably noticed them at some point during the past couple of days here at the conference, but I had no idea who they were. There was no one else in the suite that I could see.

Lisa saw me, nodded in my direction to acknowledge me, and

continued with her conversation. I took the opportunity to glance around the suite. The layout was exactly as I remembered it. The bar against the outside wall, with a large window next to it, a table that could seat six comfortably on one side of the room, and two sofas and a couple of armchairs, with a coffee table in their midst. Small tables at each end of the sofas held lamps, all dark at the moment, because Lisa had the overhead lights on.

I walked over to the bar and found a can of diet soda in a large basin full of ice and drinks. I found a napkin on the bar to wipe excess moisture from the can, and then Diesel and I walked over to one of the armchairs. He stretched out near my feet while I opened the can and took a sip.

I knew I should be more sociable and join Lisa and the women with her, but at the moment I wanted to sit and think, at least while the room was still relatively quiet. I needed to consider what I had learned from my conversation with Marisue and Randi.

Bob Coben had suddenly emerged, at least in my mind, as the chief suspect in the murders. That bothered me, because he had stepped forward quickly after the altercation I had with Gavin on Thursday, offering to support me if Gavin tried to sue or cause any other unpleasantness. The next day, however, after Gavin's shocking death, I had overheard Coben in conversation with Harlan Crais. From that I'd gathered that Coben thought Gavin had kept him from getting a better job. Given what I'd learned about Coben's plans for a PhD and the need for money to pay for that degree, I figured he must have been deeply angry with Gavin.

Angry enough to kill him? That I didn't know, but I wondered how tempted Coben might have been, working in the chemistry lab, knowing that one solution to his desire for revenge lay so close within his reach. The means was there, but did he avail himself of it?

That lay in Kanesha's province, not mine. Working with the Mississippi Bureau of Investigation, she could contact its equivalent in Alabama, I reckoned, and ask for their cooperation. That might take a time to arrange, but it would no doubt happen.

Mitch Handler, the librarian-turned-writer, had a degree in organic chemistry and worked as liaison with the chemistry department. What kind of access did he have to dangerous chemicals? Perhaps he had a crony in one of the labs who would help him out, maybe turn a blind eye and cover it up if Handler helped himself to a pinch or two of cyanide.

Sources of cyanide were always easier in Golden Age English detective stories. Everyone had cyanide on hand in the potting shed to get rid of rats and wasps and other unwelcome intruders. Or they had connections with an industrial concern where cyanide was used in various processes. This case wasn't that simple.

Lisa and the other two women interrupted my cogitations on cyanide and murder, and I stood while Lisa performed the introductions. Both women made charming remarks about Diesel, and he, the ham, ate it up. They patted his head and stroked his back, and he adored it. We chatted for a few moments longer, and then the two excused themselves and left the room.

Lisa, Diesel, and I were alone for perhaps three minutes after that. More people began to arrive, and among them, I was pleased to see, were Cathleen Matera and Nancy Dunlap. They made a beeline for the bar and helped themselves to wine. Then Nancy Dunlap spotted Diesel, and she came immediately over with Cathleen Matera.

I suggested that they take seats on the sofa that stood at a right angle to the chair I'd been occupying. They made themselves comfortable, and I resumed my seat. Diesel, happy with more attention, sat on the floor at their feet and meowed at them while they told him how handsome he was, and so on.

After a couple of minutes of attention to the cat, though, both women focused their attention on me.

"We've been hearing some interesting stories about you, Mr. Harris." Cathleen Matera smiled. "Apparently you're quite the amateur detective."

Nancy Dunlap nodded. "We heard about what happened recently at Athena, with the murder in the library."

I winced inwardly. I really didn't like talking with people I barely knew about the murders that I'd had the misfortune to encounter. I had to be polite, however. "Call me Charlie, please. And, yes, I suppose I've had more experience with murder than most people. Not something I like to talk about much, frankly."

Nancy Dunlap laughed. "No, I imagine not. Don't worry, we're not going to press you for the lurid details. I prefer my murders to be fictional. Are you a mystery reader?"

"Yes, since childhood," I said. "What about you, Cathleen?"

She shook her head. "Occasionally I'll read one, but most of the time I like fantasy and science fiction."

We chatted for a few minutes about favorite authors, and I discovered that Nancy and I had similar tastes. She was a big fan of two Mississippi writers, Carolyn Haines and Charlaine Harris. Cathleen agreed that she loved Charlaine's work as well. When I mentioned a couple of historical mystery writers I particularly enjoyed, Nancy dove into her purse, pulled out a small notepad and a pen, and started jotting down names.

All the while we discussed books, I wondered how I could introduce the subject of Gavin and do a bit of discreet probing. Finally, I figured out a way, taking a lead from Cathleen's mention of two of her favorite writers. Nancy and I had hardly given her time to talk before.

"Their work does sound interesting," I said. "I discovered that one of the librarians at the conference writes science fiction. Mitch Handler, that's his name, but I think he uses a different name for his novels."

"Berger Mitchell," Cathleen said promptly. "I've read a couple of his novels. He's really good, and he writes women characters who are real women, not like the caricatures you find in some male writers' books."

"I'll have to give him a try," I said. "I do occasionally read science fiction. I think somebody told me he once worked with Gavin, too. Have either of you ever worked with him?"

Nancy and Cathleen exchanged a glance, then Nancy spoke. "With Mitch, you mean?" At my nod Nancy continued. "No, I've not worked with him, and I don't believe Cathleen has, either."

Cathleen shook her head.

Nancy smiled briefly. "Look, Charlie, I know you're wanting to ask us something about Mitch and Gavin, so why not come right out with it?"

I could all too easily imagine my sheepish expression when I responded. "You're right. Okay, here it is. Gavin had a habit of doing nasty things to people he worked with when they tried to move on to other jobs. Does that ring any bells?"

Both women were obviously startled. "How do you know about that?" Cathleen asked, then immediately appeared to regret it.

"Two friends who worked with Gavin before told me," I said. "One of them said she'd heard Gavin had done something nasty to Handler, but she couldn't remember."

Nancy's eyes widened as she seemed to be looking over my shoulder. She opened her mouth to speak, but she was interrupted before she could say anything. At the same time Cathleen shrank back and stared down at her wineglass.

A deep voice spoke from somewhere near my shoulder. "I can tell you myself. Although why it's any business of yours, I don't have any idea."

Startled, I turned in my chair to see Mitch Handler frowning down at me.

THIRTY

That's what you get for sitting with your back to the door, you nitwit. The snide voice in my head made me want to squirm. What an idiot I was sometimes.

Repressing a sigh, I stood, being careful not to trod on Diesel. "I'm truly sorry, Mr. Handler. My curiosity gets the better of me sometimes."

Handler's response to that was a stony gaze. Behind me, I heard Nancy and Cathleen getting to their feet.

"Nice talking to you, Charlie," Nancy said, and Cathleen nodded. "See you later, Mitch."

I envied them their quick escape. At the moment I wished I could crawl under the sofa. I looked back at Handler with what I hoped was a suitably hangdog expression.

The stony gaze softened a minute amount.

"Why don't you sit back down?" Handler moved past me to the sofa and seated himself.

I resumed my former place and waited for Handler to speak. For the moment, he seemed more interested in Diesel than in continuing to chastise me. Diesel, after first trying to hide between my legs and the chair, soon responded to the soft chirps Handler made. He moved close enough to sniff at the stranger's extended fingers for a moment. He evidently decided Handler was okay, because he allowed the man to rub his head.

Handler appeared calm when he spoke to me again. "I've heard about you and your cat, Mr. Harris. Your penchant for getting involved in murders had gotten around this weekend. Frankly, I'm surprised that local law enforcement hasn't done something about that."

Despite my earlier embarrassment over being caught gossiping about this man behind his back, I was starting to feel irritated at his patronizing tone. I wasn't about to explain myself to him or share with him the unusual relationship I had with Kanesha Berry. I let his remark go without response.

Handler shrugged after a silence of several seconds and evidently decided his bait had missed its mark. "You are trying to find out what happened between Gavin and me, I presume because you plan to share it with your law enforcement contact. Deputy Berry, right?"

I nodded. At the moment I didn't trust myself to speak.

"As I've already told the deputy my story, I might as well tell you, I suppose. No doubt she will tell you herself eventually. You seem to be in the loop on everything, from what I've heard."

Now I had to speak, and I did my best to restrain my anger with him. I wanted to wipe that smug expression away. "I don't appreciate your sarcasm, Mr. Handler. Yes, I am nosy, and yes, I've been involved in a few murder investigations. But let me set you straight on one thing. Kanesha Berry is a principled, ethical investigator. She shares with me only the things that have direct bearing on an investigation when I have provided the basic information that has helped her. I don't see autopsy reports, the results of forensic tests, or witness statements, *ever*."

Handler had the grace to look slightly abashed by the time I concluded my mini-rant. "Okay, sorry, I went too far. These murders have me on edge, like they do everyone. I didn't care for Gavin Fong any more than anyone who'd ever worked with him." Suddenly he grinned. "Evidently you and I have one thing in common, according to a story I heard from one of your old library school friends. I punched him out like you did, and for the same reason."

"He was harassing your wife?" I didn't like the fact that one of my library school friends had gossiped about me, but I couldn't get on a high horse over that. That horse had no legs in this instance.

"Girlfriend at the time," Handler replied. "Now my wife. He was slime when it came to women, and I caught him with his hands all over her and her trying to get away from him. He never made that mistake again."

I understood the gleam of satisfaction in Handler's eyes. "Did he try to retaliate? Sue you, press charges, anything like that?" I asked. "He was threatening me with that after we brangled on Thursday."

"He did, at first, but when he found out there was another witness besides me who saw what he was doing, he backed down quickly." He laughed. "Gavin ignored the library cleaners as if they were invisible, but one of them saw him and spoke up on my behalf. Gavin found another job—with encouragement from our boss, frankly—and was gone six months later."

Handler sounded sincere, and I supposed if Kanesha tried to verify the story, she might be able to. It could be a clever fiction, though. This man was a novelist, and apparently a good one, to judge by what Marisue and Cathleen said. He could make up a plausible story without thinking all that hard about it.

I had to accept what he told me at face value, and he probably was telling the truth. I couldn't forget his background in chemistry, though, and that left me with a niggling doubt about his story and his motives for sharing it with me. I wondered why he hadn't simply told me to go to hell and be done with it.

"Thank you for telling me," I said. I thought about adding another apology but decided I'd apologized enough. He hadn't acknowledged the first one anyway.

Handler shrugged before he pushed himself up from the couch. "Whatever," he said before he walked off.

The room had continued to fill while I spoke with Handler, and I estimated there must be about twenty people here. A couple, a woman and a man, sat on the sofa away from me and Diesel and chatted with each other after a quick nod in my direction. Diesel seemed not to be stressed by the number of people, and I relaxed a bit.

I needed to visit the bathroom, however, and I took Diesel with me. We made our way past a small knot of people near the table where the hotel staff had laid out several choices of finger food. I spotted some cream cheese and spinach spirals that I particularly liked, and I hoped there would be some left when we came back from the bathroom.

I took my time in the bathroom, which I had fortunately found unoccupied. Despite the lure of food, I was in no hurry right then to rejoin the crowd. Once I'd washed and dried my hands, however, I had no reason to linger. "Come on, boy," I said. "Back into the fray."

The crowd had thinned by five or six people in the few minutes I was in the bathroom. I breathed a little easier as Diesel and

I approached the food table. I picked up a plate and napkin and helped myself to two—well, three, since there were still plenty left—of the cream cheese and spinach spirals. Thus far I'd avoided making eye contact because I knew I was too distracted by my thoughts to want to make conversation with strangers. I was sure people thought I was strange or standoffish or both, but I wasn't in the mood to repeat over and over information about Maine Coon cats and respond to remarks on Diesel's size. Maybe I was turning into a curmudgeon and didn't realize it. Or maybe I was just tired.

I found a seat, this time facing the door, and cleaned my plate. Diesel kept gazing at me with hope in his eyes, but I thought I detected garlic or onion in the spirals, and neither of those was good for cats. I promised him a treat when we got home.

I finished my diet soda and decided I wanted water now. The bar was near my chair, and I left Diesel where he was while I retrieved the water. Relieved to see that it was a different brand than the one Gavin favored, I brought it back to my chair and resumed my place. Diesel decided to climb into my lap, and suddenly I had large feet treading on tender places. I grimaced until the heavy weight in my lap found a comfortable position, head on one arm of the chair and tail hanging over the other.

"My goodness, that is the largest cat I think I've ever seen."

I remembered that voice. It was either Ada Lou or Virginia. I couldn't remember which was which, but they stood about five feet away from me, staring at Diesel.

"Don't you think that's the largest cat I've ever seen, Virginia?" Ada Lou nudged the woman beside her in her ribs.

Virginia scowled. "How on earth should I know whether that's the largest cat you've ever seen, Ada Lou? You've been to a zoo, haven't you? They've got much larger cats there. Surely you've seen lions and tigers."

"Well of course I have." Ada Lou appeared cross. "You know what I meant. That's the largest pet cat I've ever seen." She stared at Diesel, then her eyes seemed to travel upward to his face. "Oh, so you're the one people have been talking about."

"I suppose so," I said, resigned to conversing on the subject of my cat. "His name is Diesel, and he's a Maine Coon. They're the largest American breed of house cat, and the only truly American breed."

"You don't say," Virginia said. "I've heard of them, but I don't think I've ever seen one in person before. Does he bite?"

"How much does he eat a day?" Ada Lou talked right over Virginia's last few words, and for a moment I couldn't sort out what either of them had asked. Once I did, I answered them.

"Well, that surely is interesting," Ada Lou said. "Don't you think that's interesting, Virginia? He's so big he looks like he could be ferocious, but this man is telling us he's gentle."

"If I found everything interesting that you asked me about, Ada Lou," Virginia snapped in response, "I'd spend every waking hour finding something interesting, and frankly that's exhausting. I'm thirsty. Do you find that interesting?" She grimaced at her friend and walked around my chair to the bar.

Ada Lou appeared to be contemplating Virginia's statement. I wondered if the woman understood sarcasm at all, or whether she was one of those people who are too literal-minded to get it.

"I don't think I ask you about finding things interesting *that* much, Virginia," Ada Lou said as she walked past me to join her friend at the bar. "You do like to exaggerate, and I've never understood that about you, although I do find it interesting."

Oh dear Lord, do they go on like this all the time? My head had begun to ache, and I was contemplating getting up and moving when I noticed a new arrival to the party, Harlan Crais, standing in the doorway. I decided to remain where I was and keep an eye on Crais. I wanted to talk to him, and I needed to think up the best approach.

Virginia and Ada Lou continued to chatter behind me at the bar, and I strove to block out their voices while I watched Crais. He advanced into the room and walked over to a group of three women who stood at the table, casually grazing from the food there. They appeared to know him, and he hugged one of them.

I thought about possible conversational gambits to use with Crais, all the while Virginia and Ada Lou kept nattering away. Then I realized they were talking about Crais, and I tuned in.

"I tell you, Virginia, that *is* the clumsy man we saw at the table where Gavin Fong was sitting at lunch yesterday. Don't you remember? I think sometimes you're starting to get dementia when you can't remember something like that."

"I remember him," Virginia said. "He's the one who introduced Gavin, Ada Lou."

"Yes, that's right, Virginia, you're doing good. If you can remember that, then you ought to be able to remember how clumsy he was at the table. After all, you're the one who pointed it out to me."

"Maybe I did, and maybe I didn't," Virginia replied. "I do remember him knocking those things over on the table. It's a good thing that the only thing that fell off was that water bottle. At least the klutz didn't break any of the china."

I tensed the moment I heard mention of the water bottle. So Harlan Crais knocked Gavin's water bottle off the table. Was that how it was done?

221

THIRTY-ONE

|||||||||||||||||||||||||||||||||||||||||||||||||||||||||||

I listened, riveted, as Ada Lou and Virginia continued.

"He did manage to knock that gravy boat over, though, and that gravy went everywhere from what I could see. I don't guess anyone got it on them, but I remember a couple of people did get up and leave the table. Do you think, Virginia, that they did get gravy on their clothes?"

"Why on earth would you possibly care whether any of those people got gravy on their clothes, Ada Lou?"

"Well, it's happened to me at a conference, and you know how it is at conferences—you don't always have extra clothes to change into, and of course you don't want to go around wearing gravy or something else on your clothes all day, especially if you can't rinse it out in the bathroom sink. I remember a time at ALA in New Orleans . . ."

At that point I decided I had heard enough. The sound of those two voices had already begun to make me want to butt my head against a brick wall. I eased Diesel off my lap as gently as I could, but I was determined to get out of sound range of Ada Lou and Virginia. I was thankful to them, though, for the interesting information they had unwittingly shared with me. I hoped that Harlan Crais hadn't heard any of it, and that the two elderly women had sense enough not to talk to him about it. They could be in danger, if what I suspected was the solution to the two murders. Kanesha, however, had promised to make sure they were safe.

I hesitated. Maybe I should try to talk to them and warn them anyway. There was one point that needed clarification, if I could get it from them. Was Gavin one of the people who'd left the table after the spilled gravy incident? And was that when Crais knocked the water bottle off the table so he could switch it with a poisoned one?

Another question occurred to me. Why hadn't Crais stashed the poisoned bottle among the bottles in Gavin's suite? Was he concerned about the wrong person getting hold of one? If he hadn't put the poisoned bottle among those in the suite, where did the bottle that killed Maxine Muller come from?

The solution hinged largely on two things, I thought. How the killer obtained the cyanide and how the two victims ended up with poisoned bottles of water. I wondered if Kanesha was thinking the same thing.

If only Randi, Marisue, and I had sat at a table near Gavin's that day. I could have observed this for myself and immediately have brought it to Kanesha's attention. I realized that Crais might simply be clumsy and was always knocking things over and so on, and what Virginia and Ada Lou witnessed was normal behavior for him. I'd not seen any signs of clumsiness from him, however.

At the moment he stood balancing a wineglass atop an empty

plate. As I watched he turned slightly to pick up a couple of small wedges of cheese from the table, and when he did so, the plate and glass remained steady.

As a somewhat klutzy person myself, I would never have attempted that, because as sure as I had, I would have tilted the plate and wine would have gone everywhere. Crais's balance was better than mine. I continued to watch him for a few minutes longer, but nothing happened in the way of klutziness. I concluded that Crais had staged the little *accidents* at the luncheon table to suit his own purposes.

I spotted Nancy Dunlap and Cathleen Matera at the end of the table away from where Harlan Crais stood talking to the same three women he'd been chatting with for probably the last ten minutes. Now would be a good time to rejoin Nancy and Cathleen and finish our conversation.

"Come on, Diesel," I said in a low voice. "Let's go talk to those nice ladies again, okay?" He chirped in response. He still seemed all right, but before much longer, I knew we'd both be ready to head home.

"Hi, Charlie." Nancy grinned when Diesel and I walked up to her and Cathleen. "Our little chat earlier got cut off pretty dramatically." She bent to scratch Diesel behind one ear, and he purred.

"I'll say it did." Cathleen chuckled as she watched Nancy and Diesel. "Your expression was priceless when you realized Mitch Handler had overheard you." She chuckled again.

"Not one of my more shining moments," I said. "It was awkward, but he actually talked to me and told me what I was trying to find out."

"We aren't going to ask you what the story was, even though we're dying to know," Cathleen said.

"Thanks," I said. "If you do have a few more minutes to talk, could I ask you a few questions about Gavin's party the other night?"

Cathleen groaned. "And here I was, trying to forget the whole darn thing."

Nancy rolled her eyes. "It wasn't *that* bad. We've both been to worse. Gavin was an obnoxious twit on Thursday night, but he didn't seem to be as intent on malice as he usually was."

"Really?" That struck me as interesting. "I would have expected him to be in full-on attack mode. Didn't he basically force you all to attend the party?"

Nancy shrugged. "He didn't force me. He had no power over me anymore. I only went because Cathleen begged me to."

"I knew Nancy could make him back off if he started in on me," Cathleen said. "I just couldn't deal with him."

"I can understand that," I said. "I couldn't, either. In my case, I ended up hitting him. That's not really the way to handle a problem like the one Gavin presented."

Nancy quirked her eyebrows at me. "I bet it felt good, though. There were a few times I longed to let go and slap the you-know-what out of him, the smug little twit."

Her voice had grown heated, and her body language tense, as she spoke. Nancy didn't seem as immune to Gavin as she might want others to think. The anger hadn't disappeared, obviously.

I let that pass, however. By now I was pretty sure who killed Gavin, and it wasn't either Nancy or Cathleen.

"Back to the party," I said. "Will you tell me what you observed, in the order that it happened, if you can?"

They exchanged a glance, and both of them shrugged.

"Why not?" Cathleen said, and Nancy nodded in agreement.

"You start," Nancy said.

Cathleen launched into a summary of her observations of the party. Much of what she told me tallied with what I'd already heard from Randi and Marisue. Cathleen and Nancy had stayed on after my two friends left, however; that was the time that interested me the most.

Nancy took up the narrative from Cathleen at the point when Randi and Marisue left. "Sylvia, that odd woman who was such a close friend of Maxine's, left soon after your two friends did. Mitch Handler didn't stay more than five minutes after Sylvia left."

"So at that point, the only others there besides you and Cathleen were Harlan Crais, Maxine, and Gavin. Is that correct?" I asked.

"No, Bob Coben was still there, I think." Cathleen frowned. "Wasn't he?"

"Yes," Nancy said. "He was, for maybe another ten minutes or so. Said he had to meet someone. Sounded like a hookup to me." She shook her head. "I don't see the attraction myself."

Cathleen rolled her eyes. "You can't get past the earrings and the tattoos. He's really good-looking, I think." She sighed. "I'd've gone out with him, but I'm probably old enough to be his big sister."

Nancy snorted. "Big sister, yeah. More like his mother, you mean."

Cathleen bridled at that, and I was afraid they were going to get into an argument if I didn't intervene. "When Coben left, there were just five of you still at the party."

Cathleen gave Nancy one last speaking glance before she said, "Yes, that's right."

"Anything unusual happen from then until you left the party?" I asked.

"Not that I can recall," Nancy said. "We were ready to go ourselves, and I think Harlan was, too. I said something about being tired and ready for bed, and Harlan chimed in. Said he was pretty exhausted, too."

"Gavin was a little annoyed, I think," Cathleen said. "But he didn't make a big fuss like he usually did at one of his forced gatherings. He liked to keep everyone there as long as possible so he could torture us more."

"No, he didn't make a fuss." Nancy frowned. "That was a bit odd, and then he did another odd thing."

"You mean the food," Cathleen said, and Nancy nodded.

"What about the food?" I asked.

"There was quite a bit left over," Cathleen said. "And it was good stuff, too. I guess the hotel catered it."

"It wasn't the usual cheese tray Gavin picked up at the local discount warehouse, that's for sure," Nancy said.

"No, thank goodness." Cathleen eyed the food that remained on the table near us. "In fact it was pretty much the same as this."

I wasn't sure where this was leading, and they were taking too long to get to the point. I tried not to sound irked when I asked, "So what was it about the food that was odd?"

"Oh, just that usually Gavin made sure nobody took any of the leftovers with them," Cathleen said.

"He always wanted to keep them for himself," Nancy said. "That's how cheap he was."

"This time, though, he told us to help ourselves to whatever we wanted, even his precious bottled water," Cathleen said.

The mention of bottled water startled me. "Did any of you take food and water with you?"

"I took some food. I love those pinwheel-looking things with the cream cheese and spinach," Cathleen said. "So I took several of those, and a couple of those little Greek pastry things with the spinach inside. What are they called? I can't remember."

"You mean spanakopita?" I asked. "I love it, too."

"Yes, that's it," Cathleen said. "So I took that and the other. I love spinach, in case you couldn't tell."

I looked to Nancy, and she shook her head. "I don't care for spinach, and I wasn't particularly interested in any of the other stuff. I didn't even take any of Gavin's precious water."

Nancy laughed suddenly. "Maxine was always like a squirrel around a table full of nuts, though. She stuffed several napkins full of food into her knitting bag, along with a bottle of water."

"Yes, she did," Cathleen said. "You'd think the woman hadn't eaten in days. I took a bottle of water, too, and so did Harlan."

My heart started racing. I worked to keep my voice steady when I asked Cathleen whether she had opened the water bottle.

She looked at me strangely, then nodded. "Yes, I drank it yesterday. Why, did you think it was poisoned?"

THIRTY-TWO

||||||||||||||||||||||||||||||||||||||||||||||||||||||||||

I nodded in response to Cathleen's question.

"Oh, my good heaven, you *did* think it might be poisoned," Cathleen said, suddenly looking a bit green. She shuddered. "But why? Why would you think the water was poisoned?"

Nancy stared at me, obviously confused. "Did you think the killer poisoned more than one of Gavin's water bottles?"

"He—or she—poisoned two of them, at least." They obviously didn't know how Maxine Muller died.

Nancy's eyebrows shot up. "You mean Maxine?"

"Yes," I said. "The killer might only have poisoned a couple of them, although I'm not sure why he'd need to have poisoned more than one."

"Because Gavin never shared with anyone," Nancy said. "The killer could have, with almost overwhelming certainty, counted on the fact that Gavin, and Gavin only, would drink the poisoned water."

"Exactly," I said. "But there were at least two poisoned bottles. So why poison a second one? And maybe a third or a fourth?"

Nancy paled suddenly. "Thank the Lord I didn't take one of those bottles. What happened to the rest of them?"

"I imagine the authorities have them now," I said. "I suppose they will test all the remaining ones, that they know about, of course."

Cathleen seemed to have recovered from her earlier shock. "Somebody needs to talk to Harlan, then, since he took one of the bottles. Maybe his was clean, though, like mine."

"Either it was, or he hasn't opened it yet," Nancy said with a certain grim humor. "Charlie, maybe you'd better go ask him."

"Yes, you should," Cathleen said.

Given that I was pretty sure now that Harlan Crais was a double murderer, I wasn't all that keen on approaching him. If he were the killer, I reasoned, he would know which bottles were poisoned. If he weren't, though, he could be in danger if he'd somehow been given a poisoned bottle. *What should I do?*

I realized that both women were now watching me closely. They exchanged a glance, then focused on me again.

Nancy spoke first. "You're reluctant to talk to him, aren't you?" She didn't give me a chance to answer and continued in a low tone. "That's because you think he's the killer, don't you?"

"That's it," Cathleen said, speaking a little too loudly in her excitement. "But *why*? *Why* would Harlan kill Gavin? And poor, harmless Maxine? I don't understand."

"Keep your voice down." Nancy glared at Cathleen, who mimed an apology.

I found myself in a quandary. I didn't want to confirm these women's guesses that I had decided that Harlan Crais was the murderer. But could I deny that I had and make them believe me? If

Kanesha knew about this, she'd have my guts for garters, as the old saying went. I had to respond to them, but what was I going to say?

In desperation I said, "Look, I don't know if he's the killer. I can't talk about his possible motives for the same reason I couldn't tell you what Mitch Handler told me. For a couple of reasons, though, I can't just go up to him and ask him whether he still has that bottle of water."

"Then what are you going to do?" Cathleen asked. "If he still has it and opens it, he might not be as lucky as I was."

"I know that," I said, trying not to sound as aggravated and worried as I felt. "I have to have a minute to think about this. Please."

Neither of the women spoke after that. They stood waiting, quietly, and I had a few moments to think about what to do. When all else failed, I reckoned, summon the cavalry.

I pulled out my cell phone and sent Kanesha a text: *911 found out Fong gave away couple bottles of water from his suite. One harmless; other one status unknown. Given to Harlan Crais. Right now at party in my sight.*

I added the suite number and sent the message. I could only hope that Kanesha read the text and acted on it immediately.

"Who did you text?" Nancy asked.

"Deputy Berry," I said. "I think she needs to handle this." I didn't take my eyes from the cell phone screen. *Come on, Kanesha.* The words ran like a litany through my head for at least thirty seconds. Then my phone buzzed: *On it.*

"Thank you, thank you," I whispered. I took a couple of deep breaths to release some of the tension. I saw that the two women were watching me closely. "She's on it," I said.

"Thank heavens," Nancy murmured.

"What will she do?" Cathleen asked.

"I don't know." Now I had my gaze focused on Harlan Crais. Would Kanesha call him? Send one of her men to the suite? Come herself?

Somewhere in the room a phone rang and continued to ring. It took me a moment to locate the source of the sound. It was the room phone. Even as I found it, Lisa Krause was answering it. She was too far away, and there was too much noise around us, for me to hear her part of the conversation.

After a moment I saw her scanning the crowd, then she moved in the direction of Harlan Crais. The phone was cordless, and she simply took it to Crais and handed it over. He appeared startled as he accepted the phone.

I watched, along with Nancy and Cathleen, as he alternately spoke and listened. After a moment he shrugged and handed the phone back to Lisa. He turned to the women with whom he had been talking, and a few seconds later he made his way to the door and disappeared into the hallway.

Lisa returned the phone to its cradle and once again scanned the room. When she saw me she came right over.

"Excuse me, ladies, but I need to talk to Charlie for a moment," she said.

"No problem," Nancy said. "I think we're both about ready to go anyway. Thanks for the lovely party."

"Yes, thanks," Cathleen said. "I won't soon forget this one."

With that somewhat cryptic remark—cryptic to Lisa, that is— she and Nancy made their way out of the room.

Lisa didn't appear to have paid attention to Cathleen's words. Instead, as soon as the two women left us, she said, "What's going on? That was Kanesha Berry on the phone, insisting that she had to talk to Harlan Crais immediately. How did she even know where he was?" She regarded me, obviously suspicious that I was somehow involved. I couldn't really tell her the complete truth, so I told her part of it.

"I knew she needed to talk to him," I said. "I texted her to tell her where he was."

Lisa's eyes widened. "Oh my gosh, does this mean she's going to arrest him? Did you tell her he was the murderer?"

At least she had the sense to keep her voice down, I thought. Aloud I said, "No, I told her no such thing. I'm sure she has a few questions for him, that's all. She doesn't tell me when she's going to make an arrest, you know." I hoped that last sentence didn't come out as snarky.

Lisa stared at me, the doubt obvious in her expression. "Well, if you say so. Anyway, I wanted to thank you for coming. Do you want to take any of the food or drinks with you? Looks like things are winding down, and there's too much left to put in the tiny refrigerator."

The irony of the situation struck me, and I wanted to laugh. I restrained myself, because I wouldn't be able to explain to Lisa what I found funny about her offer. Instead, I checked out the plate with the spirals I liked so much and saw that there were half a dozen left.

"Well, I could take those, I guess." I pointed to the plate.

"Go ahead," Lisa said. "Better grab them, though, before anyone else does. I'm about to offer the people still here whatever they want to take with them. I'm hoping they'll take the hint and go. I'm about ready to drop."

I had thought earlier that she looked tired, and now that I looked again more closely, I could see that she really was more than ready to clear the room and go to bed.

"Thanks," I said. "Let me help with the cleanup."

"No, I appreciate the offer, but there won't be that much to do. I'll shove whatever's left in the fridge and leave the room for the hotel staff. They'll be getting a healthy tip, I promise you."

"All right, then, I guess I'll wrap up my goodies, and Diesel and I will head home. Ready to go home, boy?" He looked up at me and chirped. He wasn't exhausted like Lisa, but I could see that he had finally begun to tire. I had tried to keep him out of the main flow of the party so that he wouldn't be overwhelmed with people, and I thought my strategy had worked pretty well.

While I helped myself to the food I wanted to take home, Lisa gave Diesel a few strokes down his back and told him how well-behaved he was. He meowed and purred for her until I was ready to leave.

"Get some rest," I said.

"Don't worry, I will," she responded.

As Diesel and I headed for the door, Lisa called for everyone's attention and began her announcement about the food. We made it to the elevator before any of the other guests came out of the suite, so we had the car to ourselves. I imagined that Diesel enjoyed the quiet as much as I did. The older I got, the more I found noise—the kind at parties or in restaurants—ultimately exhausting. Perhaps it was an extension of my claustrophobia, or maybe it was a product of aging. Either way, I was grateful to be away from it.

Lack of hubbub around me allowed me to think more clearly. I thought about Harlan Crais and wondered about the bottle of water he'd accepted from Gavin at the party on Thursday. I still couldn't figure out why at least *two* bottles had been tampered with. There could have been more, but only the authorities would know that. I supposed that, at some point after the case was solved, Kanesha might be willing to share some of those details with me. Either that, or I'd have to read about them in the media like everyone else.

Diesel was intrigued by the napkin-wrapped food that I carried in one hand. As we made our way through the lobby and out to the parking lot behind the hotel, he kept looking at it. He meowed every so often, and I told him that this food wasn't for him. He would get a treat as soon as we got home.

In the car I made sure to put the food out of reach in the glove compartment. I didn't think he would try to get at it if I left it in the open car, but with felines, even one as well-behaved as Diesel, I had learned you could never be absolutely certain what they would do in any given situation.

The house was quiet when we entered. Stewart's car wasn't in the garage, so that meant no one was home, except possibly Dante in his crate up in Stewart and Haskell's apartment on the third floor. Once I released Diesel from his leash and harness he scurried to the utility room. I took my food out of the napkins in which I had wrapped it and transferred it into a plastic refrigerator bag. I was tempted to eat a couple of the spirals and stared at them for a moment, then put them in the fridge. A small victory for willpower. I needed more of them.

When Diesel came back to the kitchen I had his treat—or rather, treats—ready for him. I told him again what a good boy he had been at the party, and he gobbled down the treats as if I hadn't fed him in three days. He looked at me hopefully when they were gone, but I told him, "No, that's all for tonight."

He stared at me a moment before he turned and walked back to the utility room. I knew he would make do with dry food to fill the bottomless pit that was his stomach.

Shaking my head and smiling, I headed upstairs to get ready

for bed. I was tired and hoped I could go to sleep soon. I felt a little guilty that I'd left Lisa with the cleanup, but I hadn't argued when she told me she'd handle it. After all, she was around twenty years younger than I.

Diesel hadn't come upstairs when I was ready to climb into bed. I lay there with the bedside lamp on until he appeared a couple of minutes later. He climbed on the bed and stretched out beside me in his usual position. I thought about calling Helen Louise, but she wouldn't be home from the bistro for at least another hour or two. She was always exhausted on Saturday nights.

Instead, I turned out the light, got comfortable, and waited for sleep to overtake me.

And I waited.

The moment the light went out, my brain started cogitating on the murders. I knew then it would be a while before I could go to sleep. So I let my mind roam over the various questions I had and sought answers to them.

The question that I kept returning to was the two poisoned bottles. Why two?

I had a feeling that there *were* only two, but I couldn't figure out why. I started thinking about what had happened, about the scanty information Kanesha had shared with me, and all at once I had a possible answer to the riddle of the two poisoned bottles.

No, I thought, *that can't be it. It's too bizarre a solution.* But the more I thought about it, the more convinced I was that I had stumbled on the answer.

How on earth would I—or rather, Kanesha—prove it?

THIRTY-THREE

I shifted my position in the bed and squinted at the clock on the nightstand. The luminous numbers told me it was nine twenty-one.

Not too late, then, to get in touch with Kanesha.

I reached for my cell phone but drew back my hand before I touched the phone. No, what I was thinking was too wild. Kanesha would think I'd finally gone completely round the bend.

It was possible, I thought. Maybe not probable, but possible. Weirder things had happened in the annals of crime. Without thinking too hard about it, I could remember at least two crime novels that had solutions as improbable as the one I'd come up with in the present case.

I doubted, however, Kanesha would have any interest in that. She needed facts, evidence that could prove beyond a reasonable doubt the identity of the killer.

I had conjecture, mostly, no hard facts that could be considered evidence. *But maybe with my theory—okay, I'll call it that, a theory—to work with, Kanesha might* find *the evidence that would prove I'm right.*

I considered a couple of things she told me when we talked face-to-face about the investigation. I needed to figure out how certain things fit into my wild scenario.

Maxine Muller had told Kanesha that Gavin had received anonymous death threats and was frightened.

Maxine had seen a couple of the threats. One through an anonymous e-mail account, the other through the regular mail. She wasn't sure if Gavin had kept the envelope. She also wasn't sure how many threats he'd received. He had told her *multiple*, that was all.

He had told her one other thing, however. He was pretty sure who was behind the threats, but he refused to tell her who it was. He did finally admit to her that he knew the person would be attending the SALA conference, and he planned to confront him there.

Gavin had specifically said *him*, Maxine recalled, so she figured a man was behind the threats. When pressed by Maxine, however, Gavin got nasty with her and wouldn't confirm the gender of the culprit.

Kanesha couldn't ask Gavin about any of this, of course. I wondered if she had found any evidence of these threats when she and her people searched Gavin's room. I had asked her when we talked, but she said they hadn't, at that point. They were still going over his suite looking for evidence. I figured he might have brought any sent through the regular mail with him to use when he confronted the person he thought was responsible. Any others he received electronically would be found in his e-mail, surely.

Why had Maxine been given a tainted water bottle? I thought I knew the answer to that, too. Maxine knew too much about Gavin's activities, the nefarious ones, and she posed a threat to the killer. The killer wanted her completely out of the picture. Tying up the loose ends, as it were.

Maxine had told Kanesha one other thing, and it fit in with my solution. Gavin had applied for four different jobs over the past nine months, all of them at larger, better known schools than his current institution. Two of the schools appeared interested and set up phone interviews. A day or two before the scheduled phone calls, however, Gavin had received e-mails telling him that they regretted it, but he was no longer being considered for the position. From the other two schools he received fairly prompt responses to let him know they weren't interested.

He had been livid, Maxine told Kanesha, over the rejections. Particularly the two with the canceled phone interviews. Gavin was convinced someone had blackballed him. Again, he seemed to be sure who was responsible, or so Maxine thought. But he wouldn't say who. She figured it must be the same person who was sending the threatening letters. Gavin had started receiving them around the same time he received the rejections for his job applications.

I thought I knew who had blackballed Gavin, and I found it amusing, in a macabre sort of way. *Hoist by his own petard*, or *the biter bit*. Poetic justice, I'd call it. And more to come.

I reached for the phone again, and this time I picked it up. I thought about calling, because I doubted she was even at home, let alone in bed. No, a text would do. That way she could text me back and tell me I had lost what mind I had or she would call me to hear me out.

I tapped the keyboard slowly so I wouldn't have to go back and correct any misspellings or stupid auto-correct changes.

Think I have figured it out. Too complicated to explain in text. When can we talk?

I hit Send and waited.

Five minutes passed, then ten. Fifteen, and I was getting drowsy. Was she ever going to respond?

I thought about sending another text, one that I knew would grab her attention. Perhaps something like *the killer was the first to die*. That ought to get results.

I put the phone on the nightstand. Kanesha would respond when she was ready to. In the meantime I was getting drowsier by the minute. Diesel slept soundly beside me, and soon I drifted into sleep myself.

The ringing of my cell phone woke me out of a deep sleep. I fumbled for the phone, dropped it on the floor, and had to scramble to retrieve it before it stopped ringing. I knew it had to be Kanesha.

I noticed the time as I answered her call. Six fifteen. Sunday morning, then.

"Hello, this is Charlie." I yawned right into the phone the moment the words left my mouth. "Sorry."

"Guess I woke you up," Kanesha said. "I've been up most of the night. Could sure use some coffee."

I was suddenly wide awake. "I'll make the coffee. Come on by, and I'll have it ready."

"On the way." She ended the call.

"Come on, Diesel, time to get up." I glanced at the bed and realized I had been talking to the air. No Diesel on the bed. That meant Stewart must be downstairs with Dante.

Good, that meant the coffee was already made. Bless Stewart, I thought, and not for the first time, as I stumbled out of bed and into my bathroom to splash cold water on my face.

A few minutes later, after having exchanged my shorts and tee shirt for clothes suitable for talking to the law, I walked into the kitchen. Stewart sat at the table, reading the newspaper and drinking coffee. Diesel and Dante wrestled on the floor near him. The wrestling didn't amount to much, because whenever he wanted, Diesel could call a halt to the proceedings by sitting on the dog. He was at least three times the dog's size and weight.

"Good morning, Charlie." Stewart lowered the paper. "You're up earlier than usual on a Sunday morning."

"Good morning," I said. "Not by choice. Kanesha is coming over for coffee. I think I've figured out the solution to the two deaths, and I suppose she's coming to hear me out."

"There's plenty of coffee," Stewart said. "I made a whole pot, and I've had only one cup so far. Haskell is still in bed. He didn't get in until around one this morning."

"He must have been totally worn-out." I took a mug from the rack near the coffeemaker and filled my cup. I pulled out my usual chair and sat.

"Yes, he was knackered, as the Brits would say." Stewart smiled. "He's off duty today, so I plan to let him sleep in as long as he wants."

"Lucky Haskell," I muttered. I couldn't really complain, however, because I was the one who wanted to talk to Kanesha.

"Should I make myself scarce?" Stewart asked. "Is this meeting with Kanesha confidential, or can anyone sit in?"

"Probably confidential," I said. "Considering that the investigation isn't closed yet."

"No problem." Stewart rose from the table and went over to the coffeemaker. "I'll take my refill and the newspaper up to our sitting room. You're not going to be reading the paper anytime soon, right?"

"Right, you're welcome to it," I said.

"Okay, toodles, then," Stewart said. "Come on, Dante, let's go upstairs." He headed out of the kitchen. Diesel got up off the dog, and Dante scooted after his master.

I grinned at my cat. "You love having that dog to torment, don't you?"

Diesel gave me one of those feline-trademarked supercilious looks and started cleaning his right front paw. The doorbell rang moments later, though, and he abandoned his pose of indifference to follow me to the front door.

Kanesha looked as if she hadn't slept in two days, but her manner was as brusque as ever.

"Come on in, coffee's ready," I said.

"Thanks, I could use a gallon or two right about now." She headed past me to the kitchen, Diesel ambling alongside her, meowing the whole time.

While Kanesha chose a seat at the table, I poured coffee and gave it to her. She gave Diesel a couple of absentminded pats before downing about half her coffee at one go.

"Oh dear Lord, that is good," she said. "Stewart must have made it. He's the only one I know can make coffee as good as my mama."

"Yes, he did. Let me know when you want a refill."

In response she drained her mug and held it out to me. "Thanks, Charlie, I appreciate it."

I returned the mug full, and she took a couple of sips. She looked better now for having caffeine coursing through her system. I waited, though, for her to initiate our conversation about the case.

I didn't have to wait all that long. A few more sips of coffee, and she appeared to be ready to talk. "You think you've got it all figured out. Go ahead and tell me your solution."

"I will, but first I have at least one question," I said. She nodded, and I continued. "Did you find any evidence of the threats Gavin alleged to have received?"

"We did," Kanesha replied. "Several in his e-mail inbox, and he had a folder with seven printed ones in his laptop case. And, before you ask, the printed ones weren't copies of the e-mail messages. They were different."

"I'm willing to bet you'll find that Gavin wrote them himself," I said. "I don't suppose you've been able to trace any of them yet."

"Not yet," Kanesha said. "I've turned them over to the MBI. They have people who can do the necessary electronic forensics on the e-mails. They're also looking at the printed ones."

"There were no envelopes with the printed ones, were there?" I asked.

Kanesha shook her head. "If he kept them, he didn't bring them with him."

"I assume the police in Alabama, or their bureau of investigation, will be searching his house for evidence."

"Naturally. Already done," Kanesha said. "After you've told me your solution, I'll tell you what they found. We'll see if it corroborates what you're going to tell me."

"Okay, fair enough." I paused for a sip of coffee and a deep breath or two. I was preparing myself for being laughed at.

Kanesha sipped her coffee and regarded me with that laser stare of hers. I hesitated, because all of a sudden I was certain I'd gotten it all wrong. *It wouldn't be the first time you've made a fool of yourself.* I told my inner voice to shut up. Not aloud, of course.

"Well, go on," Kanesha said. "I'm listening."

"Here goes," I replied. "Gavin was the poisoner. He killed himself accidentally, but Maxine Muller deliberately."

THIRTY-FOUR

||||||||||||||||||||||||||||||||||||||||||||||||||||||||||||||||||||||||

Kanesha didn't laugh. Didn't even blink, in fact.

I wasn't sure how to interpret that lack of response. I found it unnerving, but I couldn't let it rattle me or I wouldn't remain coherent enough to explain my theory.

"Okay, well." I cleared my throat. "Gavin didn't intend to die, of course. He wanted to kill two people but make it look like they died accidentally while he himself was the actual target. He'd set it up so that his victims *accidentally* got the water bottles that were poisoned instead of him."

If Kanesha's eyes hadn't been open I'd have thought she'd gone to sleep on me. Then she drank more coffee.

"I think he probably prepared the two bottles—and I'm guessing that there *were* only two—with poison back home in Alabama. Maybe the investigators there found evidence of that in his home, but I guess you're not going to tell me that right now."

Kanesha shook her head. "Go on."

"So Gavin brings the poisoned bottles to Athena with him. He told Lisa Krause, the chair of the local arrangements committee for the conference, that he had to have a certain kind of bottled water in his suite. He demanded it as a keynote speaker. Lisa got the water bottles for him. They were his *cover*, so to speak, for the doctored ones." I paused for a sip of coffee.

"Next, all he had to do was get the right people to his suite, and he did that by having a party. One that he basically stuck the conference with the bill for, incidentally, but that's another issue. He knew he could force people to come, all people he'd worked with before, ones who knew what he was capable of if he was crossed. He needed a number of people there so that it wouldn't look like, later on, he had singled anyone out.

"Now, this devotion to one brand of bottled water wasn't a new thing, and I reckon that most of his guests knew that little idiosyncrasy of his. He was counting on that, in fact, because it was an important part of his plan. He would be able to say, after his intended victims died from the water he'd doctored, that the killer brought the bottles to the party and managed somehow to put them with the others, the ones that weren't doctored. Gavin would have been relieved at his lucky escape and wasn't it terrible, blah blah blah. And the whole time, he'd be congratulating himself on how smart he was and what idiots the rest of us were. He always thought he was the smartest person in the room. Hubris, because he outsmarted himself in the end."

"Why was he determined to kill two people in this scenario of yours?" Kanesha asked, her tone bland. "Maxine Muller apparently was one of them, but who was the other?"

"Harlan Crais," I said. "Do you remember what you told me about Gavin's attempts to find another job? How two places scheduled phone interviews with him and then canceled at the last minute? According to what Maxine Muller told you, he knew who blackballed him. He was sure it was Harlan Crais."

"Why was he so sure?" Kanesha asked.

"Because he'd done the same thing to Crais, and more than once, I suspect." I told her what I'd heard from Marisue and Randi and about the conversation between Crais and Bob Coben that I'd overheard. "I think Gavin, out of sheer spite, kept him from at least two good jobs. Crais must have taken some satisfaction in returning the favor.

"Now, back to the party. Last night, in talking with Cathleen Matera and Nancy Dunlap, both of whom had been at Gavin's party, I learned that Gavin had behaved in uncharacteristic fashion. They told me that he'd held these little gatherings before, and when the party was over, he'd made sure to keep any leftovers for himself. He never offered any of them to his guests. At the last party, though, he suddenly became generous, insisting that people help themselves. He even offered bottles of his precious water to them. Cathleen Matera took one, and she drank it and lived, so it was obviously fine. Nancy Dunlap turned it down, but both Harlan Crais and Maxine Muller left with a bottle apiece."

"After you found that out, that was when you texted me about Crais last night, correct?" Kanesha said.

"Yes, I wasn't quite sure what to do. Up until then I was sure he was the murderer, and I didn't want to give anything away by talking to him about bottled water. If he were innocent, however, and still had that bottle unopened, then he might be in danger if the killer had poisoned more than two."

"So you passed the buck to me."

I nodded. "Under the circumstances, I figured it was the only thing I could do."

"I see. Well, continue. Tell me why Fong wanted to kill Maxine Muller, and then you can explain how Fong ended up with a poisoned bottle himself." Kanesha drained her mug and set it on the table.

"More coffee? No?" I asked. "All right. Maxine knew too much about Gavin's sideline in extorting money out of people, I think. He couldn't trust her not to turn on him after he'd committed murder. Once Harlan Crais was dead, Maxine might be frightened enough to talk, because she knew Gavin well enough to figure out what he'd done. I'm guessing at that, but I think it's probably the reason."

Diesel had remained remarkably quiet during all this, but he chose now to demand attention. I felt that large paw on my thigh, and when I looked down at him, he meowed loudly. I patted his head, hoping that would quiet him, but it didn't. He meowed again, and I recognized the tone. He wanted food.

"I'm sorry," I told Kanesha. "He's hungry, and he'll keep this up till he's been fed. It won't take a minute."

"Sure," Kanesha said. "Think I'll help myself to a little more coffee after all while you do that."

I followed Diesel to the utility room and added more dry food to his not-empty bowl. I gave him fresh water and opened a can of wet food. "Starvation averted," I said. He was too busy eating to pay any attention to my smart comment. I went back to join Kanesha at the table.

"Where was I?" I thought for a moment. "Oh, yes, how did Gavin end up with the bottle instead of Crais? The problem with Gavin was that he was never that subtle. He was always so sure he could outsmart anyone that he continually underestimated a person's intelligence. I think Crais is a sharp guy, and he became suspicious over Gavin's sudden burst of generosity at the party. I think he probably examined that water bottle closely when he got back to his room, instead of just sticking it in his bag and leaving it there. He found evidence of tampering and then decided to effect a switch somehow with Gavin. Let Gavin have the bottle and see what happened. I don't know whether he suspected Gavin was trying to kill him, or maybe only make him sick.

"The luncheon on Friday was the best time for Crais to switch the bottles. He was introducing Gavin for the keynote speech, and he would be sitting at the table with him. All he had to do was act clumsy, knock over a few things, and then wait for Gavin to leave the table. He figured Gavin would have at least one bottle of water with him. After Gavin left the table, Crais got clumsy again and knocked that bottle off the table. He switched bottles when he bent down to pick up the one on the floor."

"How do you know about this? I thought you told me you sat at the back of the room by the doors. You couldn't see it, surely."

"I did sit at the back, and I couldn't see Gavin's table clearly from there." I reminded her about the two retired librarians, Ada Lou and Virginia, whose last names I didn't know. "I overheard them last night discussing Crais and his clumsiness. They were sitting at a nearby table and saw it all." I paused. "Well, I don't think they saw him actually switch bottles, but they saw him knock a bottle off the table. I'm sure if you talk to them, they'll tell you all about it. It might take a while, but they'll talk."

I glimpsed a brief smile before Kanesha raised her mug to her lips. She had already talked to Virginia and Ada Lou. They were eccentric enough to make even Kanesha smile.

"After the switch, all Crais had to do was wait. Gavin would open that bottle and drink, never suspecting that it was the bottle he'd poisoned and given to Crais. He went up to the podium without it, started talking, then realized he'd left the bottle at the table. He gestured at Lisa to hand it to him. He opened it, drank, and then of course realized he was going to die. Lisa was watching him, and she told me she thought he looked shocked in the split second or two before the cyanide hit him and he collapsed behind the podium."

"Where did he get the cyanide?" Kanesha asked.

I shrugged. "That I don't know. He might have gotten it through Bob Coben. Coben had access to chemicals at the lab. I told you he's working on a master's degree in chemistry. Gavin could have black-mailed Bob to get it for him, or he could have ordered it himself online from overseas. Stewart told me it was obtainable that way."

"Have you figured out how the cyanide was put into the bottles?"

"I think so. Make a hole in the bottom of the bottle where it's far less likely to be seen, insert the cyanide, and then stop up the hole with some kind of superglue."

"I see. You've got it all worked out pretty neatly." Kanesha leaned back in her chair and regarded me like a professor who'd been questioning her student.

"Well, how did I do?" I almost added *teacher* but that wouldn't have gone over well. Kanesha didn't appreciate flippancy. "Did I get it right?"

Kanesha didn't respond right away. The silence between us lengthened, then suddenly she laughed.

You did make a fool of yourself after all. It was too far-fetched to be believable.

I sighed and waited for her to tell me how big an idiot I was for wasting her time.

"I don't know how you do it," Kanesha said. "How you manage to figure these things out without all the other information that goes into solving a case."

"Do you mean I'm right?" I was astonished. I'd prepared myself to be laughed at, and she did laugh, but not for the reason I expected.

Kanesha nodded. "Based on information I have, I'm pretty sure you are. We've traced the cyanide to Fong's house in Alabama. We don't know yet how or where he got it, but investigators there found where he'd hidden it." She shook her head. "He was incredibly careless to go off and leave the evidence right there in his house."

"Sounds like typical Gavin to me," I said. "Always thinking he was too smart to get caught."

"I guess you're right about that," Kanesha said. "We'll find out where he got the cyanide eventually, but it will take time. Now, about those little old ladies, Miss Ada Lou and Miss Virginia. They were hard to track down, but they finally showed up in the room we were using at the hotel about six o'clock last night. Seems they realized that what they had seen at the luncheon might have some bearing on the case, and I had an officer watching them from then on. I guess they were talking about it again when you saw them later."

"Harlan Crais came into the suite where we were having a small gathering," I said. "I guess that set them off again."

"They didn't see the actual bottle switch, but I have confirmation of that from another source."

"Harlan Crais himself?" I asked.

"When you texted me last night, I'd been trying to track him down for almost an hour. He wasn't answering his cell phone or responding to messages left on his room voice mail. Thanks to you, though, I was able to question him further last night."

"So he admitted to switching the bottles?"

"Not right away," Kanesha said. "He was nervous. Pretty sure he thought he was about to be arrested for murder because he didn't think I'd believe his story. I finally convinced him to tell me."

"Was he the one who had blackballed Gavin and kept him from getting interviews?"

"Yes, and he explained why," Kanesha said. "It never occurred to him that Fong would try to kill him, he said, but he got suspicious at that party when Fong suddenly turned generous. He didn't actually examine the bottle until the next morning, and that's when he found the evidence of tampering. You figured that out, too—how Fong got the poison into the bottles."

"Did you charge Crais with anything?"

"Not yet," Kanesha said. "That's going to be up to the district attorney and the grand jury. Frankly, I believe him. He might have suspected there was poison in the bottle, and in that case he should have gone to the police. He didn't, however, and switched the bottles, and that led to Fong's death. Based on everything I've learned about Fong's personality, I have little doubt that he was the murderer. Just his bad luck he ended up killing himself."

"I'm really sorry poor Maxine Muller died," I said. "After she saw Gavin die right in front of all of us from drinking poisoned water, why on earth did she open that bottle?"

"My guess is that she believed someone else murdered Gavin and didn't suspect the truth. She wouldn't have suspected that her water was poisoned until it was too late."

I shook my head. "I can't say that I'm all that sorry about

Gavin. He was a terrible person, but I am sorry that he killed the one person who actually cared for him."

Kanesha rose wearily from her chair. "I'm going home now and getting in bed. The last time I saw a bed was a cot in my office, for about two hours yesterday morning." She yawned.

"You've earned your rest." I escorted her to the door, assisted by Diesel, and watched until she drove off in her car. I shut the door, and Diesel and I headed upstairs. I decided bed was where I wanted to be, at least for a couple more hours. Now that the investigation was done—at least my self-appointed part of it, that is—I had some decisions to make, and I figured postponing them in favor of a little rest wouldn't hurt.

THIRTY-FIVE

||||||||||||||||||||||||||||||||||||||||||||||||||||||||||||

After I woke up from my morning nap at around eight forty-five, I remembered that the conference hadn't officially ended. There were a couple more sessions this morning, and then a final luncheon. As much as I would have liked to, I couldn't skip it all. Stewart had no plans for the morning and could look after Diesel for me, so I hurriedly showered, dressed, grabbed a bite to eat, and then headed to the hotel.

I was only about twenty minutes late for the first session, a presentation on evaluating electronic resources using a particular tool available through one of the vendors exhibiting at the conference. I wasn't particularly interested in the subject, but it sounded more interesting than the other presentation scheduled for the same time—a session on career development. My career was in no need of development at this point, I decided.

I don't think I actually absorbed much from that presentation, or the one I attended in the following session. My thoughts were occupied with the decision about my job, the forthcoming discussion with Helen Louise about her decision to cut back on her working hours, and the still-pending decision by my son-in-law and daughter about a potential move to Virginia.

I chatted casually with the people at my table during the luncheon, but afterward I couldn't clearly recall who the people were or what we talked about. I vaguely remembered the keynote speaker talking about new models for the digital academic library of the future, but what those models were I couldn't tell you. After the keynote ended, Lisa Krause took the podium to thank everyone for their attendance, expressed hope that they had found the meeting worthwhile and enjoyable, despite the unfortunate events. She then shared a message from Kanesha Berry, stating that the investigation was nearing a conclusion and an announcement would be made soon. Everyone could now relax and enjoy what was left of their stay in Athena.

I had a brief, final visit with Marisue and Randi in the latter's room. Randi was still in pain but in a better frame of mind today. They pressed me for details about the investigation after I told them about the message Lisa shared at the end of the keynote address. I promised them that as soon as the results of the investigation were made public, I would tell them all that I knew about it. Until then, I said, I had to keep what I knew to myself. They were disappointed, but thankfully, they didn't press too hard. I hugged them both before I left, and we promised to keep in touch more often from now on.

I spent the afternoon relaxing with a good book while a large cat snoozed by my side. I napped for a little while. The tension of the last few days had drained mostly away, and I was able to sleep soundly. I looked forward to Sunday dinner and seeing Helen Louise away from the bistro. Stewart had taken over preparing dinner on Sunday, and I didn't argue.

Helen Louise arrived half an hour earlier than usual so that we would have time to talk in private before Sean and Alexandra arrived. Laura and Frank were dining tonight with Frank's department chair. I didn't want to place too much hope on that dinner and what inducements the chair could offer to keep Frank in Athena. But I could hope at least a little, and I did.

After greeting Stewart and Haskell in the kitchen, Helen Louise and I left Diesel playing with Dante there and retreated to the den where we could discuss our decisions with each other.

We got comfortable on the sofa, my arm around her shoulders, and her nestled against me, her hair brushing my cheek.

"So," I said after a short silence, "you're going to cut back your work hours." I loved the feel of her silky hair against my cheek.

"I am," she said. "As much as I love the business, I need to take more time away from it. I have other ways to spend my time, important ways that mean even more to me." She squeezed my hand.

"I feel the same way," I said. "That's why I've decided to turn down the job offer at the college. I don't want to tie myself down to a full-time schedule that would probably end up being more than forty hours a week."

"I'm glad," Helen Louise said. "That was one reason I made up my mind to cut back myself. I knew you were wavering, and I figured if I made a commitment like this, it would help you in your decision." She hesitated for a moment. "And also help us figure out where we go from here."

I smiled. We understood each other well. We hadn't talked specifically about marriage yet as the ultimate destination for our relationship, but it looked like now might be a good time to start.

Helen Louise pulled gently away from me so that we could see each other's faces. "Just so you know, I'm not expecting you to drop down on one knee right this minute. I think we need to spend more time together, and now we'll have the opportunity. This will help us decide if the *Big M* is what we both want. What do you think?"

"I think you're right," I said. "We do need to spend more time alone together. We've known each other most of our lives, but this phase of our friendship, if we can call it that, is different. We need time to explore it."

"I'm glad we're agreed." Helen Louise leaned in for a kiss.

We spent several agreeable minutes not talking, and we remained in the den until we could hear the sounds of new voices. Sean and Alexandra had arrived, and we went to greet them.

After hugs had been exchanged and Alexandra's baby bump—a phrase I didn't really care for—had been commented upon, we hung out in the kitchen. Alternately assisting Stewart and getting in his way, we had an enjoyable time chatting.

Sean had only heard about the investigation into the deaths at the Farrington House this morning. I was surprised he hadn't called me the minute he heard about them to fuss at me for getting involved. Impending fatherhood was giving him other things to fuss over, I reckoned. He hovered around Alexandra as if she would shatter apart without his constant attention. She bore it with better grace than I would have. The baby wasn't due until later in the fall, but to watch Sean one would have thought the delivery could happen any minute.

Because he was more preoccupied with his pregnant wife than with his trouble-seeking father, I escaped more easily than usual from the lawyer-ly lecture he often gave me. He did pull me aside at one point, however, and ask in an undertone, "Has Laura talked to you yet?"

"You mean about Frank's job offer in Virginia?"

He nodded.

"Yes, she's told me. You haven't heard anything about a firm decision yet, have you?"

"No, not yet. Frank promised her he'd listen to what his department chair has to say at dinner tonight before they decide."

"That's what she told me," I said. "Still hope."

"Yes," Sean said. "I'd hate to see them move that far away. I know Alex was looking forward to having Laura nearby, going through the same things as she will be, before and after the baby comes." He paused. "I'd miss them, too. Frank's a good guy."

"He is, and I know he considers you a good friend," I said.

Stewart announced that dinner was ready, and we took our places at the table Haskell had set for us. I said grace, and then the meal began. Conversation flowed about subjects other than my latest adventures in sleuthing, I was happy to observe. As we approached the time for dessert, I claimed everyone's attention.

"I have a couple of things to tell you, now that we're all gathered together. Laura and Frank couldn't be here with us. They're having dinner with one of Frank's colleagues." I left it at that because I didn't know how much Laura had said to Stewart or Helen Louise. I didn't want to risk violating her confidence by letting anything slip.

"I was called to a meeting on Friday morning by the president of Athena College and the search committee who have been trying to find a permanent library director. They offered me the job at that meeting."

"That's great, Dad," Sean said.

"Well done, Charlie," Stewart said, and Haskell nodded.

"You must be so excited," Alex said.

"I was quite flattered by the offer," I said. "I told them, however, that I needed time to think about it and promised them I would give them my answer first thing on Monday morning."

"And what answer are you going to give them?" Sean asked.

"I will not be accepting the job." I held up a hand to forestall comments and questions. I could tell Sean badly wanted to say something, but I didn't give him an opportunity. "I was ambivalent. There were things about the job I liked, but other things I didn't. One of the main issues is the time commitment. For various reasons—like the imminent arrival of grandchildren, for example—I don't want to work full-time." I smiled down at Helen Louise, who was sitting on my right. I held out my hand, and she grasped it.

"Another important reason is that Helen Louise told me she is going to cut back her hours at the bistro. She wants more time for us to spend together, and that offer was irresistible." I gave Sean a hard look. "And, no, that doesn't mean we're about to run off to get married. We simply want to spend more time together before we decide what we want for the future. Understood?"

"Understood, Dad." Sean raised his glass. "Here's to you and Helen Louise." The others picked up their glasses and toasted us as well. I bent to give Helen Louise a quick kiss. Somebody whistled, and I suspected Stewart. He winked at me when I glanced his way.

I resumed my seat. "Now, how about dessert?"

Later on, after dessert and coffee, with the table cleared, we remained in the kitchen, talking. I told them more about the strange deaths, and Sean, as always, had numerous questions. In the back of my mind the whole time, however, I wondered when I would hear from Laura and, more importantly, *what* I would hear.

Around seven thirty, my phone buzzed to alert me to a text. I pulled the phone out of my pocket and glanced at the screen. The message was from Laura. Just two words, two beautiful words: *We're staying.*